"I want you to bring me in.

"Guarantee my safety and I'll surrender myself to the space service. I just want to talk to someone and straighten things out."

"Max, I'm just a lawyer. You sound like you want someone from our Covert Operations branch."

"I don't care who you get. I just want people — my *own* goddamned people — to stop trying to kill me."

"Do you want to come to my place?" asked Magnussen. "I guarantee no one will try to kill you while I'm a witness."

Becker shook his head. "Jim, if you're on their side, there'll be a killer waiting for me at your house ... and if you're not, I honestly don't think they'd flinch at killing the both of us."

"Deft, clever, a real fast good read. Resnick knows what he's doing, and he does it well."   —*Analog*

"An exciting blend of detection and SF with a couple of Resnick's more memorable characters, it's his most relentlessly gripping story line yet. One of those books you keep telling yourself you'll only read a portion of at a time, and then finish in a single sitting."

—*Science Fiction Chronicle*

TOR BOOKS BY MIKE RESNICK

MIKE RESNICK
SECOND CONTACT

A TOM DOHERTY ASSOCIATES BOOK
NEW YORK

SECOND CONTACT

Copyright © 1990 by Mike Resnick

A Tor Book
Published by Tom Doherty Associates, Inc.
49 West 24th Street
New York, NY 10010

Cover art by David Hardy

ISBN: 0-812-51113-1

First edition: March 1990
First mass market printing: November 1990

Printed in the United States of America

0 9 8 7 6 5 4 3 2 1

To Carol, as always

And to Pat and Roger Sims—
intrepid travelers,
dedicated gourmets,
damned good friends

PROLOGUE

The Menninger/Klipstein Tachyon Drive, without which Man would never have been physically able to explore his galaxy, was theorized in 2029 A.D., created in 2032, and successfully field-tested in 2037 after a number of minor mishaps.

Mankind's first contact with an alien race was made on March 5, 2042 A.D., on the outskirts of the Epsilon Eridani system.

Nobody knows what precipitated the events that followed, nor in what order they occurred, but this much *is* known: within a matter of minutes both the Earth starship *Excelsior* and the alien ship, name and class unknown, had completely destroyed each other.

To this day no one knows which ship fired first. There is no record of any action by either side that might have invited such a reaction. No messages were sent back to base during the ensuing battle. Neither ship tried to escape once the conflict began. There were no survivors.

It took Man almost a decade to regroup, and by that time all space exploration was under the control of the military. Only the United States, the Soviet Union, the People's Republic of China, and the Republic of Brazil continued to send ships into deep space. By 2065 A.D. there were fourteen starships exploring the galaxy, each mapping and charting the stars and planets while fruitlessly searching for signs of alien life. Five of these ships belonged to the United States, four to the Soviet Union, four to China, and one to Brazil. Of them, the largest was the *Lenin,* a massive Soviet ship. The best-armed was the one-year-old Soviet starship *Moscow.* By far the fastest was the Chinese ship *Confucius.*

But the ship that made all the headlines in 2065 was the *Theodore Roosevelt,* which was currently orbiting the Earth while the fate of its captain was being decided hundreds of miles below it.

Max Becker rode the airlift up to the fifth floor of the Pentagon, walked rapidly past a row of holographs of former chiefs of staff, and finally came to the office he sought. The door's sensors scanned and identified him and allowed him to enter.

"Good morning, Major Becker," said the gray-haired man who bore three stars on his shoulders and was seated behind a large chrome desk. "I've been expecting you."

"May I request the meaning of this, sir?" demanded Becker, waving an official-looking document in the air.

"I should think it would be self-explanatory," answered the general. "It's your next assignment."

"I haven't had a furlough in more than two years," said Becker. "I've already bought my tickets and paid for my hotel."

"We've arranged for your money to be refunded," said the general.

"May I respectfully point out that I don't want a god-damned refund? I want a vacation!"

"Respectfully?" repeated the general, arching an eyebrow.

"I've worked my tail off for this department for two years. I've got five weeks' leave coming to me, and I want it!"

"I'm afraid that's out of the question, Major."

"Why?" demanded Becker. "And, more to the point, why *me*?"

"You're the best man for the job."

"I'm not even navy!" protested Becker. "This guy ought to be defended by one of his own."

"There is no differentiation of services in the space program, Major," replied the general. "I'm sure you'll find the navy eager to cooperate with you in every way."

"I doubt it, sir."

"Why should you say that, Major?"

"Because if this case is as open and shut as it's supposed to be, anyone can handle it," answered Becker. "So when you bypass three hundred navy lawyers who work in this building and choose me, I can't help feeling just a bit suspicious." He paused. "May I respectfully ask why I was selected?"

"It wasn't my choice," responded the general. "We asked the computer to select a name." He stared at Becker. "You look dubious, Major."

"If it was programmed to select the best criminal lawyer in the service, it would have picked Hector Garcia."

"It did. You were its second choice."

"Well?"

"Garcia's on leave."

"And I'm about to go on leave."

"He outranks you."

"May I point out to the general that I outrank two hundred other lawyers who can handle this case in their sleep?"

"The computer picked *you*."

"What if I refuse?"

"If you refuse with cause, we'll give the case to someone else—but I personally guarantee that it'll be at least a year before you get that furlough," said the general. "If you refuse without cause, I'll demote you a rank and offer you the job again. I can keep that up all the way down to private."

"May I speak frankly, sir?"

"I thought that was what you were doing, Major," said the general wryly.

"There must be hundreds of would-be Clarence Darrows who actually *want* to defend this fruitcake," said Becker. "Why don't you just ask for volunteers?"

"We don't need any Clarence Darrows making grandstand speeches for the press, Major," said the general. "We want this affair wrapped up as quickly and quietly as possible."

"Then why try him at all?" persisted Becker. "He's already confessed, hasn't he? Why not just lock him away?"

"There *must* be a court-martial," said the general. "It's too late to cover anything up." He paused. "The whole world is watching us, Major."

"I think the general will find that nine-tenths of the world doesn't give a damn, and the rest probably thinks he didn't kill enough of his crew."

"That will be quite enough, Major Becker!" snapped the general. "This is your assignment, and you're damned well going to accept it!"

Becker stared at the general and sighed deeply. "All right. When is the trial due to begin?"

"A week from Tuesday."

"Does the general seriously expect me to prepare a defense for murder in less than two weeks?" said Becker disbelievingly.

"Every day that we *don't* have the court-martial, the press becomes more critical of the entire military establishment."

"May I point out that they'll be even more critical of a poorly prepared defense?"

"You'll be given all the material you need," said the general. "As I see it, Commander Jennings' only possible defense is temporary insanity, and we have three psychiatrists who are willing to swear that he was quite insane when he committed the acts in question."

"I'll have to interview Jennings immediately."

"This afternoon, if you wish."

"And if he's half as crazy as he's supposed to be, I'll want an armed guard with me."

"No problem."

"Where are you keeping him?"

"Bethesda."

"The same Bethesda that treats congressmen and senators?"

The general nodded.

"That figures," muttered Becker.

"I didn't quite hear that, Major."

"It confirms my opinion that Jennings isn't the only madman involved in this case."

"Oh?" said the general ominously.

Becker nodded. "Whoever put him in Bethesda is as crazy as Jennings. What if he gets loose? You've got lawmakers and ambassadors on every floor of the damned building."

"He presents no threat," the general responded. "He's under round-the-clock surveillance."

"Is he on any tranquilizers? I can't interview him if he's all drugged up."

"No," said the general. "He hasn't been on any medication for almost a week."

"All right," said Becker. "If we wrap this up in ten or eleven days, maybe I can still get some skiing in."

"That's a much more reasonable attitude," said the general.

"Who's prosecuting?"

"Colonel James Magnussen," replied the general.

"Jim Magnussen?" repeated Becker, surprised. "From San Diego?"

"Do you know him?"

"About five years ago we spent a few months together, preparing a case against some military contractors. He's a good man. I thought he was still in California."

"He was."

"Why does *he* get to prosecute?"

"He requested the assignment."

"I suppose it's too late for me to request to assist him?" asked Becker.

The general stared at him. "I admire your sense of humor, Major."

"I wasn't joking."

"Of course you were," said the general. "Now get to work."

"How? You just told me I can't visit Jennings until this afternoon."

"But Colonel Magnussen is waiting for you in his office. He wants to go over some details with you. I told him you'd be there as soon as we were finished talking." He paused. "We're finished. Magnussen's office is down the hall, third door on your left."

Becker saluted and walked to the door.

"I commend you for making the proper decision," said the general.

"I had so many attractive alternatives," said Becker dryly.

Becker stopped at the washroom first and ran a styler through his thick auburn hair. Then he walked to a sink, muttered "Cold," and rinsed his face. Then, refreshed, he stepped out into the corridor and rode it to Magnussen's office.

He stepped off before the door, waited for it to identify him, and entered.

The room was as cluttered as the general's office was neat. A number of law degrees hung on the walls, most of them at infuriatingly odd angles. Piles of transcripts and computer disks and cubes, all marked for disposal, sat atop three file cabinets. A late-model voice-activated computer took up one corner of the room. Magnussen was a smoker, and though Becker knew the office had been cleaned by the night staff, two ashtrays overflowed with cigar butts, and there were ashes on the floor.

Perched atop an uncomfortable-looking stool in front of

the file cabinets, a sheaf of papers clutched in a meaty hand, was Colonel James Magnussen. He was short, stocky, and powerful, with the build, if not the height, of a football player. Just beside his eyes were a pair of relatively recent surgical scars, but in spite of them he wore extremely thick glasses, as if the operation, whatever it was, had been a failure. His dark hair was streaked with gray and seemed resistant to brushes and combs. He peered out from behind a thick cloud of cigar smoke.

"Max!" he said enthusiastically. "How the hell are you?"

"I was fine until twenty minutes ago," said Becker. "And yourself?"

"Doing great," said Magnussen. "I'm married now. Got two little girls, three and two. How about you?"

"Married and unmarried."

"I'm sorry to hear it."

"Ancient history," said Becker with a shrug.

"We've got a lot to catch up on," said Magnussen. "Grab a seat."

Becker looked around. "Where?"

Magnussen walked over to a chair and pushed a pile of papers onto the floor. "Right here will do. They just gave me this office two days ago," he added apologetically. "I'm still throwing out junk from twenty years ago."

"Thanks," said Becker, sitting down.

Magnussen went back to his stool, grabbing an ashtray along the way.

"Why the hell are you here, Jim?" asked Becker.

"I begged every brass I knew to get this assignment," chuckled Magnussen. "It's the biggest case to come along in years."

"I thought it was open and shut."

"I mean big in terms of publicity," replied Magnussen. "And to be perfectly honest, it's about time I left the service and went back into private practice—I'm not fourth-genera-tion military like you—and this case ought to get me into any law firm I choose."

"You're really quitting the service?"

Magnussen nodded. "I'm not a kid anymore, Max. I've got responsibilities, and to be quite blunt about it, I can't support my family on a colonel's pay—not the way I want to, anyway."

"Well, good luck to you," said Becker.

"Getting this assignment was all the luck I needed."

"Getting this assignment was all the *bad* luck I needed," said Becker. "I was going up to Aspen for a couple of weeks. I even had my bags packed."

"I'm sorry."

Becker shrugged. "It's not your fault."

"Have you met your client yet?" asked Magnussen.

Becker shook his head.

"Strange man," said Magnussen.

"Of course he's a strange man," said Becker. "Normal men don't come out of their cabins and blow two crewmen away for no reason at all."

Magnussen stared at him for a moment, then spoke. "What, exactly, do you know about the case?"

"Just what I've heard," replied Becker.

"And what is that?"

"I gather he woke up one morning, walked up to two crew members, shot them, and then confined himself to his quarters and turned over command of the *Roosevelt* to his executive officer with orders to return to base immediately."

"That's about it." Magnussen paused. "Ready to deal?"

"So soon?" asked Becker with an amused smile.

"The sooner we wrap this up, the better."

"I thought you wanted publicity for your new career."

"Just putting him away will be publicity enough."

Becker leaned back on his chair. "Make me an offer," he said, waving some of the smoke away with his hand.

Magnussen smiled. "The prosecution is willing to accept a plea of insanity."

"Temporary or permanent?" asked Becker.

"Take your choice," said Magnussen.

"Sounds good to me," said Becker. "We plead insanity, you accept it, and we all go home half an hour later. I might even get some skiing in after all." He paused thoughtfully. "Besides, he *has* to be crazy to do what he did."

"He is," replied Magnussen. "Though he does have his moments of lucidity."

"Oh?"

"What I mean to say is that he's not a raving lunatic."

"You've spoken to him?"

"Once," answered Magnussen. "I took his deposition. He wasn't cooperative, but he wasn't ranting and raving."

"What's the prosecution's position if he doesn't want to plead insanity?" asked Becker.

"We'll accept a guilty plea—but we'd much prefer insanity, for the good of the service." Magnussen paused. "Have we got a deal?"

"I'll have to speak to Jennings first," said Becker.

"Of course. But you'll urge him to plead insanity?"

"Probably," said Becker.

"Good!" said Magnussen with obvious satisfaction. "*That's* settled!"

"Not necessarily," said Becker. "What if he wants to plead not guilty?"

"You've got to be kidding."

"It's not up to me," said Becker with a shrug. "Ultimately it's *his* decision."

Magnussen exhaled a cloud of smoke and stared at his old friend. "If he pleads not guilty, I'll crucify him."

"I don't doubt it."

"I'm not kidding, Max. We've got his own log, the ship computer's account, and more eyewitnesses than you can shake a stick at. If Jennings pleads not guilty, I'll nail him up and hang him out to dry."

"The general tells me you've got three shrinks who will testify that he's gone off the deep end," said Becker. "Is that right?"

"Not exactly," said Magnussen carefully. "But they *will* testify that he was temporarily insane when he committed the murders."

Becker frowned. "But not before or since?"

Magnussen shrugged. "Psychiatry's an inexact science."

"Not *that* inexact," said Becker. "What makes a starship commander go crazy for only five minutes in the middle of a lifetime of perfect sanity?"

"Ours is not to wonder why," replied Magnussen. "Ours is just to take their testimony and run with it."

"All three shrinks are in agreement?" persisted Becker.

"*These* three are."

"There were others?"

"One other."

"And he thinks Jennings is sane?"

"He doesn't know," replied Magnussen. "At least he was honest about it."

"Jim, I'm going to need copies of all four statements," said Becker.

"Certainly," said Magnussen. He got up, walked to a pile of holographic disks, withdrew one, and tossed it to Becker before sitting down again. "Is there anything else I can do for you?"

"I'll need Jennings's service record," said Becker. "And I'll want copies of his log and the eyewitness statements."

"I'll have them delivered to your office before the end of the day," said Magnussen.

"And the record of the ship's computer."

"No problem. Anything else?"

Becker lowered his head in thought for a moment, then looked up. "Yeah. I'd like the service records of the men he killed." He paused. "Also, I want any psychiatric profiles that were done on Jennings prior to his appointment as commander of the *Theodore Roosevelt.*"

"That may take a couple of days."

"I'll need it by the weekend at the latest," said Becker seriously. "Otherwise, I'll probably have to ask for a postponement. We may be sending this guy to the funny farm, but I'm still an officer of the court, charged with protecting his interests."

Magnussen frowned.

"They'll never give you a postponement, Max. Too many people are anxious to get this one over with fast."

"Which people?"

"Important ones," said Magnussen noncommittally. He took a puff on his cigar, then got to his feet. "I admire your thoroughness, Max. I'll instruct my staff to make sure you get what you need. Do you still have that cute little blonde secretary? You know, the one with the big—"

"No," said Becker. "I lost her about the same time as I lost my wife." He grimaced. "These days I've got a middle-aged woman named Karla who spends all her time reading espionage novels and wondering why nothing exciting ever happens in the Pentagon. Not exactly the kind of secretary who makes you want to get to the office early, but damned efficient. Just send everything to her, and tell her it's for the Jennings case. It'll make her day."

"Right."

"Thanks. Is there anything else I should be asking for?"

"Not that I can think of at the moment."

"By the way, who's sitting on the tribunal?"

Magnussen shrugged. "They haven't told me yet. As soon as they do, I'll let you know." He paused. "Why don't you stop by for a drink at about 6:30 tonight? I might have some information on it by then."

"Thanks," said Becker. "Maybe I'll take you up on it."

"We can sit around and talk about old times."

"I thought you had a family to go home to."

"They're visiting her parents in Montana. The vidphone hasn't stopped buzzing since I got here, and I practically have to beat the press off with a stick every time I go in or out of my townhouse. No sense putting my family through all that—though once this is over, I'd love to have you meet them." He grinned. "You'll never forgive me for having spotted Irene before you did."

"Spotting pretty women never did me all that much good in the long run," replied Becker. He paused. "Speaking of the press, are they going to be allowed in?"

"Probably," answered Magnussen. "It's a military court-martial, and theoretically we can keep them out, but the service is very sensitive about being charged with a cover-up."

"How the hell can it be a cover-up if you lock him away for the rest of his life?"

"You know the press. They always think we're hiding something."

"They're usually right."

"Not this time, Max. Anyway, I think they'll probably allow a dozen senior correspondents in to cover the trial." Magnussen smiled. "Think of it—billions of people hanging upon our every word."

"Wonderful," muttered Becker.

"Cheer up, Max. I guarantee it'll be worth at least a million dollars in publicity if you ever quit the service and go into private practice."

"As the shyster who defended the Mad Butcher of the Fleet?" replied Becker sardonically. "Or as the totally immoral son of a bitch who helped him beat an open-and-shut murder rap on a technicality?"

"There won't be any technicalities on this one, Max."

"Don't be so sure of yourself," said Becker with a smile. "I'm a pretty good lawyer."

"So am I," said Magnussen seriously. "And I'm not allowed to lose this case."

"Oh?"

Magnussen nodded. "It's been explained to me that we can't have this maniac walking the streets."

"Explained by *who*?" asked Becker sharply.

"By *whom*, Max," Magnussen corrected him.

"Am I to assume you're ducking the question?"

Magnussen smiled. "I was beginning to wonder if you'd noticed."

Becker stared at him for a long moment, then checked his timepiece. "Well, I've got about an hour to grab some lunch before I visit Jennings. Care to join me?"

Magnussen shook his head. "I wish I could, Max, but I've still got to make some sense out of this filing system."

Becker got to his feet, and Magnussen escorted him to the door.

"Remember—tonight at 6:30."

"Right," said Becker, fighting back an urge to cough as a cloud of cigar smoke engulfed him.

He left the room, then took an airlift down to the third floor, where he stopped at the commissary for a sandwich and a cup of coffee. He spent the next few minutes eating and skimming through the psychiatrists' reports. Then, still wondering why such an open-and-shut case had to be tried at all, he descended to the main floor, walked outside, and went off to meet his newest client.

2

Becker stood directly behind his military escort as the walkway transported them through the sterile white corridors of the Maximum Security Wing. The windows were barred, the doors triple-latched, the atmosphere oppressive. After a few minutes they stepped onto another walkway that went off to the left, and soon found themselves approaching a door that was guarded by two armed men standing at attention.

"End of the line, sir," said his escort, stepping from the walkway onto the solid floor.

"Thank you, Lieutenant," said Becker, following him.

"Do you want anyone to come inside with you?" asked the officer.

"I'm not sure," said Becker. "Do you think it's necessary?"

"That has to be your decision, sir."

"He hasn't been violent?"

"Not to my knowledge, sir."

"May I assume someone will be observing us?"

The lieutenant nodded. "At all times, sir."

Becker shrugged. "Then I'll go in alone. It may put him more at his ease."

The lieutenant saluted, unlatched the door, then touched a five-digit code on the computer lock and stepped aside as Becker entered the room.

Despite all he had been told, he had half expected to find himself inside a padded cell, facing a wild-eyed man wrapped in a straitjacket. Instead, the room seemed more like a first-class hotel accommodation—bed, chairs, desk, even a television set, and a door leading to a separate bathroom. Commander Wilbur H. Jennings was sitting on an upholstered chair, smoking a cigarette and staring out the barred window. He wore a white shirt with the collar open and his cuffs unbuttoned and rolled halfway up to his elbows, and a pair of neatly pressed blue trousers.

Jennings got to his feet and stared at Becker questioningly. He was a stocky man in his mid-fifties. His steel gray hair was clipped quite short, and his nose had been broken at least twice in his youth. His teeth were white but uneven.

"Commander Jennings?" said Becker.

"Yes?"

"My name is Max Becker. I'm your attorney."

Becker extended his hand and Jennings took it after a momentary pause.

"Have a seat, Major," he said at last, indicating an empty chair a few feet away from his own.

"Thank you," said Becker, walking over to it.

Jennings sat down on his own chair, snuffed his cigarette out in an ashtray, and immediately lit another, studying Becker all the while. "So you're my lawyer."

"That's right."

"Who are you working for?"

"I'm working for you, sir," said Becker.

Jennings shook his head irritably. "*Why* are you here—to help me, or to keep me quiet?"

"To be perfectly honest, I'm here because I didn't have any choice in the matter," replied Becker bluntly. "I was preparing to take a long-overdue furlough when I was informed that I had been selected as your attorney."

"Why should I believe you?"

"Look," said Becker, "for better or worse, we're stuck with each other. You might as well trust me; I guarantee they're not going to take me off the case."

"You've tried to get reassigned?" asked Jennings.

"Frankly, sir, yes."

"Good," said Jennings.

"Good?" repeated Becker.

"My life is at stake here," said Jennings. "I don't want it to depend upon a stupid lawyer, and only a stupid lawyer would *want* to take this case." He paused. "Have they set a date for the trial?"

"Yes, sir. It's less than two weeks off."

"That's not a very long time to prepare a case," noted Jennings.

"If I may speak frankly, sir," said Becker, "I get the distinct impression that your case is considered open and shut, and that I am expected to strike a bargain rather than prepare a defense." He paused. "Under the circumstances, it seems the most reasonable course of action."

"I'm sure it does, Major," said Jennings irritably. "They want a nice, tidy whitewash for the media." He paused. "They're doomed to be disappointed."

Becker studied him closely for a long minute without speaking.

"What are you staring at, Major?" demanded Jennings.

"You're not quite what I expected, sir."

"You would prefer someone foaming at the mouth and screaming about how God told him to do it, no doubt?"

"It might make matters easier," admitted Becker with a smile. "The prosecution has agreed to accept a plea of temporary insanity, but permanent insanity is much easier to prove."

"Don't worry about it, Major."

"Oh?"

"I have no intention of pleading insanity."

"You don't?"

Jennings shook his head. "No."

Becker frowned. "You're making a serious mistake, sir. If you plead guilty, the death penalty is mandatory. The prosecution has already expressed its willingness to deal."

"I'm not pleading guilty, either."

Becker grimaced. "If you wanted to plead innocent, you shouldn't have confessed to killing two members of your crew."

"But I *did* kill them."

"Then how am I to convince the court that you're innocent?" asked Becker.

"I intend to plead justifiable homicide."

"Justifiable homicide?" repeated Becker, unable to hide his surprise.

"That's correct."

"Did the two men you killed attempt to mutiny?"

"No."

"Did they threaten you physically?"

"No."

"That's going to make killing them awfully difficult to justify."

"Put me on the stand and I'll explain my actions."

"Perhaps you'd better start by explaining them to me."

Jennings shook his head. "Not until I'm sure I can trust you."

"Right at this moment, I am probably the only person in the world that you *can* trust."

"Perhaps," said Jennings. "But I have to be certain. I have to make sure you're not here just to silence me."

"I'm your attorney," repeated Becker. "If you're going to plead innocent, I'm legally compelled to present your story to the court, whether I believe it or not."

"Maybe," said Jennings.

"Why wouldn't I?" demanded Becker in exasperation.

"Because once I explain my actions to you, Major, you'll demand that I plead insanity, and when I refuse to, you'll drop the case and they'll just give me another lawyer who won't believe me either."

"I'm ethically predisposed to believe you," said Becker patiently. "You're my client." He paused. "Now, if you can't convince *me* that it was justifiable homicide, how are you going to convince the court?"

"That's *my* problem, Major."

"It's supposed to be *our* problem," Becker corrected him.

"It's *my* problem," repeated Jennings firmly. "I'm the one who's facing a death sentence."

"This is no good," said Becker. "We're going to have to come to an understanding right here and now." He paused again. "I'm your attorney, and if you want to plead innocent, then I'll prepare the best damned case for innocence that I can. But I can't do it in a vacuum. You've got to give me some information that I can use."

Jennings stared at him again, then seemed to come to a decision.

"Do I seem irrational to you, Major?"

"Not at the moment."

"And you want me to confide in you completely?"

"I insist upon it."

"What if I were to tell you that if you try to prove my story, you may be putting your life at risk?"

"I wouldn't believe you," said Becker bluntly.

"I have no reason to lie to you. It is in my best interest that you try to prove my innocence."

"Why don't you just tell me your story, and we'll worry about the rest of it later?"

Jennings sighed deeply, then opened a desk drawer and pulled out a notebook. "It's all in here, Major," he said. "What I did, why I did it, why I'm convinced that I was acting in the best interests of my ship."

He handed the notebook over to Becker, who thumbed through it briefly and then placed it inside his briefcase.

"I'll read it tonight," promised Becker. "But right at this moment, I'd rather hear it firsthand, and interrupt with any questions that may occur to me."

"All right, Major. Where shall I begin?"

"You can begin by telling me why you killed Crewmen Greenberg and Provost."

"I didn't."

Becker frowned. "Just a minute. You just admitted to killing them."

"That is incorrect," said Jennings. "You asked me if I killed two members of my crew, and I said I did."

"Well?" asked Becker, confused.

"You didn't ask me if they were Greenberg and Provost."

Becker pulled a paper out of his briefcase. "It says right here that you shot and killed Robert Greenberg and Jonathan Provost, Jr."

"I know what it says—and it's wrong."

"All right," said Becker. "Who *did* you kill?"

"I don't know—but they *weren't* Greenberg and Provost."

"You don't know?" repeated Becker.

"No."

"All right. Who do you *think* they were?"

Jennings drew a deep breath and exhaled it slowly.

"Two aliens."

"Oh, shit!" muttered Becker. "It had to be *aliens*? It couldn't be spies?"

"They almost certainly were spies as well."

"Aliens?" repeated Becker.

"Aliens."

"Well, let's follow it through," said Becker grimly. "Did they look like humans?"

"Yes."

"Did any of your staff ever suggest they might be aliens?"

"No."

"Did they pass their weekly physical exams during the mission?"

"Yes."

"They didn't speak with an accent?"

"None."

"Do you know the odds against an alien race evolving to the point where they could pass for men?"

"Millions to one, I suppose," answered Jennings.

"*Billions* to one," Becker corrected him.

"Nevertheless, that's what they were," said Jennings firmly.

"And you're the only one who was able to recognize them as aliens?"

"As far as I know."

"How did you spot them? What did they do?"

"Little things," said Jennings. "There was no single thing you could put your finger on and say that it was conclusive evidence."

"Give me an example."

"One evening Greenberg brought me a cup of coffee while I was on the bridge. He kept his thumb in it the whole time he carried it—and I had him wait while I issued some commands to adjust our course—but when I tried to drink it, it was still so hot that I burned my mouth. And when I examined his thumb, it wasn't even red."

"And you blew him away because he had a thumb that was insensitive to heat?" demanded Becker incredulously.

Jennings shook his head. "No, of course not. There were other things, lots of them. Like the fact that the computer in the crew's lavatory said Provost hadn't urinated in more than a week."

"Maybe he was a bed-wetter," said Becker. "Maybe he used the officers' lavatory. Maybe he used the toilet instead of the urinal. Maybe he got drunk every night and pissed in the sink. Maybe . . ."

"I told you it wasn't any single thing," explained Jennings testily. "But during our four months in deep space I kept noticing little things. Any one or two of them could be explained away, but not ten or twenty of them. They're all listed *there*," he continued, pointing to the edge of his notebook, which was visible inside Becker's briefcase. "When I was finally convinced that I was right, I decided that the safety of the ship and the security of Earth itself required me to terminate them as quickly as possible."

"Why not simply place them under arrest?"

"They were aliens. I had no idea what their physical or mental capabilities were. It was possible that our brig couldn't hold them, or that they were capable of damaging the ship even from detention."

"You did something else, too, didn't you?" said Becker, scanning still more sheets that he had withdrawn from his briefcase. "Besides killing them, I mean."

"Yes," said Jennings. "I turned over command of the *Roosevelt* to my executive officer and confined myself to my quarters."

Becker shook his head. "Before that."

"I relieved Chief Medical Officer Gillette from duty and placed him under arrest."

"Right," said Becker. "Why?"

"I suspected that he was an alien, too."

"Then why didn't you kill him?"

"I had made no firsthand observations of any aberrant behavior."

"Then what made you think he was an alien?"

"Because when he examined the bodies of Crewmen Greenberg and Provost after I killed them, he made no mention of the fact that they were aliens."

"Possibly because they weren't."

"They were," said Jennings firmly, "and he must therefore have been in collusion with them, whether he was a human *or* an alien." He paused. "I asked him point-blank if they were humans and he answered in the affirmative. I couldn't allow him to remain on duty after that."

"And your exec backed you up?"

Jennings shook his head. "No. I gather he freed Gillette a few hours later."

Becker paused, considering his next question. "If I choose not to believe your story, will you think that *I* am an alien?"

"No."

"Or that I'm in collusion with them?"

"No," said Jennings. "You have only my word and my observations, and I realize how farfetched they must sound." He paused again. "But," he continued, "if you had had the opportunity to examine the bodies of Greenberg and Provost, and *then* you doubted my story, I would have to conclude that yes, you were in collusion with them."

Becker leaned back in his chair, made a frustrated gesture with his hands, and sighed deeply.

"Do you really want to go into court with that story?"

"It's the truth," said Jennings. "I know it sounds bizarre, but—"

"Bizarre isn't the word for it," interrupted Becker. "Frankly, it's the most indefensible piece of paranoia I've ever heard—and I'm on *your* side. I hate to think of what Magnussen is going to do with it." He looked across the small room at Jennings. "Are you sure you wouldn't rather plead insanity?"

"I'm sure."

"I was afraid you'd say that," said Becker. "All right," he added with a shrug of defeat, "if that's your story, we'll just have to work with it—for the moment, anyway. Had either Greenberg or Provost ever served under you prior to the voyage in question?"

"No."

"What about the doctor—Gillette?"

"No." Jennings shifted his weight on the edge of the bed. "Excuse me, Major, but . . ."

"Yes?"

"What if I were to submit to a lie detector?"

"It's not acceptable evidence."

Jennings shook his head. "I don't mean for the court. I mean to convince *you* that I'm telling the truth."

"It wouldn't make a bit of difference," replied Becker bluntly. "If you're crazy, you'll pass with flying colors."

Jennings smiled wryly. "Yes, I see your point."

"Did you mention your suspicions to anyone else aboard the *Roosevelt* before you killed Provost and Greenberg?"

"When I first began suspecting the truth, I skirted the subject with a couple of my officers. I never addressed it outright."

"Why not?"

"They would have thought I was crazy," replied Jennings.

"The prosecution has three psychiatrists who are willing to swear to it."

"Only three?" said Jennings, surprised. "I must have convinced one of them."

"The fourth one is undecided. He won't do us a bit of good." Becker paused. "Let me ask you once more: are you *sure* you wouldn't rather plead temporary insanity?"

"I'm not crazy!" snapped Jennings. "And more to the point, I *must* alert our military to the fact that we have been infiltrated and are at hazard. They've taken away my command and denied me access to the press, so the only way I can do so is in court."

"There's no way you're going to convince the court that two of your crew members were aliens when 237 other crew members plus the examining medical officer will swear they weren't. If you plead insanity, you'll be given treatment at government expense, and you'll keep your commission and your pension."

"And if I convince them I'm sane?"

"Then they'll try to figure out what kind of grudge you had against Greenberg and Provost, find you guilty of premeditated murder, and put you in front of a firing squad."

"They were aliens," said Jennings stubbornly.

"The court will buy murder before it'll buy aliens," replied Becker. "Believe me."

"I know what they were, and I performed the proper action in my capacity as commander of the *Theodore Roose-*

velt," said Jennings adamantly. "Moreover, it is essential to our security that I convince my colleagues that I am correct; if there were three of them on *my* ship, God knows how many of them have infiltrated the entire military establishment." He turned to Becker. "Now, are you going to defend me on a plea of not guilty or aren't you?"

"I really don't know how to go about it," admitted Becker truthfully. "I'll talk to your medical officer, but he's going to tell me he examined two perfectly normal human bodies. He's already signed a statement to that effect, and the medical log shows nothing out of the ordinary. I can't bring in any defense witnesses who might corroborate your observations, because you never discussed it with anyone else. There's simply no way I can build a cogent defense based on the premise that you killed two alien beings who were masquerading as humans." Becker's expression reflected his frustration. "Even if they *were* aliens, how did they pass for human? Why didn't the medical staff spot them? How did they get aboard the *Roosevelt* in the first place? Each of them had served on other deep-space missions; why weren't they spotted before? If they were deep-cover agents, when was the switch made? Who knew about it? Who authorized it? Why didn't their friends and families report it? How did they learn the language?" He shook his head. "The more questions they ask, the more implausible your story's going to become."

"I don't have any of the answers," said Jennings grimly. "I'm a military man. I saw a military problem. I solved it in a military manner. I'm willing to be tried by my peers."

"The men who will sit in judgment on this case aren't your peers," said Becker.

"What are you talking about?"

"Your peers, if you have any, believe that aliens look exactly like human beings and can avoid being spotted by their crewmates during four months of close daily contact in deep space." Becker stared at him. "There is a strong possibility that you may not have a peer in the whole world. In fact, now that I come to think of it, I have a feeling that the quickest way to lose your case would be to put you on the stand. They'd have you wrapped up in a straitjacket five minutes into the cross-examination."

"You *must* put me on the stand! It's the only way I can explain my actions and warn the world about what's happening!"

"Not smart," answered Becker. "I've worked with Jim Magnussen before. He's as good as they get at breaking down a witness's credibility."

"I don't care!" said Jennings. "I'm pleading not guilty, and I insist that you place me on the stand to defend myself."

"That's your final word on the subject?"

"It is."

Becker sighed and got slowly to his feet. He extended his hand, which Jennings ignored.

"Thank you, Commander Jennings," he said formally. "It's possible that I may have to consult with you again."

"Just remember what I said," replied Jennings.

Becker walked to the door, which slid back to allow him to pass through, then quickly closed behind him.

Three hours later Becker was in the general's office, standing at attention.

"Out of the question," said the general irritably.

"But, sir . . ."

"You heard me, Major. You're the man we selected, and you're the man we're going with. You didn't volunteer *for* this case, and there's no way you're going to volunteer *off* of it."

"Sir, I simply cannot prepare a competent defense given the restrictions that Commander Jennings has placed on me."

"Could anyone else?"

"I don't know."

"Well, until you *do* know, you're his attorney."

"Have you read any of the notes on the case, sir?" continued Becker.

"I'm acquainted with it, yes."

Becker paused for a moment. "Commander Jennings wants to plead not guilty."

The general frowned. "We'd prefer a plea of temporary insanity."

"You'll get a *verdict* of insanity," Becker assured him. "He insists that I put him on the stand."

"Oh?" The general drummed his fingers on the desk. "That would be most unwise. The press would have a field day with his story."

"If I don't do it, my guess is that he'll fire me and defend himself."

"We won't permit that. He *must* have counsel, whether he desires it or not. And *you* must prevent him from embarrassing the service."

"He's already killed two members of his crew," said Becker. "How much more embarrassing can it get?"

"I don't want that ridiculous story about aliens coming out," said the general firmly. "If it sees print, do you know how many nut cases will shoot their neighbors on the assumption that *they're* aliens?"

"Why not just close the trial to the press?"

"We've already invited them to cover it. If we reverse ourselves at this late date, they'll be sure we're covering something up."

"Sir," said Becker, finally relaxing his posture, "the problem still remains: whether Jennings takes the stand or not, how can I present a case for not guilty without his story about aliens coming out?"

"Then don't allow him to plead not guilty."

"There's no way I can prevent it, sir. If I get up in court and say that he agrees to a plea of insanity and he corrects me, they'll remove me and postpone the trial until he gets a lawyer who will do what he wants. I'm simply suggesting that you get that lawyer now and save a lot of time and trouble." Becker paused for breath. "You know he's crazy, Jim Magnussen knows he's crazy, and now that I've talked to him *I* know he's crazy. Why not take me off the case and at least give him a lawyer who thinks he's sane?"

"Find me one and I'll consider it."

"I've been trying all afternoon," admitted Becker wryly. "No one wants any part of this defense."

"Who gave you permission to find a replacement?" demanded the general. "*You're* the defense attorney."

"Yes, sir."

"Then perhaps you'd better start preparing his defense."

"I won't be able to shut him up, sir."

"Then go through the motions of trying to prove his case. When you show him that it's hopeless, maybe then he'll agree to an insanity plea."

"I doubt it," said Becker. "Couldn't you—"

"That will be all, Major."

Becker stared at the general, started to say something, changed his mind, saluted, and walked out of the office. At least, he reflected wearily, the whole damned trial ought to take less than half a day . . . and it was probably worth a little public humiliation if he could salvage part of his furlough.

|3|

"What happened?" asked Magnussen as Becker entered his office the next morning. "I thought you were stopping by for a drink last night?"

"Problems," muttered Becker, flopping down on an empty chair.

"Women?"

"I should be so lucky."

"Well, then?" asked Magnussen.

"Jennings," said Becker. "And I'll have that drink now."

"Now? It's ten o'clock in the morning."

"Better late than never," said Becker.

Magnussen stared at him for a moment, then shrugged, got to his feet, walked to a chrome cabinet, and pulled out a bottle of vodka. "You want a little tomato or orange juice with it?"

"Whatever you've got."

"Whatever you want," responded Magnussen.

"What I want is a drink. With coloring, without coloring, it makes no difference."

"Just a minute," said Magnussen, opening a container of tomato juice and mixing up a Bloody Mary. "I can't stand to

watch anyone drinking straight vodka this early in the day."
He walked over to Becker, handed him the glass, and returned to his desk.

"Thanks," said Becker, downing the drink in a single swallow. "I never thought I'd say 'I needed that'—but by God, I needed that!"

"Are you going to tell me what this is all about?"

Becker nodded. "That's what I'm here for." He fell silent again.

"Well?"

"You're about to become a national hero," said Becker. "When this trial is over, they're going to ghostwrite your autobiography and make you into a video series."

"I'm gratified, of course," said Magnussen sardonically, "but what the hell are you talking about?"

"He's pleading innocent."

"You're kidding!"

"Do I look like a comedian?"

"I don't believe it!" said Magnussen.

"If that strains your credibility, you're gonna *love* his defense," said Becker wryly.

"Are you willing to tell me what it is?" asked Magnussen seriously.

"Why not?" replied Becker. "Before I do, I want you to know that I tried to quit the case yesterday. The general won't let me off the hook."

"It's *that* flimsy a defense?"

"It's so flimsy that I spent half the night pulling every string I could to get myself reassigned."

"Unsuccessfully, I presume?"

"Unsuccessfully."

"I suppose I should ask what you did with the other half of your night?"

"Nothing. I spent it reading his diary or journal or whatever he wants to call it." Becker paused. "All you have to do is sit back and watch me make a fool of myself."

"The devil made him do it?" suggested Magnussen.

"The devil's big and red; these guys were probably little and green."

"I don't think I follow you."

"Greenberg and Provost were aliens, and he was protecting his crew by killing them."

"Aliens? He never mentioned aliens in his deposition." Becker stared at him. "You're sure?"

"Of course I'm sure."

"Then why does the general know about it?"

"Jennings is under constant surveillance; Security probably told the general what he said to you."

"Well, now Jennings wants to tell it to the world."

Magnussen started chuckling. "I can't wait to see you try to convince the court that the *Roosevelt* was infested by men from Mars."

"Thanks for your sympathy," said Becker.

"I can't help it!" laughed Magnussen. "*Aliens!* Have you seen the medical reports?"

"Yes."

"I'm dying to hear you get up in court and explain how aliens wound up with fingerprints identical to Greenberg and Provost!"

"I can hardly wait."

"God, what I'd give to get him on the stand!"

"How much would you give?" asked Becker.

"What are you talking about?" asked Magnussen, confused.

"Ten bucks and he's yours," said Becker, holding out his hand.

"You're not serious!" said Magnussen incredulously. "You're going to let him testify?"

"Let's say, rather, that I can't stop him."

"This is too good to be true! Jesus, Max, give me six months to set up my practice and you can come in as a partner. I'll owe you that much."

"I may not be able to wait six months once this fiasco is over."

"I can't believe it!" continued Magnussen. "He's actually going to testify that he thought he was killing aliens?"

"Right," said Becker. "Now, if you can control your elation for a minute, I've got a serious question."

"Go ahead."

"What do we do about it?"

"What do you mean?"

"If he pleads innocent, all they can do is convict or acquit," said Becker. "If they convict, he's going to get the death sentence. You and I both know he's as crazy as a loon—so how do we save him from the firing squad and get him committed to an asylum?"

"It shouldn't be a problem. As prosecutor, I can request a commutation of sentence and ask that he be remanded to the proper facility for psychiatric treatment."

"Are you sure there'll be enough time?" asked Becker. "The court is going to be under considerable pressure to execute him immediately."

"Nonsense," said Magnussen. "Once his story gets out, everyone will *know* he's crazy."

"I hope so," said Becker. "In the meantime, I still hope I can get him to change his mind."

"About what?"

"About pleading insanity."

"How do you convince a crazy man that he's crazy?" asked Magnussen with a smile.

"I try to put together a case for not guilty, reporting back to him every step of the way, and when he sees that it'll be laughed out of court, maybe he'll opt for free medical treatment and a pension."

"And if he doesn't?"

"Then I go to court and try to convince you that we've been infiltrated by aliens who look and sound exactly like men."

"I'll look forward to it."

"Personally, I'd rather have my teeth drilled."

*   *   *

By noon, Becker had been on the vidphone to Cornell, Stanford, and the University of Chicago. Cornell and Stanford thought the odds against an alien being able to pass for a human were in the neighborhood of five billion to one. The University of Chicago thought the odds were so high that they couldn't be computed.

He had a quick lunch, then returned to Bethesda, where he requested copies of the autopsy reports on Greenberg and Provost.

The Department of Forensic Medicine kept him waiting in the outer office for an hour, then transferred him to the Public Information Division. He spent another twenty minutes there, then was sent to the pathology laboratory, which wasn't expecting him, didn't quite know what to do with him, and finally sent him to see Juan Maria Greco, a tall, dark, ascetic civilian who was in charge of all problems that couldn't be handled at a lower level.

"Major Becker, is it?" he asked when Becker entered his plush, elegant office.

"Right."

"Won't you please have a seat, Major?" said Greco. "Can my secretary bring you anything to drink?"

Becker shook his head. "I've spent the past three hours trying to get my hands on the autopsy reports for Greenberg and Provost. If you'll just give me copies of them, I'll be on my way."

"Copies of the autopsy reports?"

"That's right."

"We seem to have a minor problem here," said Greco.

"You seem to have a *major* problem," Becker corrected him. "I've been all over the damned hospital, and nobody seems to know who has the reports."

"In point of fact, no postmortems were ever performed on either Greenberg or Provost."

"Even though they'd been murdered?" said Becker. "I find that difficult to believe."

"It *is* most irregular," agreed Greco. "But as there were witnesses to the murders, the ship's Chief Medical Officer thought it unnecessary."

"Isn't that against regulations?"

Greco shrugged and smiled a tight little smile. "There are no regulations concerning murder aboard a starship, Major."

"Come on," said Becker irritably. "The military has regulations for everything."

"Not for that, I'm afraid," said Greco. "Why are you so interested in autopsy reports, Major?"

"I'm a lawyer. My client is Commander Wilbur Jennings— and a large part of his defense rests on the postmortems of those two crewmen."

"Really?" said Greco, his face suddenly alive with curiosity. "I wonder why?"

"Come to the trial and you'll find out," said Becker. "In the meantime, it's essential to our case that the bodies be examined by a competent doctor." He paused. "Is there any reason why an autopsy can't be performed now, if I were to get a court order to exhume the bodies?"

"There's an excellent reason," said Greco. "They were jettisoned into space."

"Why?"

"That *is* a regulation, Major. A starship has no excess storage capacity."

"So you're saying that a murder was committed—two murders, in fact—and not only weren't autopsies performed, but also that the bodies were immediately disposed of?"

"You make it sound like some deep, dark conspiracy," said Greco. "The simple fact is that two crewmen were murdered in cold blood in front of several witnesses, the examining medical officer gave them a perfunctory examination—which included, I believe, taking their fingerprints and their weights at the time of death—and their bodies were jettisoned in accordance with regulations."

"And no action was taken against the Chief Medical Officer?"

"There's nothing in the record to indicate that any action *should* have been taken. But now that you have brought the matter to my attention, I will look into the possibility of officially reprimanding him for not performing thorough postmortems on the two deceased crewmen."

"I can't tell you how gratifying I find that," said Becker irritably.

"I'm sorry, Major Becker, but please do not mistake the bearer of unfortunate information for the creator of it. I am merely reporting what I know." He paused. "Would you like a copy of the fingerprints and the death weights?"

"I've got them."

"Then have we anything else to discuss?"

Becker glared at him, couldn't think of another thing to say, and stalked out of the office. It was a good thing, he decided, that he was just going through the motions to show Jennings how hopeless it was to plead innocent: he might go as crazy as Jennings if he actually had to build a defense.

"It may work to our advantage in the long run," concluded Becker, summing up his conversation with Juan Maria Greco.

"How can the fact that the bodies were jettisoned work to our advantage?" asked Jennings dubiously.

"Because now they can't be used as evidence against you," explained Becker, sitting on the edge of Jennings' bed while the former commander of the *Roosevelt* leaned against a sterile white wall.

"They never could," said Jennings patiently. "I told you:

any thorough examination would have shown that they were aliens."

"I know what you told me, sir," said Becker. "But if you were wrong, the autopsy reports would have condemned you. Now it's just your word against Gillette's. If I can break him down, show him to be incompetent, get him to lose control of himself, then you've got a chance. A small one," he added, "but a chance."

"He's *not* incompetent," responded Jennings firmly. "He's highly competent. He's one of *them*, and when he saw what I had done, he realized that he had to get rid of the bodies before anyone could examine them too closely. He couldn't take the chance that another medic might be looking over his shoulder while he performed the autopsies."

"Look," said Becker, trying to keep the exasperation out of his voice, "it would be asking too much for Gillette to admit that he's an alien, even if he is. But he screwed up by not performing the autopsies. I'd like to be able to show that he messed up his other duties so much that you became suspicious of him."

"But it was Greenberg and Provost I first suspected."

"I know—but they're dead and he's alive. He's the weakest link in the prosecution's chain of evidence. He's also the *only* link we can attack." Becker pulled out a miniaturized audio recorder. "I want you to tell me everything you can about him."

"Where shall I begin?" asked Jennings.

"Anywhere you want."

"His name is Franklin Gillette; he's about six feet two, and—"

"I can get that stuff off his service record," interrupted Becker. "What is he *like*? What turns him on? What makes him mad? What does he think of the military? Does he drink too much? Who did he associate with on the *Roosevelt*?"

"He always kept pretty much to himself," answered Jennings. "With a crew of more than two hundred operating in zero gravity, we always had at least half a dozen men in the sick bay at any given time. He took most of his meals there."

"When he came out of the sick bay, who did he spend his time with?"

Jennings shrugged helplessly. "I don't know."

"Why not?" demanded Becker. "You thought he was an alien, didn't you?"

"Not until he examined the bodies and didn't report that *they* were aliens," repeated Jennings.

"Did he have much of a temper?"

"Not that I recall."

Becker grimaced. "This is getting us nowhere. Let's try a different approach. He examined the crew every week, right?"

"Yes."

"That's because they were subjected to zero gravity on a prolonged deep-space mission?"

"That's right."

"Okay. Who examined *him*?"

"I don't know."

"Someone must have," persisted Becker. "With as many sick crewmen as you had, it wouldn't do to have a sick doctor."

"There were other doctors aboard the *Roosevelt*," said Jennings. "Doubtless one of them examined him."

"How many other doctors?"

"Two."

"Then why do you think he and he alone was an alien?"

"Because he was the one who examined the bodies."

"Did he ever get into an argument with either of the other doctors?" asked Becker.

"I'd have no way of knowing."

"Is he married? Does he have a family?"

"I believe he once told me he was a widower, and that he didn't have any children."

"Did he ever mention his family?"

"I just told you: he didn't have one."

"I mean brothers and sisters, or maybe his parents?"

"No. Whenever we spoke, it was strictly about ship's business."

"Did you ever expressly discuss Greenberg or Provost with him?"

"No."

"Why not? If you suspected they were aliens, wouldn't the Chief Medical Officer be the most likely person to consult?"

"They were just suspicions. They would have sounded ridiculous if I had voiced them."

"Did you ever go to the sick bay to find their health records, just to satisfy your own curiosity?"

"I wouldn't have had to. All medical records were kept in the ship's computer."

"And as commander of the *Roosevelt,* you had access to them." Becker paused. "You suspected that these two men were aliens. Why didn't you try to access their physical readouts?"

"I assumed that if they had abnormal readings, it would have been reported to me," said Jennings. "Of course, that was before I realized that Gillette was one of them."

"All right. You killed the two men and tried to arrest Gillette. Why didn't you access the records *then,* if for no other reason than to justify your actions to yourself?"

"I *did* access them, just before relinquishing command."

"And?"

"What do you expect?" retorted Jennings. "I keep telling you that he was one of them."

"In other words, the records showed them to be perfectly normal human beings."

"He falsified his reports."

"Did any other doctor ever examine Greenberg or Provost?"

"Not to my knowledge."

"Good. Then once we get into court, my first job will be

to make Gillette look crazier than Magnussen makes *you* look."

"Thanks," said Jennings wryly.

"If you want me to start lying to you, just say the word," replied Becker.

"I apologize," said Jennings. "I realize that you're doing your best to help me. But I won't win my case by having you make Gillette look like a madman. I'll win it by convincing the court that my actions were correct under the circumstances."

"You don't object to my trying to discredit the prosecution's witnesses, do you?"

"Not at all. But eventually it will depend on what I say on my own behalf."

"I read your notebook, and frankly, it won't convince anyone. It's all suppositions and suspicions and conclusions—but there isn't any *proof* in it."

"I'm sorry you don't believe me," said Jennings sincerely.

"I'm being paid to defend you, not believe you," replied Becker. "Which means that my next step is to take Gillette's deposition. I don't suppose you know where he lives?"

"Somewhere out west," answered Jennings. "Wyoming, Colorado, somewhere out there."

"Well, let's hope that he hasn't been reassigned yet. Maybe I can catch him at home and get this done over the vidphone. If it looks promising, I'll subpoena him."

"He wouldn't have been reassigned," replied Jennings. "It's standard operating procedure for deep-space crews to serve a minimum of six months on Earth when they return from a mission. Their bodies need that long to readjust, and the Psychology Department also insists on it."

"All right," said Becker, rising to his feet and deactivating his recorder. "I'll check back with you after I've spoken to him, and let you know where we stand."

He walked to the door, waited for it to slide into the wall, and then followed his armed escort to the elevator.

*   *   *

Becker suspected something was wrong when he called Information and found out that Gillette's vidphone had been disconnected. After a futile five minutes trying to trace him through the vidphone company, he activated his computer and tied in to the space program's duty roster.

Please transmit current whereabouts of Franklin Gillette, formerly Chief Medical Officer aboard the Theodore Roosevelt.

The machine hummed and whirred for almost a full minute, and then flashed its message across the screen.

GILLETTE, FRANKLIN WILLIAM, M.D., CHIEF MEDICAL OFFICER ABOARD THE STARSHIP *MARTIN LUTHER KING*. TOUR OF DUTY TO END JUNE 22, 2066.

He stared at the answer for a moment, then asked his next question.

How long was Franklin William Gillette on Earth before being reassigned from the Roosevelt *to the* King?

The computer answered much more rapidly this time.

ELEVEN DAYS.

He began typing again.

Isn't reassignment in less than six months an unusual procedure?

The computer spat out a quick reply:

I POSSESS INSUFFICIENT DATA TO ANSWER THAT QUESTION.

He typed one last question.

Who issued the order reassigning Franklin William Gillette to the King?

The answer came back immediately.

CLASSIFIED.

Becker frowned. He was still frowning long after the message had disappeared from the computer screen.

|4|

Becker knocked on the frame of the open doorway.

"Yes, Major?" said the general, looking up. "What can I do for you?"

"I need to discuss a potential problem with you, sir," said Becker.

"Other than your client's story?" asked the general wryly.

"Yes, sir. It concerns Franklin William Gillette."

"Never heard of him."

"He was Chief Medical Officer aboard the *Roosevelt*, sir," said Becker.

The general frowned. "The name still means nothing to me. What's your problem, Major?"

"My problem is that I may need him as a witness."

"You don't need *my* permission to subpoena him."

"It's not quite that simple, sir," said Becker. "May I sit down?"

"Certainly," said the general, indicating the chair across from his desk. "Can I offer you a drink?"

"No, thank you, sir."

"Cigar?"

Becker shook his head.

"All right, Major," said the general, leaning back and pressing his fingertips together. "You say things aren't as simple as they seem. That's usually the case in the military. Why do you need this Gillette as a witness?"

"I didn't say I needed him, sir," replied Becker carefully. "I said I *might* need him."

"Why?"

"He jettisoned the murdered men into space without performing an autopsy."

"Was there any question about the cause of their deaths?" asked the general. "It's my understanding that there were more than a dozen witnesses."

"No, sir, there was no question about the cause of their deaths."

"Well, then?"

Becker shifted uneasily in his chair. "There is some question concerning their identities, sir."

"Jennings still claims they were aliens?"

"Yes, sir."

"I thought we agreed that you were going to get him to change his story."

"*You* and *I* agreed to it, General," said Becker. "So far Jennings hasn't agreed."

The general frowned. "I see."

"And if I'm to defend him," continued Becker, "I may need to subpoena Chief Medical Officer Gillette."

"So you said." The general took a puff of his cigar. "Well, go ahead and subpoena him if you wish. I don't see what the problem is."

"He's currently aboard the *Martin Luther King*."

"Impossible."

Becker got to his feet and approached the general's computer. "May I?"

"Be my guest."

He requested Gillette's current whereabouts and received the same answer that he had gotten from his own computer.

"That's highly irregular," said the general at last.

"You see my problem, sir," said Becker. "Right now Gillette is somewhere between Uranus and Neptune. Even if the *King* were ordered to return to base immediately, we would have to postpone the trial . . . and the cost would be prohibitive."

"True," said the general. He stared at his cigar for a moment, then looked up. "I don't suppose there's any reason why we can't contact the *King* by radio and let you take his deposition."

Becker shook his head. "I don't need his deposition. I need his *testimony*, in front of the court."

"I see no reason why the court shouldn't agree to let you question him via radio."

"He will almost certainly be a hostile witness, sir. I can't cross-examine him with a lag time of twenty minutes between each question and answer."

"Then you'll have to go to trial without him," said the general firmly.

"I can't do that, sir," said Becker.

"I'm not going to spend tens of millions of the taxpayers' dollars recalling a ship to provide you with a witness who is certainly going to testify that Crewmen Greenberg and Provost were human beings."

"Then can we postpone the trial until the *King* completes its mission?"

The general shook his head vigorously. "The *King* won't be back in port for more than a year, and the press is already hinting that we're trying to protect Jennings because he's one of our own. I won't allow the trial to be postponed for that long. It goes ahead as scheduled."

"I'll have to file a protest."

"You do that, if it'll make you feel any better. Hell, that's just what I'd do in your place. I'd petition for a postponement, and a change of venue, and a mistrial, and everything else I could think of—and nobody will blame you for doing the same thing." The general paused, and his face hardened.

"But Jennings goes to trial a week from Tuesday, and nothing's going to prevent or delay it."

Becker sat motionless for a moment, then leaned forward. "I have another question, sir," he said at last.

"About the trial?"

"About Gillette."

"What about him?"

"Why would he be reassigned to the *King* when it's standard procedure for space-going personnel to spend at least six months on Earth between missions?"

"Perhaps they needed another medical officer."

"Perhaps they did," agreed Becker. "But why would that be classified?"

"Classified?" repeated the general. "I don't think I understand you."

"When I asked the computer to tell me who reassigned Gillette, it replied that the answer was classified."

The general shrugged. "Probably it was just some officer protecting his tail for ordering Gillette back into space too soon."

"There has to be a very small number of officers who were in a position to issue that order," said Becker. "Can you find out who it was?"

"Perhaps. Why?"

"As of this moment, Gillette is my only witness. If someone is trying to get him out of reach before the trial, I want to know who's doing it and why."

The general snorted derisively. "You've been talking to Jennings too much, Major. You're starting to sound like *you* think there were aliens aboard the *Roosevelt.*"

"No, sir, I don't," replied Becker. "But I do think there were irregularities. Two dead men were jettisoned into space without an autopsy, and the presiding medical officer, who should be spending the next five months being debriefed and relaxing at his home in Wyoming, was reassigned to deep-space duty eleven days after the *Roosevelt* landed."

"I doubt that there's any connection whatsoever."

"So do I," admitted Becker. "But I've got to start somewhere, and Gillette's all I've got."

"Well, I'll do what I can," said the general, getting to his feet and waiting for Becker to do the same. "But I can almost guarantee that he was reassigned because the *King* needed a chief medical officer in a hurry." He escorted Becker to the door. "I'll let you know what I find out."

"Thank you, sir," said Becker, even as some inner voice told him that he wouldn't hear from the general again unless he himself initiated the contact.

Alone in his office, Becker activated his computer once more.

How many senior medical officers are fully qualified for deep-space duty?

The computer took almost a full minute to answer.

23.

He typed in his next question:

How many that have been stationed on Earth for more than six months are currently available for deep-space duty?

The answer came much more rapidly this time:

7.

Somehow he wasn't surprised.

"Well?" Jennings asked as the door to his cell closed behind Becker. "Did you locate him?"

"Yes and no."

"What do you mean?" demanded Jennings, getting to his feet.

"It's a long story," replied Becker, walking over to a chair and sitting down heavily. He sighed deeply. "Why the hell couldn't you have thought they were Russian spies? I could almost buy that story after this morning."

"They've gotten to Gillette," said Jennings with certainty.

Becker nodded.

"Dead?" asked Jennings.

"He might as well be, for all the use he'll be to our case," answered Becker. "They gave him another deep-space mission eleven days after the *Roosevelt* landed. He's already out beyond Uranus."

"I knew it," muttered Jennings. "Which ship is he on?"

"The *King*. I checked the available duty rosters, and there were seven able-bodied medical officers who should have been assigned to the *King* before they picked Gillette." He lit up a small cigar. "Someone's breaking a lot of rules to make sure I can't build a defense for you." He grimaced. "I could even buy Brazilian spies. Why the hell did it have to be *aliens*?"

"I didn't choose them," replied Jennings.

Becker paused, trying futilely to find a connection.

"I have a question," he said at last. "Gillette's not supposed to go into deep space again for months. How will that affect him physically?"

"I don't know. Some muscle atrophy, I suppose, and perhaps some cardiovascular problems. I'm not a medic."

"But he won't die?"

"Probably not. Some Chinese have spent four years in space."

"So if he's still alive when the *King* returns from its mission, that wouldn't prove anything, would it?"

"Like what?"

"Like he was an alien," responded Becker, feeling slightly ridiculous as the words left his mouth.

"No."

"Then we're up against a brick wall. I've been given permission to take his deposition by radio, but I can't put him on the stand. They won't recall him, they won't postpone the trial, and by your own admission his surviving the trip won't prove that he's anything except what he's supposed to be." Becker stared at his client. "I'm a damned good lawyer, but I'm running out of ideas."

"I won't plead insanity," said Jennings adamantly. "I want my day in court. I've *got* to make them understand."

"You can *have* your day in court," said Becker. "But if you plead not guilty and lose, you're going to face a firing squad, and as of this moment there's not a thing I can do to prevent it." He paused. "Gillette wasn't just our best bet; he was our *only* bet."

"There must be something else."

"There's always temporary insanity."

"No!"

"All right. I won't bring it up again." Becker paused. *"This* visit."

"Any visit," replied Jennings. "I'm as sane as you are. The only difference between us is that I realize there is a threat to our security, and you don't."

"I just wish there was one other man in the whole damned space program who could corroborate it."

"There is."

"Oh?" said Becker sharply. "Who?"

"The man who reassigned Gillette to the *Martin Luther King.*"

Becker relaxed again. "You find him and I'll cross-examine him."

"You're supposed to be my lawyer," snapped Jennings irritably. *"You* find him."

"I'll try," answered Becker, "but if the military wants to keep his name a secret, it could take months. You've got less than two weeks."

Jennings sighed. "It's not your fault," he said at last. "If we even came close to finding him, he'd disappear or be reassigned, just like Gillette."

"Nobody's reassigning *me,*" noted Becker. "And I've asked to be reassigned."

"That's because *you* don't know the truth," said Jennings.

"Who does, besides you and Gillette and the guy who re-assigned him?"

"Somebody must. Greenberg and Provost and Gillette didn't all get on the *Roosevelt* by chance."

"Who *might* know, other than those conspirators whose job is to keep everything hushed up?"

Jennings shrugged. "I don't know."

"Any other starship captains?"

"I doubt it."

"Why?"

"If they had realized what's going on, I wouldn't be the only captain awaiting trial." He paused and stared thoughtfully at Becker. "You know, I just can't understand you, Major."

"Me?" said Becker, surprised.

"You've read my notebook, you've seen them manipulate Gillette out of your reach, you keep making reasonable demands and getting unreasonable responses—and you still don't believe me."

"I believe someone doesn't want Gillette to testify, and I believe he should have performed an autopsy. That does not automatically lead me to conclude that we've got a plague of look-alike aliens on our hands." He paused. "The most obvious answer is that someone's trying to manipulate this so that the service doesn't get a black eye. After all, we've got a captain who killed two crew members in cold blood, and a medic who didn't bother to perform an autopsy, and who knows what else might come to light if I dig deep enough? Put enough scandal in the headlines and Congress might decide to kill the deep-space program. After all, there are other nations out there looking for aliens; they don't really need our help." He paused. "Anyway, that's my analysis."

Jennings lit a cigarette and both of them fell silent for a few minutes. The starship commander was the first to speak.

"I hope to hell you're thinking and not daydreaming."

"I'm thinking," Becker assured him.

"And?"

Becker shrugged. "Nothing's coming." He snuffed out his cigar and lit another. "It's as simple as this: you have perhaps the most farfetched justification for your actions that anyone has ever heard of. If we can't find someone to corroborate the facts, nightclub comics will be incorporating your testimony into their routines. We had one person who *might* have been able to help us. He'd have been a hostile witness, and the odds are that I couldn't have broken him down, but at least he was in the right place at the right time. If we can't come up with somebody else, they're going to find you insane no matter what you plead, and if you're lucky they're going to lock you away for the rest of your life instead of shooting you. Is that blunt enough for you?"

"Yes."

"Then help me come up with the name of just one other person who might have reason to think that there were aliens aboard the *Roosevelt.*"

"There isn't anyone."

"You never mentioned your suspicions?"

"No," said Jennings wearily. "As I told you, I skirted the subject with a couple of my officers, but I never actually said what I thought."

"Tell me what you mean by the word 'skirted.'"

"I asked them if they had noticed anything unusual in Greenberg's or Provost's behavior."

"And they said?"

"They were noncommittal."

"Who were these officers?"

"Mallardi and Montoya."

"Ranks?"

"They were both lieutenants, and neither was in the habit of contradicting me. They each mumbled something about how space makes some crewmen behave a little strangely, and I didn't follow up on it."

"Do you know if either of them took it upon himself to

monitor Greenberg's or Provost's behavior after you spoke to them?"

"No."

"Would it have been likely?" persisted Becker. "After all, there's not really all that much for nonscientific personnel to do on a deep-space mission, and they may have been trying to find ways to ingratiate themselves with you."

"It's possible," admitted Jennings. He considered the proposition, then nodded his head vigorously. "Yes, it's quite possible!"

"All right," said Becker. "Don't get your hopes up, because the odds are that they're going to tell me that Greenberg and Provost were perfectly normal human beings, but at least I've got another line to follow now."

He got to his feet and walked to the door, then turned back to Jennings.

"I just wish I knew why I have this feeling that both of them are aboard the *King*."

Three hours later, he still didn't know where the two officers were, and he was getting tired of running into one dead end after another. There had been no further classified restrictions; his computer simply could not find a single source that knew where Mallardi and Montoya were.

Finally he called Magnussen on the vidphone.

"Hi, Max," said the attorney, looking up from his own computer screen. "What can I do for you?"

"I'm not sure," replied Becker. "But something funny is going on."

"Does this concern the Jennings case?"

"Yes."

"Why not come on over to my office and we'll discuss it over a drink?"

Becker shook his head. "I don't want a drink, Jim. I want some answers."

The cordial smile vanished from Magnussen's face. "You sound serious."

"I am," said Becker. He paused. "Look, I know the military wants this thing packaged nice and neat, but they've gone too damned far."

"I don't think I understand."

"They hand me a madman and give me less than two weeks to prepare a case. Okay, I can understand their wanting to expedite matters. They won't let me off the case. Okay, I wave my Harvard degree around a little too much, and I've made some enemies who'd like to see me lose a big one. I can live with all that. But I'm grasping at straws to build a defense, and I resent it when they start fucking with my straws."

"What are you talking about, Max?"

"Someone is getting to my witnesses."

"I didn't know you had any witnesses."

"I don't."

"I'm a little confused," said Magnussen. "How can anyone tamper with your witnesses if you don't have any?"

"I didn't say they're tampering with them."

Magnussen smiled uncertainly. "Now I'm totally confused."

"Damn it, Jim! Every time I come up with a potential witness, someone moves him out of reach."

"Out of reach?" repeated Magnussen. "Explain yourself, please."

"I need the *Roosevelt*'s Chief Medical Officer, a man named Gillette. Do you know where he is?"

"No."

"Halfway between Uranus and Neptune!"

Magnussen frowned. "Have you told the general that Gillette's in deep space?"

"Of course I told him!"

"And?"

"He claims it's most irregular, he sympathizes with me,

and he won't lift a finger to get him back—and he won't let me ask for a postponement."

Magnussen stared into the camera. "You've got to believe me, Max—I knew nothing about this. If you want a postponement, I'll back your request for it."

"It won't do a bit of good and we both know it," said Becker. "The military wants its pound of flesh, and they want it quick."

Magnussen was silent for a moment, then spoke again. "You mentioned witnesses. Was there another?"

"Two more: Lieutenant James Mallardi and Lieutenant Anthony Montoya."

"Are they on deep-space missions too?"

"I don't know," said Becker. "I can't find out a damned thing about them."

"That's ridiculous, Max. Nobody in the military is unfindable."

"These two are."

"They may not be on any active-duty rosters, but—"

"Damn it, Jim, I know how to work a computer!"

Magnussen paused thoughtfully. "And they're important to your case?"

"How the hell do I know until I can talk to them?"

"I see," said Magnussen. He paused again. "Okay, Max—I think that we just came to the operative question: why are you telling *me* about all this?"

"Because *I* can't get any answers."

"What makes you think *I* can?"

Becker stared directly into the vidphone camera. "Because you represent the side that's hiding these guys." He paused again. "Jim, I want you to tell your people that if somebody doesn't find these two men for me by tomorrow morning, I'm going to the press and scream *Cover-up*! I really mean it."

"Why not tell them yourself? They're *your* people too, you know."

"Not in this instance, they aren't. They really *are* covering something up, you know."

"What?"

"I don't know," said Becker. "Maybe Greenberg and Provost were buying drugs from Gillette, and they're trying to hush it up. Maybe one or the other really *was* a Russian spy, even if Jennings didn't know it. Maybe Gillette flunked his medical boards and bought his degree. I don't know what they're covering up, and as long as I can present my case, I don't much care—but if they keep interfering with me, I damned well intend to find out."

"You're imagining things, Max."

"The hell I am!" said Becker hotly. "They've tied my hands in every way they can. In fact, the second I hang up I'm going someplace where they can't find me and order me not to speak to the press. I'll call you back in four hours."

"Max, that's hardly necessary."

"I think it is. Now, are you going to do what I ask, or not?"

"Why do you insist on involving *me* in this?" complained Magnussen. "I'm the prosecuting attorney, for Christ's sake."

"Because I think you're an honest man."

"Thanks a lot," said Magnussen grimly.

"Say you won't help me and I'll change my mind."

Magnussen was silent for a long moment. Finally he spoke: "Four hours, you say?"

"More or less."

"And their names are Mallardi and Montoya?"

"Right," said Becker.

"All right, Max," said Magnussen. "I'll do it."

"Thanks. And good luck."

"Oh, I'll get your answers, all right," said Magnussen. "Who in the hell is going to endanger his career over a nut case who thinks he's saved his planet by killing a couple of aliens that look just like us?"

"That's the part that's driving me crazy," admitted Becker.

"I'll pass the word and see what happens," promised Magnussen.

"You just might be surprised," said Becker.

But not as surprised as I'll be if either of them is still on Earth, he concluded silently.

|5|

Becker sat in the back of the nondescript roadside bar, halfway between the pool table and the holographic game machines, nursing his beer and sorting out the facts that he had managed to obtain. His own taste in taverns was more upscale, but he had chosen this particular bar precisely because he had never frequented it before.

Though I don't know why I'm being so secretive, he thought. So what if Jim Magnussen knows where I am? So what if he tells somebody? What's the worst they could do to me—kill me?

He shook his head vigorously. *Now you're thinking like Jennings,* he told himself irritably. Listen to a madman long enough and some of it starts rubbing off on you.

No, there were no aliens aboard any spaceships, and Jennings was less than two weeks away from being permanently reassigned to a nice, pleasant, green place in the country, where his every need would be catered to, and maybe someday some doctor might even cure him.

But *someone* was hiding *something.* Why else would Gillette have been transferred to the *King* after only eleven days? Why hadn't he performed the autopsies? Why wouldn't anyone talk about Mallardi and Montoya? These men weren't aliens, and they weren't spies; they were officers in the United States Space Agency.

Becker stared down at his beer. It just didn't make any sense. Insanity was the verdict they wanted; insanity was the only verdict they could possibly get. Hell, even if Gillette got up on the stand and corroborated Jennings' story, all it meant was that the court would lock *both* of them away. So why were they trying to prevent him from building his case? It could only make him look incompetent; it couldn't possibly alter the verdict. If there was some area they didn't want touched, all they had to do was tell him so. He was loyal to the service; he wasn't going to be the man to bring it down because of some scandal.

Unless they forced him to.

Which brought him full circle. They weren't stupid men, his unseen opponents. *Why* were they forcing him to grasp at straws? Why didn't they just give him his witnesses and be done with it?

He checked his timepiece, for perhaps the fiftieth time. Another hour, and then he would call Magnussen.

And Magnussen would tell him that Mallardi and Montoya were on the *Martin Luther King,* and before long he'd be as crazy as Jennings, just from the effort of trying to make sense out of what was happening.

He grimaced, finished his beer, and ordered another. While waiting for it to arrive, he activated the tiny video monitor in his table and spent the next few minutes trying to work up some interest in the soccer game that was being broadcast from Uruguay.

"That's a rerun, hon," the waitress informed him as she set his new beer down on the table next to the monitor. "Brazil won it, eight to three."

"Thanks."

"You expecting someone?"

He shook his head.

"I just asked, because you've been here a long time, and you keep checking your watch."

"No, just killing time."

"Fight with your missus?" she asked with a knowing smile.

"No, just with the United States Government," he replied, returning her smile.

"Tax people," she said, nodding her head. "We ought to shoot 'em all." Suddenly she stared sharply at him. "You got enough to pay your tab?"

He withdrew a large bill and laid it on the table next to him, covering most of the monitor with it.

"No offense intended," said the waitress. "You just go back to killing time."

"To hell with it," he said. "Have you got a pay phone here?"

"Vidphone's on the fritz, but we've got an old talkie in the back. No charge if it's local."

"Where is it?" he asked, getting to his feet.

"Follow me," she said, leading him behind the bar to a storeroom filled with cases of liquor. "Right here," she said, pointing to a telephone.

"Thanks," said Becker, pulling out another bill and handing it to her.

"I told you," she said, "there's no charge if it's local."

"It's also private," he said, holding the money out to her.

She took it and left the storeroom without another word.

It had been a few years since Becker had used a telephone, but he still remembered how to log onto the vidphone grid, and a moment later he heard Magnussen's voice.

"Hello?"

"Hi, Jim. It's Max."

"We've got a bad connection," said Magnussen. "I can't see you."

"I'm not using a vidphone."

There was a brief pause.

"Are you sure all this secrecy's necessary?"

"I'm not being secretive," answered Becker. "I'm being practical. The nearest vidphone is half a mile away."

Magnussen's answer was a noncommittal "Oh."

"Did you get the information I need?"

"Yes and no."

"What does *that* mean?"

"Yes on Mallardi, no on Montoya."

"Amazing how quickly they gave it to you once I threatened to go the press, isn't it?" said Becker wryly. "Where's Mallardi?"

"This is going to sound crazy, Max. . . ."

"Mallardi's aboard the *King,* right?"

"No, but for all practical purposes, he might as well be."

"Explain."

"He was just transferred to Mars Base this afternoon. His ship took off about two hours ago."

"Can we divert it or order it back to base?"

"Not a chance, Max. He's on some hush-hush security project. He can't be contacted until it's over."

"Does he have any background in security?" demanded Becker sharply.

"How the hell should I know?"

"Check his military record and his personal dossier. I'll lay ten to one that this is his first security assignment."

"All right," said Magnussen. "I'll do that." He laughed nervously. "Hell, Max, you've even got *me* half believing this conspiracy bullshit."

"What about Montoya?"

"Classified. I couldn't find out a thing."

"Then I want you to go back to them and tell them that I—"

"Hold it, Max," interrupted Magnussen. "You asked for a favor; you got one. I'm not about to become your errand boy."

"All right, Jim," said Becker. "You helped me out, and I'm grateful. Now let me repay you."

"How?"

"Have Jennings transferred to another level of Bethesda—or better still, put him in a private clinic."

"Why?"

"Because he never mentioned Mallardi or Montoya's names until today—and suddenly one of them is being sent to Mars and the other's hidden under a mountain of red tape."

"If you're implying that they've got a bug in his room, that's no secret," said Magnussen. "He's under constant surveillance."

"I *know* there's a bug in his room," replied Becker. "And whoever's at the other end of it doesn't want me to speak to anyone who might corroborate any facet of Jennings' story."

"That's awfully farfetched, Max."

"So is sending a doctor back into deep space after eleven days on Earth, or sending a junior officer to Mars on some security project less than half a day after his name first comes up."

"Maybe it's just a coincidence," said Magnussen.

"Do you really think so?"

"No," admitted Magnussen. "Even *I* can't buy it." He paused, and this time he sounded truly worried. "Just what the hell have you gotten into, Max?"

"I don't know," replied Becker grimly, "but it's more than some spaceship captain who went a little loony and killed a couple of crewmen."

"Maybe we'd better sit down and talk about this face-to-face," said Magnussen.

"Not now."

"Why not?"

"First, if they've tapped your phone and we arrange a meeting, they'll know where I'm going to show up."

"So what?"

"I need some time to find Montoya before a superior officer orders me not to."

"You had a second reason?"

"To be perfectly honest, I'm not sure that you aren't one of them."

"One of *whom*, for God's sake?" demanded Magnussen. "Are you honestly accusing me of being an alien?"

"I don't believe in aliens," responded Becker. "But I do believe that some person or group of people is trying to hamper my preparation of this case."

"Not me!" snapped Magnussen irately. "I got you the information on Mallardi, didn't I?"

"Yes, you did," admitted Becker.

"Well, then?"

"I still can't meet with you until I've found Montoya."

"He could be anywhere: on Earth, on Mars, on Ganymede, aboard the *King* . . ."

"He's on Earth," said Becker with certainty. "If he was where I couldn't reach him, they'd have told you."

"All right. Say, for the sake of argument, that he's on Earth. Where do you begin looking for him? It's a pretty big planet."

"I don't know," lied Becker, suddenly grateful that the vidphone was broken so that Magnussen couldn't see his face.

"All right," said Magnussen. "I want you to keep in touch with me."

"Not at your office."

"Then how?"

"Give Karla a secure number, and a time when I can call you."

"If my office isn't secure, then neither is my home," said Magnussen.

"Right."

"Then how do I come up with a secure number?"

"You'll figure it out."

"How soon can we meet in person?"

"As soon as I talk to Montoya and find out what this is all about."

"Good luck."

"Thanks," said Becker, signing off. "I have a feeling that I'll need it."

Becker left the bar and took a cab to D Street, then began walking through the maze of dilapidated buildings until he found the one he sought.

There was an elevator, but it hadn't been working for years. He felt very uneasy about using the stairs, especially since most of the lights had been shot out, but there was no other choice, and after pausing a moment to see if he could hear anyone above him on the staircase, he took a deep, fatalistic breath and began climbing. Five flights later, panting for breath, he pushed open a door and walked down a long corridor, the walls covered with graffiti.

Finally he came to the door he sought, pushed the buzzer, waited a few minutes, and then knocked.

"Come in, Counselor!" shouted a feminine voice from the other side of the door. A moment later the door slid back into the wall and he was confronted by a short, wiry black woman wearing a very expensive leisure outfit.

"Hello, Jaimie," said Becker. "It's been a long time."

"Could have been longer, though. Come on in, Counselor."

Becker followed her into the elegantly furnished living room. The walls displayed a collection of truly exquisite artwork, the floor was covered by a plush white carpet, and the furniture belonged in a mansion fronting the ocean. The row of computers along the back wall was the equal of anything this side of the Pentagon.

"This is a hell of a place you have, Jaimie," said Becker.

"You approve?"

"Except for the building and the neighborhood, I do more than approve—I covet."

"Come in, Counselor," said Jaimie with an easy smile. "If I moved to Georgetown, I'd get arrested again just on general principles." She paused. "Can I get you a drink?"

"That'd be nice," replied Becker, sitting down on a leather sofa.

"You got it," said Jaimie, disappearing into the next room. "Be right back."

"How have you been, Jaimie?" asked Becker, idly inspecting the magazines strewn on the coffee table in front of him. Almost half of them were business journals; the other half were devoted to the more esoteric realms of computer technology.

"Can't complain, Counselor," said Jaimie, returning with Becker's drink.

"Glad to hear it."

"Served my year's time, though it only came to four months with good behavior. Got you to thank for that, Counselor."

"I was just doing my job."

"Uh-uh," said Jaimie adamantly. "My own lawyer was gonna cut me loose and watch me sink. You're the one who arranged my plea bargain."

"You weren't a real thief," replied Becker. "You could have transferred a couple of billion dollars to your own account if you'd wanted. Instead, you just ordered six generals to show up in an Argentine whorehouse."

"They should have thanked me," chuckled Jaimie. "Anyway," she continued, "if I needed money, there were banks galore; I know better than to rob the government. I just wanted to see how good your security was."

"Nobody ever cracked one of the Pentagon's M-117 machines until you did it. We had to find out how it was done. *That's* why we arranged to let you plea-bargain."

"I knew it wasn't because of my winning personality."

Becker smiled wryly. "In the end, they decided you were such a genius that it wasn't cost-effective to keep you out. They figured there were only five people in the whole country who could have done what you did: three of them work for Uncle Sam and one's doing life at Leavenworth for being greedier than you."

"You're gonna make me blush, Counselor," said Jaimie.

"Been back in lately?"

"Is this an official visit?" she asked.

Becker shook his head. "Just curious."

"Yeah, I snuck back in, just to see if I could do it." She grinned. "I could have transferred twenty thousand tanks to South Dakota."

"I believe it."

"I didn't, though."

"I know. I would have heard of it if you had, and you would have had two dozen MPs paying you a little visit."

"So instead of two dozen MPs, I've got one hotshot lawyer who says he's not here on official business."

"That's right," said Becker.

"Okay, Counselor—why *are* you here?"

"Do you remember the day I took you into my office and offered you a reduced sentence if you'd tell us how you did it?"

"I'm not likely to forget it."

"Do you also remember that you said you'd return the favor if the opportunity ever arose?"

"I take it that the opportunity has arisen?" asked Jaimie dryly.

"It has."

Jaimie shrugged. "No problem. Jaimie Nchobe always keeps her promises." She paused. "What can I do for you, Counselor?"

"I'm trying to find a certain lieutenant."

"Have you looked in the phone book?"

"No jokes, please."

"I wasn't joking. Usually the simplest way is the best."

"He doesn't have a listing. He's been in the space service for the past few years."

"If he's in the space service, you ought to be able to track him down with no trouble."

"He's not in the computer."

"*Everyone's* in the computer, Counselor," said Jaimie. "It's just a matter of knowing where to look."

"That why I've come to you," said Becker.

"So you just want to know where this guy is, nothing else?"

"I'd also like a look at some service records, just to see if they've been tampered with."

"No problem."

"If there was no problem, I wouldn't have come to you," said Becker. "The military is trying to cover something up."

"Sounds like the military," commented Jaimie without any show of surprise. "I know things about them that would curl your hair."

"Don't tell me," said Becker. "What I don't know, I can't testify to."

Jaimie grinned. "You always did play it close to the vest, Counselor." She rubbed her hands together. "All right. Let's get started."

"Can you do it from here, or do you need my computer?"

"I don't need anything from you except the names I'm after," said Jaimie. "Of course, your access number would save me a few minutes."

"Can you get what you need without it?"

"Yes."

"Then do so."

Jaimie looked amused. "Afraid I'll use it sometime in the future?"

"No," said Becker. "But I don't want my superiors to think I've managed to find out where Montoya is."

"Montoya?"

"Lieutenant Anthony Montoya—the man we're looking for."

"Not to worry, Counselor," Jaimie assured him. "I can cover up my tracks once I'm on the way out."

"You're sure?" demanded Becker.

"Is the Pope Catholic?"

"All right," said Becker. "My access number is XB2236772439Q."

"What's this Montoya done that makes you so hot to find him?"

"I don't know," replied Becker. "Probably nothing."

"If you tell me what this is all about, I can probably find him a lot quicker."

"I wish to hell I *knew* what it was all about. I just know that they're trying to keep his whereabouts a secret."

"So for all you know he could be on one of Jupiter's moons?"

"No," said Becker, "I'm pretty sure he's on Earth."

"Any reason why?"

"Just that I've got a case coming up soon, and they don't mind telling me where my witnesses are once they're so far away that I can't pull them back in time."

"They? You mean the military?"

"Right."

"Well, you just sit back and drink your drink, Counselor, because the champ is about to enter the ring. Think hard, now—is there anything you can tell me about this Montoya besides his name?"

"Only that he served aboard the *Theodore Roosevelt* until a month ago."

"The *Teddy Roosevelt*," repeated Jaimie, frowning. "Isn't that the ship that . . . ?" Suddenly she laughed aloud. "You're not defending that loony, are you?"

Becker nodded.

"I sure don't envy you," she continued. "Is this guy Montoya gonna testify that the captain was crazy?"

"I don't know what he's going to say," replied Becker. "First I've got to find him."

"It's as good as done, Counselor," said Jaimie, activating one of her machines. "Give me that access number again."

"XB2236772439Q."

"Got it," said Jaimie, typing it into the computer's memory. "Okay, let's roll."

"I would have thought you'd use a computer that you could speak to," commented Becker.

"This may come as a shock to you, Counselor," replied Jaimie, "but there are a lot of languages that are much more complex and powerful than English, and you need a keyboard instead of a microphone for most of them."

The computer's modem came to life, and a moment later Jaimie began hitting keys with the skill and speed of a jazz pianist.

"They don't like you, Counselor," she announced after a moment.

"I beg your pardon?"

"They're hiding things from you."

"More than Montoya's whereabouts?"

"Lots more," said Jaimie.

"Like what?"

"Don't know yet. That's what I'm going to find out." Jaimie turned back to the computer. "Okay, you sons of bitches, let's see how smart you *really* are." She broke the modem connection, then dialed a new number. A flurry of commands followed, and finally she paused again. "They're *good,* Counselor, I'll give 'em that." She hit another combination of keys. "But there ain't no one as good as Jaimie Nchobe." She paused for a moment, studying the screen. "Got it! We're in!"

"Where is he?" asked Becker.

Jaimie turned to him. "It's not that easy, Counselor. You got to be subtle. Right now I've accessed their Officer Appraisal File."

"What good does that do?"

"We'll see," said Jaimie. "There's probably thirty or forty routes to the information you want: front doors, side doors, back doors, windows, chimneys. They can't have locked all of them."

A moment later she cursed under her breath. "Smart boys you got working security, Counselor—a lot smarter than they used to be."

"You came to another locked door?"

"I came to a hell of a loop. I'm back evaluating officer candidates." She disconnected, then gave the modem further instructions and sat back while it obtained a new connection.

"Now where are you?" asked Becker, walking across the room and staring at the screen over her shoulder.

"Payroll," came the answer. "Hah! See? He's cashed his last six checks."

"Where?"

"The most recent one was in Waukegan, Illinois . . . and it was countersigned by a Lieutenant MacCarron."

"Never heard of him."

"Let's see what we can bring up on him," said Jaimie, her fingers a blur of motion. "Here we go: Edward MacCarron, twenty-eight, Caucasian, Lieutenant in the U.S. Navy, currently stationed at Great Lakes Naval Base. Graduated Annapolis in 2061, two hundred and forty-fourth in class. Injured January 3, 2065 . . . seems to have lost his thumb in an accident."

"Has he ever been in the space service?"

"No."

"Damn," muttered Becker. "Another dead end."

"You're not thinking clearly, Counselor," she corrected him. "You know almost everything you need to know."

"Oh?"

"Your boy Montoya is obviously at the Great Lakes Naval Base, and he's got someone signing his paychecks for him. Why isn't he at home, wherever home is? Why can't he cash his own checks?"

"What else have you got on this MacCarron?"

Jaimie shrugged. "Nothing much. He seems to work for hospital security."

"That's it!" exclaimed Becker. "Montoya must be in the base hospital! The space service uses Bethesda, but he'd be too easy to find if they stuck him there."

"Does it jibe with whatever other information you've got?"

"Yes, it does," said Becker excitedly. "Every other potential witness I've tried to locate has been transferred off the planet. But if Montoya has had some kind of accident or contracted some disease, he's either too weak to travel or too contagious to risk putting in a closed environment."

"Sounds logical to me," said Jaimie. "Let's see if he's using his own name."

She accessed the Great Lakes Naval Hospital and asked for a list of all current patients.

"Nope. They've got him using a phony name."

"Can you find out which one it is?"

Jaimie smiled confidently. "I've just located your missing boy in something less than half an hour. Do you really think some goddamned hospital identification system is gonna stump me?"

She turned back to the machine, rapidly typed in a set of instructions, and turned back to Becker.

"Now what?" asked Becker.

"Now we wait. I've got the computer checking every name on the list against every naval and space-going officer we can access. When it's done, we should have one name that it can't identify, and that'll be Montoya—and just to make sure they're not being tricky, once we get that name, I'll make sure that two men aren't sharing it."

"Sharing it?"

"They don't *have* to give him a phony name, you know. They can give him the name of some officer who's serving in Antarctica—or on Ganymede, for that matter."

"How long will this take?"

Jaimie shrugged. "Maybe five minutes, maybe ten. It depends how many duty lists it has to access. How about another drink?"

Becker nodded, and followed Jaimie into her kitchen, which was filled with more machines than the living room.

"Jesus!" he muttered. "I've never seen anything like this!"

"What's the good of having computers if you don't make them work for you?" responded Jaimie. She touched a spot on one of the machines. "Bourbon, please." She turned to Becker. "Do you want any ice?"

"No."

She touched the spot again. "Straight up."

An instant later two robotic arms opened a small cabinet to the left of the sink, pulled out two glasses, and suddenly extended them across the room, to where another arm had pulled out a bottle of bourbon, uncapped it, and was waiting to pour it into the glasses.

"Do you know how much money you could make designing the Kitchen of the Future?" said Becker.

"Not as much as I make robbing the banks of the present," replied Jaimie smugly.

"I don't want to hear about it."

"I don't mind telling you. After all, we're probably committing some form of treason tonight. It's not as if we don't both have secrets to keep."

"If there's any treason around, *I'm* not the one who's committing it," replied Becker heatedly. "I'm just trying to defend my client."

Jaimie shrugged. "Whatever you say, Counselor." She took the drinks from the robotic arms and handed one to Becker. "Let's go see how we're doing with that name."

She led the way back to the living room and sat down at the computer.

"Problems, Counselor."

"You can't find the one under the alias?"

"I told you I could," said Jaimie contemptuously. "Problem is that they've got six guys there under phony names. You sure you're only missing one witness?"

"One that I know of."

"Then probably the other five are just sitting around waiting for fresh identities. Spies, maybe—or maybe you're not the only lawyer the military courts are messing around with." She paused. "Anyway, I need more information to identify Montoya."

"I don't have any."

"Three of these guys are under round-the-clock guard," noted Jaimie. "It might be difficult to just walk in and ask each of them if he's Montoya."

"Hunt up his service record," suggested Becker. "There's got to be a photo, or a blood type, or something we can use."

"That was the first thing I tried," she replied. "It's been classified since this morning."

"Can't you break into it?"

"I've got to find it first."

"What do you mean, find it? Like you said—it's in the computer."

"When the military wants to hide something, they don't just restrict access to it, Counselor," explained Jaimie. "They start shuttling it around."

"I don't understand."

"Let's say they think it'll take someone like me twenty minutes to get around the restriction and access it," said Jaimie. "What they do is put it in motion. It'll be in the medical file for ten minutes, and the space file for ten minutes, and the debriefing file for ten minutes, and on and on. There's about fifty ways they can categorize an officer, from age and race and rank down to some really esoteric things like blood type and retina pattern. Your boy's file isn't just classified—it's on one hell of a ride."

"If you find it, can you access it in ten minutes?" asked Becker.

"The military bets that I can't."

"That isn't what I asked."

"Probably," said Jaimie. "But it could also be on a seven-minute transfer cycle, or a three-minute . . . or they could have some file that's so obscure only three or four guys know about it and they're hiding it there."

"So we're at a dead end?"

"Yep—but that doesn't mean we're beaten. Jaimie Nchobe knows more than one way to skin a cat."

"That's a horrible expression."

"I read it in a book somewhere," she replied with a smile. "I like it. But then, I hate cats."

"What's your next step?"

"Let's access the files on your witnesses who were transferred off-planet and see what they have in common," she suggested. "Then maybe we'll be able to find one or two Great Lakes patients who have compatible files, and we can eliminate the rest."

"Do it."

"I need their names, and anything else you can give me."

Becker offered her all the limited data he had on Gillette and Mallardi.

"One more thing, Counselor."

"What?"

"This guy Jennings—do you think he's innocent?"

"He's already admitted he killed the crewmen."

"I mean, did he have some reason, or are you just going through the motions?"

"I really don't know," Becker admitted.

"Well, if he really had a reason, let's add the two dead men to the list, just in case."

"Right," said Becker, giving Jaimie all the information he could remember about Greenberg and Provost.

"That should do it," said Jaimie at last. She began issuing instructions to her computer, alternately feeding it orders and whispering encouragement, her dark eyes glued to the screen.

"Well, now, isn't this interesting?" she said after a moment.

"What have you got?" demanded Becker.

"Your boy Gillette."

"What about him?"

"He's been in the service for twenty-one years."

"So?"

"So how come he's got bank accounts in Zurich and Brussels totaling more than twelve million dollars?"

"What?"

"You heard me, Counselor," said Jaimie. "He's been doing more than telling spacemen to turn their heads and cough."

"It's got to be drugs!" said Becker excitedly. "That's the only thing that could produce that kind of income."

"Not really," said Jaimie. "But it's the most logical thing. Let's see," she mused, hitting still more commands. "There's your connection, Counselor. Greenberg and Provost both had records as addicts before they joined the service—and Provost was a pusher, too."

"So Gillette was selling drugs to Provost and Greenberg?"

"Either that, or they were his conduits to the crew," agreed Jaimie.

"Where do Montoya and Mallardi fit in?"

Jaimie shrugged. "Don't know yet. I'll have it all pieced together in less than an hour, though."

"Can you access the records of the *Roosevelt*'s medical stores? Both when it left and when it returned?"

"Given enough time," said Jaimie. She tapped a new order into the computer. "Classified," she said happily. "We're on the right track, all right."

"Let me think for a moment," said Becker. "Gillette was selling drugs. Provost and Greenberg were either addicts or they worked for him—probably both, since he refused to perform an autopsy. Jennings went crazy and killed them, but they couldn't stand an investigation, since it would show that the ship's chief medical officer was selling drugs, and probably that a hell of a lot of the crew were shooting up." He paused. "Okay, that all makes sense. Now if we can just fit Mallardi and Montoya into the picture . . ."

"What difference does it make?" asked Jaimie. "Your client's still a murderer."

"My client is as crazy as a loon," replied Becker. "Whether he pleads innocent or guilty, it's a foregone conclusion that when the dust clears, he's going to be locked away in a nice quiet home for the criminally insane."

"Then why have a trial at all?" asked Jaimie.

Becker sighed. "The military is convinced that their image will be tarnished if they don't prosecute." He paused. "But if I can show them that all of these sordid details will come out in a court-martial, I think I can convince them that a trial will tarnish their image even more than locking Jennings away right now."

"Sounds good to me," agreed Jaimie.

"If you can tie Montoya and Mallardi into this drug ring," concluded Becker, "I think I can wind up this whole mess by tomorrow afternoon."

It was a good prediction, based on reasonable expectations—but nothing was going to be that easy for Max Becker for the foreseeable future.

6

"You know, Counselor," said Jaimie, sipping her drink as her computer tried to locate Anthony Montoya, "if you actually find this guy, I think you'd better consider your next step very carefully."

"My next step is automatic: I go to the prosecution, tell them what I've found out, and let my esteemed opponent go to his higher-ups with the information. Five'll get you ten that Jennings is in an asylum by nightfall."

"I wasn't thinking of Jennings," replied Jaimie. "I think it'll be a race to see if they get him into an asylum before they plant you in the ground."

"This is just a drug case," said Becker confidently. "The military doesn't work that way."

"The military has killed a lot more people than you for a lot less justification than keeping a scandal quiet," replied Jaimie. "It occurs to me that you're going to need me even more after you find out what's going on than you do now."

"It's a possibility," admitted Becker reluctantly. "How well can you hide what I find, and how public can you make it on very short notice?"

"I can hide it where no one alive can find it, and I can put it on every computer network in the country in less than thirty seconds. That means we can distribute it to, oh, about ninety million people." She paused. "You're probably gonna need help breaking into that hospital in Illinois, too—especially if they've got guards on some of their patients."

He stared at her. "How much?"

"How much help will you need?"

"Don't pretend to be stupid, Jaimie; it's unbecoming. How much is this going to cost me?"

"Not a penny, Counselor."

Becker stared at her. "Why do I have difficulty believing that?"

"Beats the hell out of me."

"Jaimie, I *know* you. You don't do favors for free."

"I won't be doing *this* for free, either," said Jaimie. "What happened aboard the *Teddy Roosevelt* is probably just the tip of the iceberg. An awful lot of money changes hands in a well-run drug ring."

"Dirty money," said Becker distastefully.

"I'll put it to clean uses," she assured him. "What do you say, Counselor?"

"You're going to rob a dope ring, and you're worried about *my* health?" replied Becker.

"Sooner or later you're going to have to confront your enemies," she said. "Mine will never even know who I am."

He considered her proposition for a moment, then shrugged. "What the hell. Why should I care what happens to their money?"

Jaimie grinned and clapped her hands together. "You've got yourself a partner, Counselor!" She finished her drink, lit a smokeless cigarette, and turned back to the computer. "Let's see how we're doing."

She fell silent for a moment, then issued more commands.

"Closing in on you bastards," she muttered happily. "Got you in a corner now. No escape from Jaimie the Magnificent." She paused. "Nice block. Very clever. Now let's see what happens if I do *this*. . . ." Suddenly she snapped her fingers. "Got 'em, Counselor!"

"Got whom?"

"Got the records of your missing lieutenants."

"I always said you were a genius."

"Child's play," said Jaimie with a modest shrug.

"Bullshit. I could never have found them."

"You're a lawyer. I'm a hacker." She peered at the screen. "Yep, we've got our connection."

"What is it?"

"Mallardi was kicked out of college for substance abuse. He spent a year abroad, attended another college, got his degree, and joined the service as a lieutenant. Two promotions for performance, two demotions for possession of narcotics. He's got to be part of it, all right."

"And Montoya?"

"Let me check. Yeah, here it is— he was a pharmacist's apprentice before he joined the service."

"But no drug convictions?"

"Counselor, if they were *all* stupid enough to be caught and convicted, they wouldn't have so many friends in high places manipulating things so you can't question them. Montoya's got a thorough knowledge of drugs, and he's probably got a list of suppliers in his head or his computer."

"Okay," said Becker. "It all fits."

"Got another question for you, Counselor."

"What is it?"

"Now that you've put all this together, why do you want to bother talking to Montoya? Why not just use what you know to expose the drug ring?"

"First, because I'm defending Jennings, not prosecuting a drug ring," replied Becker. "And second, none of this gives me the leverage I need as long as it remains mere supposition. I need evidence."

"You doubt that it's true?"

"Not for a minute. But of the five people we suspect were

involved, two are dead, one's in deep space, and one is incommunicado on Mars. Whether I talk to Montoya about Jennings or confront him with the drug ring, the fact remains that I've still got to talk to him."

"So you can't just go to the brass and tell 'em what you suspect?"

Becker shook his head. "If they know I haven't spoken to Montoya, they'll know I'm bluffing."

"Then I guess we have to find Montoya and interview him."

"It looks like it," agreed Becker.

"Well, we're down to six candidates," said Jaimie. She stared at the screen. "Let's see if we can limit it even more." Suddenly she stiffened. "Oh-oh!"

"What is it?"

"Something very funny's going on here."

"Oh? What?"

"Those six files were locked up tighter than a drum not two minutes ago, and now suddenly the door is wide open."

"You opened it."

"Not this wide, I didn't."

A red light on the computer started flashing.

"Ah!" said Jaimie. "Time for Doctor Feelgood!"

She quickly typed in a number of exotic commands.

"Doctor Feelgood?" repeated Becker. "What the hell are you talking about?"

"Nifty little line of defense," said Jaimie admiringly. "They make you think you've broken in, and the second you step through the doorway they hit you with a virus."

"A computer virus?"

Jaimie nodded. "Not to worry, Counselor. Old Doctor Feelgood has antibodies that'll kill any virus the military ever created." She watched the flashing light intently, and a moment later it went dark. "That's it," she announced. "Healthy again."

"Thank God you don't work for the Russians."

"The Russians are even worse than the Americans," she

replied. "You want to see a virus that just won't stop, try the Chinese. Anyway," she concluded, "we're in."

She entered another command, and six names flashed on the screen. "Well, let's start with the simplest approach. How long has it been since the *Roosevelt* returned to Earth?"

"Eleven weeks, I think," said Becker. "Maybe twelve."

Jaimie punched the information in.

"Okay, Counselor," she announced. "We're down to two candidates. The other four have been in the hospital for more than three months." She paused. "What else can we use?"

"You must have Montoya's height and weight in his personnel file," suggested Becker.

"But not in the hospital file," replied Jaimie. She shrugged. "Well, let's see what's wrong with them." She hit another command. "Damn! They're both contagious. I was hoping for a pair of broken legs."

"What do they have?"

"One's got Asian flu, the other's got something akin to cholera, only more exotic."

"Let's hope it's the one with the flu," said Becker.

Suddenly Jaimie began running her fingers over the keyboard.

"What is it?"

"Damned clever system," she announced. "Someone just found out that we're online."

She hit two more keys, then sat back and smiled at her handiwork as a long column of words appeared on the screen:

WHIRLAWAY
PENSIVE
PILOT JET
MIDDLEGROUND
STAR DARK
NEEDLES

LEE TOMY

DECIDEDLY

DEBONAIR LUCKY

IMAGE DANCER'S

COMMANDER DUST

CANNONADE

SLEW SEATTLE

RISK GENUINE

HALO'S SUNNY

FERDINAND

"What's that all about?" asked Becker, as twenty-six more names scrolled down the screen.

"Code."

"Code? What kind of code?"

Jaimie grinned. "Damned if I know. It's an old standby I programmed a couple of years ago: the computer lists every third Kentucky Derby winner starting in 1941, and if the name has two words it lists them in reverse order."

"What does it mean?"

"Nothing," answered Jaimie. "But if they were expecting a code, now they've got one. I always have this ready to insert, just in case I get discovered infiltrating a system. And it's got a beautiful twist, too—I listed Dancer's Image as the 1966 Derby winner, but he was disqualified; the real winner was Forward Pass. That'll drive 'em crazy, trying to figure out what the list represents, and especially why *he's* on it."

"How will they know this wasn't meant for Montoya?"

"They won't, initially—but they can either take his word for it or give him a shot of sodium-p or scopolamine or some other truth serum, and they'll know that he doesn't have any idea what the hell it's about. That's the beauty of having five other guys in hiding there: not only won't they dope out the code, but if even one of those guys is a spy—and probably most of 'em are—no one'll ever know we were looking for Montoya."

Becker stared at the slight black woman for a long moment.

"Jaimie," he said at last, "you have qualities."

"Thank you for noticing."

"How the hell did you get to be so good with a computer?"

"Seriously?"

He nodded.

"I was a very bright girl," she said. "I still am, for that matter."

"I know."

"Yeah," she said. "Well, sexual equality notwithstanding, most boys are afraid of bright girls, and most men are afraid of bright women—which means that I've always had a lot of time on my hands. Somewhere along the way I found out that I was interested in computers, and the rest, like they say, is history."

"Criminal history, for the most part," Becker added dryly.

"Even a computer's no fun without a challenge." Suddenly she smiled at him. "Want me to transfer a quick two million or so to your Swiss account? Chase Manhattan'll never miss it."

"I don't have a Swiss account."

"You can borrow one of mine."

"No, thanks."

She sighed. "Just as well. I really ought to leave Chase alone for a while."

"I'm glad you're on *my* side," he said earnestly.

"You could do worse," she agreed.

"Modest, too," said Becker. He returned to his chair. "Well, now that they've spotted you, I assume they'll be waiting for you to sneak back in, right?"

"Right."

"Can you get past them anyway?"

"Probably, but not without their knowing it."

"So what do we do now?"

"Now we get a good night's sleep and fly to Chicago tomorrow to see what kind of security they've really got before we break in," replied Jaimie. "Separate planes, of course, just in case they're watching you."

"I suppose so," said Becker wearily. "I can't believe that I'm actually contemplating breaking into a heavily-guarded military installation."

"Relax and have another drink, Counselor," said Jaimie with a reassuring smile. "That's what you've got *me* for." She paused. "Besides, it's not an installation. It's a hospital."

"Whatever we call it, getting past armed guards isn't quite the same thing as breaking into a computer."

"Actually it's easier."

"Sure it is," replied Becker sarcastically.

"Did I ever tell you that I used to be a cat burglar?" said Jaimie innocently.

|7|

Becker woke up at 6:00 A.M., shaved and showered, and drove to the airport. While waiting for his flight, he phoned ahead and reserved a single room at the suburban motel he and Jaimie had selected the previous evening.

Then he called Karla.

"Yes, Mr. Becker?" she said as soon as she recognized his face on the vidphone screen.

"Just called to tell you that I'm not going to be in the office today," he said.

"Where can I reach you?"

"You can't," he said. "Save all my messages, and I'll answer them when I come in tomorrow."

"Are you feeling all right?" she asked solicitously.

"I'm fine." He forced a guilty smile to his face. "There isn't likely to be any movement on the Jennings case, so I'm going to get in one last round of golf before the trial begins."

"Then you'll be at your country club?"

"No. I'm joining a friend at *his* club. See you tomorrow."

He broke the connection before she could say anything more, feeling rather proud of his cover story. There were more than forty private country clubs in the area, and there was every possibility that he'd be back from Chicago before anyone tapping his office line had checked them all out.

He walked around the airport for half an hour, trying without success to spot someone, anyone, who might be following him. Finally his flight was called for boarding, and he proceeded immediately to the gate. He was among the first to be seated, and he scrutinized each passenger that entered, wondering which of them had business in Chicago and which had business only with him. There was one, a small, wiry man dressed in a well-tailored brown suit, who met his gaze for a moment, smiled at him, and then proceeded to the back of the cabin. Another, built like an athlete, passed him so quickly that Becker was sure he was hiding something. Finally a young blond man sat down next to him, closed his eyes, and went to sleep. He snored gently for the entire trip, his hands clasped tightly around a magazine featuring three of the newest superstar singers on the cover.

When Becker landed in Chicago, he immediately summoned a cab and spent the next half hour taking it out to the Inn By The Lake, a sprawling, half-century-old Lake Forest hostelry that had been added onto at least three times and somewhere along the way had given up all hope of ever appearing to be a unified structure. His own room—considerably more elegant than it appeared from the outside—was on a bluff overlooking a broad expanse of Lake Michigan beachfront. He tossed his suitcase onto the bed, rinsed his face, memorized the combination to his door, and walked out into the corridor, which was lined with old English sporting prints. It conveyed him to the lobby, where he found the oak-paneled lounge and entered it.

There were two dowagers sitting at a table by the window, each with a pair of binoculars slung over the arms of their chairs, avidly comparing notes and drawings of birds they had seen during their morning walk.

A whiskey salesman, his case full of bottles, was standing

at the bar, attempting to interest the bored bartender in his wares, while the bartender kept explaining patiently that he really had to speak to the day manager, who was on sick leave and wouldn't be back for another three or four days.

The only other patron was a small, wiry black woman, clad in an expensive-looking green and white dress. Jaimie had her nose buried in a Chicago newspaper and didn't even give him a glance as he walked past her and sat down a few tables away.

He lit a small cigar, looked around for an ashtray, found one on the next table, reached over, and appropriated it. The lone waitress managed to tear herself away from the game show on the holovision long enough to approach Becker and ask what he wanted.

"Whatever that young lady is drinking," he replied, gesturing toward Jaimie. "And bring her another one, and put it on my bill."

The waitress nodded, and a moment later presented Jaimie with her drink. She whispered something to the waitress, who indicated Becker, and she stood up and brought her drink over to his table.

"Thank you very much, whoever you are," she said with a smile.

"Smith," he replied, half rising. "John Smith."

"I hope you showed a little more creativity at the hotel desk," she said softly.

"What's wrong with Smith?"

"You've been dealing with the criminal elements in our society for years," she said. "Hasn't anything rubbed off?"

"I was trained as a lawyer, not a spy," he responded irritably. "Are you sure this charade is necessary?"

"Are you sure it isn't?" she shot back. "Can you swear that you weren't followed?"

"No," he admitted.

"Then let's get down to business."

"Fine." He paused uneasily. "Do you have to smile at me like that?"

"Yes. And if you can't smile back, at least try to produce something resembling a lean and hungry look. You're supposed to be a lonely guy who's talking his way into my bedroom."

"I'll do my best," he said.

"Good. And loosen up. We're not gonna get to the naval hospital for at least two hours."

"Why so long?"

"Because we have to sneak off to my room to use my computer, and unless you want your sexual reputation to suffer, we're gonna have to spend at least ninety minutes there."

"What do I care about my sexual reputation in Lake Forest, Illinois?"

"Because if we have to stay an extra day or two, I'd be more likely to invite you back to my room again if you didn't break any track records the first time."

He nodded. "You win. Why do I get the feeling you've done this before?" he asked wryly.

"I haven't," she replied. Suddenly she grinned. "But I have a duplicitous nature."

"I'll vouch for that," he said. "Have we talked long enough, do you think?"

She shook her head. "I'm not that easy, Counselor. Order us each another drink, and tell me a couple of dirty jokes. That ought to loosen you up and get you laughing."

"My store of dirty jokes is extremely limited, I warn you."

Fifteen minutes later she decided that they had put on a good enough show, and they left the bar and headed off to her room, which was much smaller and less elaborate than his.

"Where's your computer?" he asked, looking around the neat, empty room.

"Right here," she said, patting her purse. She withdrew a small leather packet, about four inches on a side and half an inch thick, and opened it up.

"There's no keyboard," he noted.

"You're so observant, Counselor," she said dryly. "I brought this little baby because it doesn't set off any alarms at the airport. Ever since that hijacking in Buenos Aires two years ago, they haven't been allowing even laptops on airplanes."

"How does it work?" he asked.

"You'll see," she replied. "Wheel the holovision over, will you, please?"

While he was following her instructions, she disconnected the vidphone on the night table, did something to its interior with a small pin, attached the wire to her tiny computer, and pulled another wire out of her purse, which she used to connect the computer to the phone.

"Thanks," she said when she noticed Becker standing beside her. "Disconnect the cable in the back of the set, please."

He did so, and let it drop to the floor.

She pulled another wire out of her purse. "Now take this and connect it where the cable was."

While he worked on his end, she worked on hers, attaching it to the computer.

"Well, so much for the preliminaries, Counselor," she announced a moment later. "We're ready to roll."

"Call me Max," he said.

"Why?"

"Because I don't want you to get in the habit of calling me Counselor once we get inside the hospital."

"Then why don't I call you John, since that's the name you're using?"

"Because I probably won't respond to it," he answered. "I'm used to Max."

"Then you shouldn't have used John Smith."

"I can be Max Smith when we go to the hospital."

"You're probably better off being Max Becker, since you're wearing a military uniform that can probably be traced to him," she replied.

"I've packed a suit," he noted.

"The uniform will probably do you more good. First, though," she continued, pressing a button on the computer that brought the holo screen to life, "we'd better find out if you can get into the hospital under any name at all."

She picked up the vidphone and keyed the front desk.

"Yes?" said the clerk a moment later.

"I've had a very tiring trip," she said, "and I'm going to take a nap. Please give me a wake-up call at six this evening."

"Yes, ma'am."

She hung up the phone. "I hope he got a good look at you, Max."

"Why?"

"For the money this joint charges, they should know enough to be discreet, which means they won't bother us with maid service or anything else for a few hours."

"They'll know you're using the phone," he replied. "It'll show up on the hotel's switchboard."

She looked at him, smiling and shaking her head. "Sweet, innocent child."

He sighed. "You have a way around that, of course."

"Of course."

She pressed two buttons on the computer, then dialed a number on the vidphone. Another button was pressed, she dialed again, there was a wait of perhaps ten seconds, and suddenly the holovision screen came completely to life, displaying a complex mathematical readout that was incomprehensible to Becker.

"Nothing to it," Jaimie announced.

"What did you do?"

"I had the pay phone in the ladies' room make our call for us," she replied. "It bypasses the hotel switchboard that way."

"You can do that?" he asked incredulously.

"I just did."

"What if someone tries to use it?"

"I rigged it so they won't get a dial tone, and eventually

they'll go use some other phone. By the time they get a repairman out here to see what's wrong, I'll be disconnected and it'll be working fine again."

"And what's all this stuff on the holo screen?"

"Pay no attention to it," she said. "I haven't got a keyboard, so we're going to talk English to it."

"I thought you told me keyboards were better than speaking."

"True," she agreed. "But not getting stopped at the airport is even better than keyboards." She paused. "Now, if you're ready to be quiet, we can get started."

"Go ahead."

"I mean it, Max. You say one word and you can screw up the works. I have to speak very precisely to this machine, and it can't differentiate between your voice and mine."

"I understand."

She turned back to the screen. "Computer, access all patient records."

"Accessed," said a metallic voice emanating from the holovision set."

"Display."

"Displayed," was the response as some six hundred names scrolled down the screen.

"Display all data on patients Jones and Benares."

"Displayed," replied the voice, as two medical biographies appeared on the screen.

"Go to pause mode."

"Acknowledged."

She turned to Becker. "You can speak now. As you can see, Jones is the one with the cholera, and Benares has the flu."

"And Montoya is definitely one of the two?"

"Right." She paused. "Do you see anything in the medical biographies that would lead you to choose one over the other?"

Becker studied the screen. "No," he said at last. "Montoya is an Hispanic name, but both of these guys have black hair and dark eyes. Is there any way you can call up their prior medical histories? If one of them was in the hospital while we know the other was aboard the *Roosevelt*, then we've got our man."

"Computer?" she said.

"Yes?"

"Display all previous medical histories of patients Jones and Benares."

Further data was added, but neither man had been treated for any illness during the *Roosevelt*'s most recent deep-space mission.

Becker signaled her that he wished to ask another question.

"Go to pause mode," she commanded.

"Acknowledged."

"What is it, Max?"

"Nobody knew I was interested in Montoya until yesterday morning. Can you see if there's been any change in their status in the past thirty hours—new name, armed guard, transfer of rooms, anything like that?"

"We'll see," she said. "Computer?"

"Yes?"

"Has there been any change in either patient's non-medical status during the past two days?"

"Yes."

"Which patient?"

"Patient Benares."

"Nature of change?"

"Transferred from third floor to sixth floor."

"Reason for transfer?"

"Security."

"Reason for security?"

"Classified."

"Go to pause mode."

"Acknowledged."

"Well, Max," she said, turning to him, "it looks like Benares is your man."

"That wasn't so difficult," remarked Becker.

"That was the easy part," she answered. "Now we've got to find out the nature of the added security, and how to get around it."

"You're on a roll," said Becker. "Go ahead and ask."

Jaimie shook her head. "A direct question concerning security would set off every alarm the system has—and unlike the machine I used last night, this one won't be able to cover our tracks. They'll know exactly where the call came from." She paused. "This is gonna require a little thought."

She pulled out a smokeless cigarette and walked over to a large easy chair, where she sat down, tucking her feet beneath her, and stared out at the beach.

Becker watched her, feeling totally useless. He had a number of suggestions he wanted to make, but he was sure that she had already considered and rejected each of them. Finally he sighed, lit another of his small cigars, and sat down on the bed, propping his back up against a couple of pillows.

Jaimie remained motionless for so long that Becker thought she had fallen asleep. Then, just as he had finally made up his mind to cross the room and shake her into wakefulness, she stood up and returned to her computer.

"Computer?"

"Yes?"

"How many means of access are there to the sixth floor?"

"Two public elevators, one service elevator, one medical elevator, and one stairwell."

"Differentiate between a service elevator and a medical elevator."

"The medical elevator can accommodate two hospital beds on wheels, and has oxygen supplies built into the walls. The service elevator, while larger, is not sterile, and is exclusively for the use of the maintenance crew."

"Can patients on the sixth floor receive guests?"

"Yes, with restrictions."

"What restrictions?"

"Ground-level security must approve their visitors' passes."

"Can patients on the sixth floor receive vidphone communications?"

"Yes, with restrictions."

"What restrictions?"

"Hospital security must approve the calls before they are connected, and all calls are monitored."

"What level of authority is required for security approval?"

"It varies with the patient."

"Are you empowered to answer the previous question with regard to individual patients?"

"I am not."

"Go to pause mode."

"Acknowledged."

She turned to Becker. "That's about as explicit as I can get without tripping an alarm. We know that we have to be approved by security on the ground level, we don't dare ask how many armed guards are watching Benares, and we know that any attempt to get him on the vidphone will be tapped, even if we manage to break through the security system."

"Then how the hell am I supposed to get in to see him— disguise myself as a maintenance man?"

"Too obvious," she said. "Or not obvious enough."

"What are you talking about?"

"Along with the fact that this hospital, like any other, has a large store of drugs, it also has a number of people in it that the military wants to keep safe and private. Just take my word for it—they count their maintenance people, and they've got the maintenance elevator rigged with half a dozen scanners. You walk into it half an inch too tall, or with too many fillings in your teeth, or three pounds too light, and you're going to find that a reception committee is waiting for you when the doors open." She shook her head. "No, if you go to the hospital, you'll go in your military outfit and use your own name, and we'll see just how far we can bluff our way."

"You sound as if there's an alternative."

"There is: Lieutenant Edward MacCarron."

"Who the hell is Lieutenant Edward MacCarron?"

"He's the man who cashed Montoya's last paycheck," answered Jaimie. "Obviously he has access to him."

"Even now that he's been transferred to the security floor?" said Becker dubiously.

"I don't know—but tomorrow's payday, and I'll bet Montoya has MacCarron cash his check again."

"He can just have it deposited directly into his account," objected Becker.

"He could have done it last week, too," replied Jaimie. "But he didn't. What does that imply to you?"

"That he needs cash, I suppose."

"Right," she agreed.

"But why the hell would he need cash in a hospital ward?"

"There's a bunch of healthy spies up there waiting for new identities. Probably they've got an around-the-clock poker game going, or something like that."

"But Montoya's sick."

"Wouldn't you risk a little flu for a few hundred dollars, especially if you were bored to tears sitting around waiting for reassignment?"

"I suppose so," admitted Becker. "So our next step is to find MacCarron before the paychecks are passed out tomorrow."

She nodded. "Once we talk to him, we'll have a much better picture of the set-up at the hospital, and how to get around it."

"What makes you think he'll talk to us?"

"Because he owes money all over town," she answered. "I don't know if he's a gambler and a junkie, or if he's keeping a woman on the side, but he obviously spends more than he makes—which means that for the proper bribe, he ought to be willing to talk to just about anybody."

"How much do you think it will take?"

"Oh, I wouldn't offer him much more than five hundred dollars. We could give him a million just as easily, but that would set off every alarm in his empty little head."

"I don't have that kind of money with me," said Becker, "and somehow I doubt that he'll take a credit card."

"I'll pick it up tomorrow morning."

"Where can *you* get it on such short notice?"

Jaimie grinned. "Do you really want to know?"

"No, I really don't," he said with a sigh.

8

They had an early dinner in the hotel's restaurant, and Becker, feeling slightly silly, did his best to look like a sexual predator. Finally Jaimie went back to her room to locate MacCarron, while Becker wandered into the bar, where the huge holographic screen was showing a boxing match between two quick little featherweights, one from Zimbabwe and one from Pakistan, both with their fervent and very vocal rooting sections.

He ordered a martini, then sought out a small booth in the shadows at the back of the room and spent the next hour nursing his drink while watching a procession of fights leading up to the main event, which featured two Oriental middleweights whose names were unfamiliar to him.

The fight had just gotten interesting when Jaimie approached him.

"Well?" Becker asked softly.

"I know where he *should* be. There's a bar that takes his personal checks, and he's always short of money. That's where he figures to go when he's off duty."

"How will we know when he's off duty?"

She grinned.

"Silly question," he amended. "When does he get off?"

"Nine o'clock."

"Then we've got about an hour to kill."

"We've got an hour to *plan.*"

"What's to plan?" said Becker. "I'll just approach him and . . ."

"And *what*?" she demanded. "Bribe him to sneak you into Montoya's room?"

"I hadn't really thought about it," admitted Becker.

"Fortunately for you, I have."

"And?"

"And it seems to me that the quickest way to wind up in the brig is for you to bribe a friend of Montoya's to let you see him—especially when *you're* the reason he's been transferred to a security level of the hospital in the first place."

"I'll explain the problem to him."

"You tell him half of what you told me and he'll think you're drunk or crazy."

Becker sighed. "You have a better way, of course?"

"Of course."

"I'm listening."

"The key to this is that MacCarron is Montoya's friend."

"You know that for a fact?"

"It's a fair assumption. He's the one Montoya trusts to cash his check."

"He could ask any security guard."

"He could—but MacCarron's the one he *does* ask."

"Okay, so MacCarron's his friend," conceded Becker. "So what?"

She shook her head sadly. "I do wish you'd get over this notion that the shortest distance between two points is a straight line. It only works in geometry, you know."

"What particular crooked line do you plan to have me walk tonight?" he asked wryly.

"If you even mention Montoya's name, you're not going to get to first base with MacCarron; he's there to protect him. Therefore, you're not interested in Montoya. In fact, you've never heard of Montoya. It's Samuel Benares that you want."

"Why do I want Benares?"

"Because he's the father of my unborn baby, and you're my lawyer, and certain promises were made in writing. Now, we tell MacCarron that the Benares we're looking for comes from a very wealthy family, so we're more than willing to spend a few hundred dollars to see if this is the right guy. . . ."

"What kind of background have they created for Samuel Benares?" asked Becker.

She shrugged. "It doesn't matter. The beauty of this approach is that MacCarron *knows* you've got the wrong man, because he knows that this Benares is really Anthony Montoya."

Becker nodded his approval. "I see," he said. "If MacCarron is Montoya's friend, he knows Montoya can't be the guy you're looking for, so he can rationalize that he's not really disobeying his orders. All he's doing is making some easy money by letting me see that Montoya's not the man I'm looking for. He can probably even convince himself that he's actually getting paid to keep me from wrongly subpoenaing Montoya and blowing his new identity."

"You got it, Counselor."

"Max."

"Max," she corrected. "Works out pretty neatly all the way around, doesn't it?" she said.

"It sure as hell does," said Becker. He paused thoughtfully. "You realize, of course, that you can't come with me. The second you see him you'd know he isn't the proud papa-to-be, and I won't have any reason to speak to him."

"I know," she said. "I kind of hate to leave you on your own, though. You're just not used to this kind of stuff."

"To questioning witnesses?"

"To subterfuge."

"How much help will I need?" he responded. "I've got

two questions to ask him—one about the dead crewmen, and the other about the traffic in drugs."

"You realize that since he's in a security ward, his room will almost certainly be bugged."

"So what?" said Becker.

"You're breaking the law by being there."

He shook his head. "Uh-uh. MacCarron's disobeying his orders by letting me in. I'm not doing anything except working on behalf of my client."

"Speaking of MacCarron, what do you plan to do about him?"

"Nothing. Once I'm there, he's in more trouble than I am if he makes a scene, so I'll ask what I have to ask and then leave." Becker paused. "Are you absolutely sure MacCarron *can* get me in?"

"He's assigned to hospital security. If he can't, nobody can."

"And if nobody can?" continued Becker.

"Then he'll make some arrangement for you to speak to Montoya on the vidphone."

"I'd much rather do it in person. He can't disconnect me if I'm standing four feet away from him."

"Sure he can," replied Jaimie. "He can do it just by yelling for the guards."

"But then he'll be getting MacCarron in trouble."

"That's what I'm counting on—that MacCarron is a close enough friend that he won't want to do that."

They fell silent for a moment. Then Becker ordered them a pair of martinis.

"There are a lot of weak points in this scheme," he said after the waitress had delivered them. "Maybe we ought to go over it again."

She shook her head. "There's nothing worse than a rigid plan. It doesn't allow for flexibility."

"How flexible can you be when ten security guards start shooting at you?" he asked wryly.

"That's when you've got to be at your *most* creative, not

your least," she answered. "A rigid plan eliminates your options."

"As a lawyer, I build a case like a house: first the foundation, then the—"

"You're not building a case, Max," she interrupted him. "You're infiltrating the enemy's camp."

"The United States military is *not* the enemy," he corrected her. "Hell, I'm part of it."

"If they were your friends, would you be considering this?" she asked.

He stared levelly at her. "A few members of the military are hiding certain facts I need to prepare my case. It's as simple as that."

"If I thought you believed that, I'd leave right now," said Jaimie. "This is *big*, Max. They're hiding your witnesses all over the solar system, or keeping them under guard in classified locations. It takes more than two or three brass to do that."

"I know," he admitted wearily. "I just don't like to think about it."

"You'd better *start* thinking about it. More to the point, you'd better start thinking about *why* they're doing it."

He nodded, then suddenly got to his feet.

"What is it?" she asked.

"I think it's time I put in a call to Jim Magnussen."

"The prosecutor?"

"Yes."

"Why?"

"Because if I don't, he might get the idea I've found Montoya."

She smiled. "You're learning, Counselor."

"I've got a hell of a teacher." He paused. "Can you rig one of the public phones around here so they can't trace the call?"

"No, but I can fix it so it can't be traced if you're off in less than a minute. Use the one right here in the bar; no sense letting him know you're in a hotel—and give me about ninety seconds to get to my room and rig it."

He nodded, walked off to the men's room while she left the bar, waited for two minutes, and then reentered the bar and went directly to the vidphone booth.

A moment later Magnussen picked up the phone in his office.

"Hi, Max," he said, staring at the screen. "What's up?"

"Nothing much. In fact, things are so slow that I sneaked out and got in a round of golf," answered Becker. "Any word on Montoya yet?"

"No."

"Shit. I guess I'll just have to do without him."

"I'm sorry, Max. I did what I could."

"I know."

"Why don't you stop by for a drink? It's cheaper in my office than in whatever bar you're calling from."

"I'll stop by if I can—but don't wait for me. I've got a couple of stops to make in Georgetown first. See you, Jim."

He broke the connection, then checked his watch: forty-one seconds. Satisfied, he returned to his table.

"It's getting late, Max," announced Jaimie, joining him a moment later. "We'd better be going."

"You *do* know what this MacCarron looks like?" asked Becker, leaving a few bills on the table.

"Down to the dimples on his ass," she replied. "The military isn't trying to hide *his* file."

"All right," he said. "Let's go find him."

They took a cab to Waukegan, just north of the Great Lakes Naval Base, and got off at The Destroyer, a service bar filled with photos and holograms of various battleships from the past two centuries. Since Becker was in uniform, and there was no shortage of women on the premises, they drew no undue attention as they entered.

"Any sign of him?" he asked softly as they walked down the long, polished bar toward one of the few empty tables.

"Not yet," replied Jaimie. "But we're a few minutes early.

As soon as he enters, I'll point him out to you and then vanish."

"Why?"

"Because if the little mother is here, he's gonna wonder why you're not taking her to the hospital with you."

"I should have thought of that myself," he muttered, leading her to a table.

"Yes, you should have."

They sat down and ordered a couple of beers, and Becker lit up one of his small cigars.

"You're sure he comes here every night?"

"I'm sure he comes here *most* nights," answered Jaimie.

"And if tonight is one of the exceptions?"

"I've got his home address if we need it, but I'd rather not have him wondering how we got it."

Becker nodded, nursed his beer, and stared at the door. Perhaps two dozen officers and enlisted men had entered and left when he felt a sharp pain in his shin.

"That's him," whispered Jaimie, kicking him as a tall, dark-haired lieutenant entered, waved at the bartender, and made his way to the back of the tavern.

"Let's see where he winds up," said Becker.

MacCarron reached the back of the room and looked around for a table. Before he could find one, Becker realized that Jaimie was no longer sitting down, and he gestured MacCarron over to her empty seat.

"You looked like you needed a friend," said Becker.

"A seat, anyway," said MacCarron with a smile. "Thanks."

"My pleasure," said Becker, extending his hand. "I'm Max Smith."

"Ed MacCarron. Pleased to meet you." MacCarron looked around. "It's crowded in here tonight. You're sure I'm not intruding?"

"Not at all," said Becker. "As a matter of fact, you're the reason I'm here."

"Me?" said MacCarron.

"You're the Lieutenant Edward MacCarron who's stationed at Great Lakes, aren't you?"

"That's right."

"Then I might be able to do you a favor," said Becker.

"Oh?" MacCarron studied him closely. "Is this official business, Major?"

"In an unofficial kind of way," replied Becker. "What are you drinking?"

"Vodka and tonic."

"My treat."

"Thanks," said MacCarron, increasingly uneasy. "What does the space service want with me?"

"The space service couldn't care less about you, Ed," replied Becker. "Relax. You stand to make a good deal of money."

"I do?"

Becker nodded. "My client is a young woman who's stationed at Fort Dix."

"She's in the service?"

Becker nodded. "Comes from a good military family," he continued. "Her father's a colonel and her brother's a lieutenant."

"Okay, she's a pillar of virtue," said MacCarron. "So what?"

"So she's pregnant."

"I hope you don't think you can get away with coming in here and accusing *me* of—" began MacCarron heatedly.

"Nobody's accusing you of anything," said Becker reassuringly. "Believe me. The guy who got her pregnant could buy both of us with his pin money."

"Then what is this all about?" demanded MacCarron.

"I'm her family's attorney," said Becker. "The guy who did this to her made certain commitments in writing. He has chosen not to honor them. Do you begin to understand?"

"I understand," said MacCarron. "What I don't understand is what all this has to do with me."

"I've been told on very good authority that you know the father," said Becker, leaning forward confidentially. "I've got five hundred dollars for you if you'll put me together with him for five minutes."

"Five hundred, just to talk to him?"

"That's just a drop in the bucket compared to what I'm going to sue his ass for."

"Why pay me at all?" asked MacCarron suspiciously. "Why not just go to his commanding officer and demand an audience?"

"I'll be honest with you," replied Becker. "I traced the son of a bitch to Great Lakes, and now I've lost him. I can't find him in the barracks or on any of the duty rosters, and nobody there has been any help at all."

"So what makes you think *I* can help?"

"I was tipped by someone who wants his name kept out of it."

"Five hundred, you say?"

"Right."

"In cash?"

Becker nodded. "Tax free."

MacCarron shrugged. "So who's the proud papa?"

"Lieutenant Samuel Benares."

MacCarron frowned. "Samuel Benares? I don't know any—" Suddenly he put on a poker face. "Oh, yeah, sure—Sam Benares."

"You know him?"

"Yeah, I know him."

"Well, like I said, there's five hundred in it for you if you can get me in to see him long enough for me to ask him a few questions."

"That might be a little difficult," said MacCarron.

"That's why I'm not asking you to do it for free."

"There are probably a dozen guys named Sam Benares in the service," said MacCarron carefully. "How do you know this is the right one?"

"He told the girl he was being transferred to Illinois," said Becker confidently. "I've got the right man."

"But *if* you're wrong . . ." persisted MacCarron.

"Then I'll keep looking until I find him. But that won't be necessary—this is the man I want."

"If you're wrong, what about the five hundred?"

"That's yours—win, lose, or draw. When we finally nail this bastard, I'm suing his ass for three million."

"That much?" asked MacCarron, impressed.

"He's worth it."

"That's a lot of money," said MacCarron. He paused uncomfortably. "Could you maybe manage a thousand for me?"

"If I can see him within twenty-four hours."

"The money's on the front end?"

"Absolutely."

"I've got to make some arrangements first. How about tomorrow morning?"

"Name the time."

"Nine o'clock sharp."

"Where should I meet you?" asked Becker.

"Right here. It'll probably work better if we go in together."

"Sounds good. Nine o'clock at the bar."

"In front of the building. It doesn't open until noon."

Becker nodded.

"Okay," said MacCarron, getting to his feet. "If you'll excuse me, I've got some arrangements to make." He shook Becker's hand. "See you tomorrow."

"Right."

"And remember to bring the money."

Becker nodded, and MacCarron began making his way toward the front door.

"How did it go?" asked Jaimie, returning to the table and sitting down opposite Becker.

"We're in," said Becker. "Or, at least, *I'm* in." He paused. "And I'll need a thousand dollars instead of five hundred."

She smiled. "You're awfully generous with *my* money, Counselor."

"If I thought it was yours, I'd be a lot more careful with it," he replied. "Can you get it before nine in the morning?"

"No problem," she said, getting up. "I think we'd better get back to the hotel and get a good night's sleep. There's every possibility that one of us is going to need it."

"Relax," said Becker. "We're on the last lap. Once I talk to Montoya, I'll have enough on those bastards that they'll have to put Jennings away without a trial."

"You really think so, Counselor?" she asked.

"Of course. Don't you?"

"Ask me tomorrow," said Jaimie.

"I'm asking you now."

"Has it occurred to you, Counselor, that we've come awfully far awfully easy?"

"Easy?" laughed Becker. "My God, Jaimie—without your help I'd still be making meaningless threats to Jim Magnussen."

"It's not that," she said.

"Then what?"

"You told me that the army had three computer experts as good as me, remember?"

"So?"

"So if this is such a big scandal, why didn't one of them hide the data on Montoya?"

"One of them probably did."

She shook her head. "It wasn't *that* hard to find."

"Then maybe they're keeping it in a small circle of intimates, and none of your experts qualified."

"Maybe," she said.

"Okay," he said. "Why do *you* think it was so easy?"

"I wish I knew," said Jaimie.

9

Jaimie was busily trying to track down all of Chief Medical Officer Gillette's secret bank accounts when Becker finally left the hotel.

He flagged down a cab and arrived at The Destroyer just before nine o'clock. MacCarron was already there, waiting for him and looking nervous.

"Good morning," said Becker pleasantly.

"Morning," replied MacCarron.

"Is it all set?"

MacCarron nodded.

Becker handed him an envelope with ten hundred-dollar bills in it. Jaimie had gone out at seven in the morning and returned with it an hour later; he hadn't asked her where the money had come from.

MacCarron peeked into the envelope, then slipped it into his pocket.

"All right," he said. "Let's go."

He led Becker to a military car, unlocked it, waited until they were both seated, and then headed off to the base.

"You seem edgy," noted Becker.

"This may not be as easy as it seemed last night," responded MacCarron.

"Oh?" said Becker, sounding surprised.

"Yeah."

"What else has Benares done?"

"Nothing."

"But—"

"Look," said MacCarron harshly, "you don't need to know anything about it. Just keep quiet when we get there and let me do the talking."

"Whatever you say," replied Becker.

They drove the next few minutes in silence, and then MacCarron spoke again.

"If it should turn out that this isn't the Sam Benares you're looking for, what will you do next?"

"Keep looking."

"If I can hunt up another Sam Benares at Fort Sheridan or some other location, do I get another finder's fee?"

"If this isn't our man."

MacCarron grunted, and shortly thereafter they entered the Great Lakes Naval Base. He drove past a long row of barracks and a handful of administration buildings, and finally pulled up to a large building that was badly in need of a coat of paint. He parked in a space that was labeled Reserved For Officers.

"Remember to keep your mouth shut," said MacCarron tensely as they got out of the car and walked up to the main entrance.

MacCarron showed his pass to the young officer at the front door and introduced Becker as a visiting security officer who was taking a brief tour of the entire base.

The officer nodded his approval, and the two men stepped into the large, well-scrubbed lobby.

"Follow me," said MacCarron, heading off to his left, "and try to look as if you belong here."

Becker fell into step behind him, and a moment later Mac-

Carron was loudly explaining the security devices that had been installed in the bank of public elevators. Finally they edged down to the service elevator, and MacCarron led him into it, still pointing out various features. Then the door slid shut and they began ascending to the sixth floor.

"Hi, Charlie," said MacCarron to the armed guard who confronted them when they emerged from the elevator.

"Good morning, sir. Is this the officer you mentioned to me last night?"

MacCarron nodded. "This is Major Max Smith, who's here to study our security methods."

"Okay," responded Charlie, his eyes darting up and down the long corridor, "but I strongly suggest that Major Smith not waste any time. My replacement's due in about twenty minutes."

"We'll be back in five," MacCarron promised him. "Ten at the outside."

The young guard frisked Becker quickly, then saluted and stood aside. "You may pass, sir."

MacCarron and Becker both returned the salute and rode the corridor to the corner of the building, where MacCarron stepped onto the floor and Becker followed suit. They turned left and walked past two heavily-guarded rooms, saluting as they passed, then turned left again and walked halfway down yet another corridor before they entered an unnumbered room that had no armed guards in front of it.

"Here he is," said MacCarron.

An obviously Hispanic patient was sitting up in his bed, reading a magazine.

"This is the guy?" he asked.

MacCarron nodded.

"Tell you what," said the patient, handing him an envelope. "Why don't you cash this across the street? By the time you get back, I think we'll have solved our little problem."

"You're sure you'll be okay?" asked MacCarron.

The patient grinned. "Do I look like a father-to-be?"

MacCarron shrugged and left the room. Becker waited until the door slid shut behind him and then approached the bed.

"Sorry to disappoint you, Major," said the patient, "but my name isn't really Sam Benares."

"That's okay," said Becker, pulling up a chair. "Mine isn't Max Smith."

The patient frowned. "What's going on here?"

"I *am* a major and I *am* a lawyer, but my name's Maxwell Becker, and I'm representing Captain Wilbur Jennings at his murder trial. Does the name mean anything to you?"

"Of course it does."

"You *are* Lieutenant Anthony Montoya, late of the *Theodore Roosevelt*, aren't you?"

"Yeah, that's me," said Montoya.

"I want to ask you a couple of questions about the *Roosevelt*."

"Sure, why not?" said Montoya with a shrug.

"Nobody has told you not to speak to me?" asked Becker, surprised.

"Major, I never heard your name before, until you announced yourself."

Becker frowned. "Nobody has told you not to discuss the Jennings case?"

"That's right."

"Then what are you doing on the security level of the hospital?"

Montoya stared directly at Becker. "Meaning no disrespect, I don't think that's any of your business, Major."

Becker, aware of the press of time, elected not to debate the point. "All right," he said. "First question: did Jennings ever mention to you and to a Lieutenant Mallardi that crewmen Greenberg and Provost were acting strangely?"

"Yes, he did."

"Did he offer any conclusions or suggestions as to *why* they were behaving so oddly?"

Montoya shook his head. "No, he just mentioned it in

passing. In fact, I had totally put it out of my mind until he went crazy and killed them."

"You didn't follow it up?"

"I didn't have to," said Montoya. "I *knew* why they were acting that way."

Becker cleared his throat. "You really should have an attorney present for my next question, but I'm going to have to ask it anyway."

Montoya looked amused. "Here it comes."

"I beg your pardon."

"Go ahead and ask your question, Major. I have a feeling that you know a lot more than you're supposed to know."

"How deeply involved with the *Roosevelt*'s drug ring were you?"

Montoya laughed aloud. "Well, that's a new one!"

"You haven't answered my question."

"I was deeply involved—but not in the way you think."

"Then perhaps you'll enlighten me."

Montoya opened a drawer of his nightstand and withdrew a wallet. He opened it and handed it to Becker.

"You're a member of the space service's Internal Security Division?" said Becker, surprised.

"That's right, Major."

Becker frowned in confusion. "It doesn't say anything about this on your dossier."

"It does if you know where to look for it," said Montoya. "It's not the kind of thing we're anxious to make public."

"What's the story about the drugs?"

"Does this have a direct bearing on Jennings' defense?" asked Montoya.

"If it didn't, I wouldn't be asking," replied Becker, grateful for the question and keenly aware that their conversation was probably being monitored.

"I don't know if I can talk about it."

"There are a couple things I need to know."

"Tell you what," said Montoya after a moment's consideration. "As long as you you've found out on your own that there *was* a drug ring, I'll give you whatever you want on deep background. But in exchange for my cooperation, you will never subpoena me or identify me as a source."

"I may have to."

"I don't know how you discovered this, Major, but we're not ready to go public with this yet."

"Who is *'we'*?"

"Do we have a deal?"

"No."

"Then I've got nothing to say."

Becker stared at him for a long moment and finally nodded. "Okay. You've got all the answers—I guess we'll have to play by your rules."

"You might as well," said Montoya. "The military will never let you get me into court until they're ready."

"Ready for what?"

Montoya lowered his voice confidentially, despite the fact that the door was closed. "Large stores of narcotics—and I mean *large*—were turning up missing from Bethesda for the past two years, and we suspected Gillette was at the center of it. As we began closing in, he applied for deep-space duty and got assigned to the *Roosevelt*. We couldn't stop him without tipping our hand too soon, so we had to let him go. We kept his replacement under surveillance, and I was put aboard the *Roosevelt* to keep an eye on him."

"And?" said Becker.

"Major, I could hardly believe my eyes! Half the crew was stoned from the moment we took off. I've put together a pretty good case against Gillette and Mallardi—and I had one against Greenberg and Provost, too, until the Captain went mad and killed them—but what happened aboard the *Roosevelt* is small potatoes compared to what's going on back at Bethesda, at least in terms of the quantity of drugs involved, so the service is keeping me on ice until we've got our bigger case ready to go. No sense warning Gillette's people if we don't have to."

"So they're not hiding you from Jennings!" said Becker.

"They're just keeping you tucked away until they've broken the drug ring."

"Right."

"But why did they let Gillette go back into deep space?"

"It's as good a place as any to keep him until we've identified every person in the ring." He paused. "This is going to be the biggest drug case in the history of the military, and we're making sure that everything's in its place before we finally go to court."

Becker paused, trying to assimilate all that he had been told. Finally he turned his attention back to Montoya. "You've been here in the hospital since the *Roosevelt* landed?"

"No, I was on leave until a few weeks ago. I really did have the flu, and it gave them a great opportunity to hide me. They took advantage of it, too—I haven't seen or spoken to anyone except MacCarron and a couple of my fellow patients for more than a week. Then, two days ago, they moved me here after someone in the drug ring made a threat on my life." He grimaced. "It's a pain in the ass, being stuck here like this. For all I know, the President's been assassinated and we're at war."

"He's alive and we're at peace," Becker assured him with a smile.

"Well, *that's* comforting, anyway," replied Montoya dryly. He paused. "Is MacCarron going to get to keep the money?"

Becker nodded.

"Good," said Montoya. "He was scared to death about sneaking you in here."

"He had no reason to be."

"He works for security, and you gave him a bribe. That's reason enough. I figured that you weren't after the mythical Mr. Benares," said Montoya with a self-satisfied chuckle. "I didn't know exactly what you wanted, but I had to keep assuring MacCarron that no one was going to harm me, that Mallardi was the only one who might, and that he's been transferred to Mars Base." He paused. "I mean, hell, even a hit man wants to live, and there's just too damned much security around here, even if you were here to kill me, for you to get away with it. Still, it took almost half an hour to convince him."

"So how long will you be staying here?" asked Becker.

"Until we tie Gillette and his successor to a certain Italian distributor," answered Montoya. "Now that they've got me here, they're not likely to let me go."

"Are you talking weeks, months, what?"

Montoya shrugged. "Who knows? I hope it's soon, though. I'm going nuts in this place."

"It could be worse," said Becker.

"Oh, yeah? How?"

"They could keep you in the kind of cell they've got Jennings in."

"I thought I read that he was at Bethesda—or maybe I heard it on the grapevine. Either way, Bethesda is a hospital—they don't have cells there."

"I don't know what else you could call it."

"A padded room, perhaps?" suggested Montoya.

"Actually, it's not padded at all."

Montoya shrugged. "They're making a big mistake. He's mad as a hatter."

"Did he strike you as mad when he was in control of the ship?" asked Becker as MacCarron reentered the room and handed Montoya his money.

"No," said Montoya. Suddenly he smiled. "But *I* didn't kill two crew members for the good of the service and the security of our planet. Jennings did—or at least he thinks he did."

"True enough," conceded Becker.

"You all through, Major Smith?" asked MacCarron nervously.

"Yes, I think I am," said Becker, walking to the door. "Thank you for your time, Lieutenant Benares."

"My pleasure," replied Montoya.

Becker followed MacCarron out into the hall, and they

returned the way they had come, saluting at each checkpoint.

"Do you need a ride back to your hotel?" asked MacCarron as they left the hospital.

"No, thanks," replied Becker. "I'm staying with friends. One of them should be picking me up any minute."

"Then I'll say good-bye to you here. I'm due on duty in about forty minutes."

"Thanks for your help, Lieutenant."

"It wasn't the right man, was it?" said MacCarron.

Becker shook his head. "No, it wasn't."

"Do you want me to start checking for a Samuel Benares at the other Illinois bases?"

"Might as well," said Becker. "I've still got to find him before I can bring him to trial."

"How will I get in touch with you?"

"I'll be on the move, and pretty hard to contact," answered Becker. "I'll get in touch with *you.*"

"Okay, then," said MacCarron, walking to his car. "Nice to do business with you, Major."

"My pleasure," replied Becker.

As soon as MacCarron had driven off, Becker walked to the gate and hailed a cab. Fifteen minutes later he was back at the Inn by the Lake.

Jaimie was working with her computer as he entered her room.

"I hope things went better for you than for me," she said, looking up from her screen.

"I wish I knew," he replied.

"What do you mean?" asked Jaimie. "Wasn't he willing to talk to you?"

Becker frowned. "He was *too* damned willing. He confirmed everything we suspected about the drug ring."

"Well, then?"

"Did you ever listen to one of those talk shows on radio or holovision, and wish to hell that the host didn't agree with your position because he was such a son of a bitch you hated being on the same side with him?"

"Once in a while. So what?"

"Well, I had that feeling again this morning," he replied. "I'd have been much happier if Montoya had denied that there was any dope at all aboard the *Roosevelt.*"

She stared at him curiously. "What are you getting at?"

"I'm not exactly sure," said Becker, "but I think we're in *big* trouble."

"Maybe we'd better sit down together and start comparing what we learned this morning," said Jaimie, a hint of nervousness in her voice.

"All right," said Becker, looking around the room. "Have you got anything to drink?"

"Let's stick to water until we know exactly where we stand," she replied.

He nodded and sat down on an easy chair, while she sat cross-legged on the bed and lit a smokeless cigarette.

"While you were at the hospital," she began, "I spent the morning trying to follow the money trail."

"Following it where?"

She shrugged. "Wherever it led. Gillette doesn't grow or manufacture the drugs; he's just a middle-man. If he's got twelve million dollars in his Swiss and Brussels accounts—and he does—then somebody's got a hell of a lot more in theirs."

"What did you find out?" he asked.

She frowned. "Nothing."

"You couldn't follow the trail?"

"It's stranger than that, Max," she said. "There *isn't* any trail."

"Same thing."

"No it's not," she contradicted him. "If it was hidden or protected, I'd know it was there even if I couldn't read it. But there's no trail of any kind. That money wasn't transferred to his account. Somebody came into those two banks about six weeks ago and deposited twelve million dollars, cash, in his accounts."

"It couldn't have been Gillette. He's been in deep space aboard the *Martin Luther King* for longer than that."

"It shouldn't have been *anyone.* People just don't walk around with briefcases filled with cash, not even drug dealers. Hell, especially not drug dealers."

"That's interesting, but I don't know what it means," said Becker.

"I didn't know, either, so I did some more checking."

"And?"

"The Swiss account has only been open for six weeks. Ditto for his account in Brussels."

"And before that?"

"If he had twenty thousand dollars to his name before that, I'll be damned if I can find it."

"He *had* to," said Becker. "He only signed on aboard the *Roosevelt* when things got too hot for him here."

"Yeah?" she said, picking up her computer. "Take a look at this, Counselor." She activated the speaker and leaned forward. "Computer, bring up Franklin Gillette's financial statement one week prior to his assignment as Chief Medical Officer aboard the *Theodore Roosevelt.*"

Two columns appeared on the screen.

"The left-hand column contains his assets, and the right-hand one lists his indebtedness," she continued.

"I can read a financial statement," said Becker irritably as he searched fruitlessly for any sign of the drug money.

"Then you know that his net worth was about two hundred and sixty thousand dollars, including his house."

"Did you run credit checks on Mallardi, Provost, and Greenberg?" he asked.

She nodded. "The three of them together weren't worth as much as a new car. Provost had bill collectors on his ass for years, Mallardi was just starting out and didn't own much more than the shirt on his back, and Greenberg had managed to save eight thousand dollars during the three years he was in the service."

"Something's very wrong here," muttered Becker.

"I take it this doesn't jibe with what Montoya told you?"

"No, it doesn't." He pressed his fingers against his temples. "Let me think."

He tried to recall his conversation with Montoya, tried to reconstruct just what it was that had made him so uneasy, so nervous that he didn't want even MacCarron to know where he was staying.

"Well?" she said after he'd been silent for a full minute. "Was he telling the truth?"

"I don't know."

"You said he was *too* willing to talk. What did you mean?"

Becker spent the next few minutes relating his conversation with Montoya—the young officer's secret mission aboard the *Roosevelt*, his confirmation of Gillette's connection to a major drug ring, and his explanation for the military's complex manipulation of personnel once Becker tried to put together a defense for Jennings.

"Well, it all fits nice and neat," said Jaimie when he was through. "I suppose I'm just gonna have to try harder to find out where the money came from."

Becker shook his head. "It's *too* neat."

"What do you mean?"

"I don't know. I'm missing something, but I don't know what it is."

"Missing what?" she asked. "Information? Is there something Montoya didn't tell you?"

"He told me *too* much," replied Becker. "Something's wrong."

"Like what?"

He shrugged helplessly. "I don't know. It's been bothering me all morning, but I can't put my finger on it."

"Well, let's go over it step by step," she said, putting her cigarette out and lighting another. "You walked into the room and there he was. Should he have been surprised to see you?"

"No. MacCarron had told him I'd be coming."

"Okay. You accused him of being part of a drug ring, and he showed you his credentials. Were they authentic?"

"I suppose so."

"You *suppose* so?"

"I don't know. They looked authentic. Hell, I've never seen any Internal Security credentials."

"But they didn't bother you?"

"The only thing that bothered me at that moment was that he was willing to give me all the details I needed."

"But you promised not to use them."

"Even so, he shouldn't have told me as much as he did."

"Did you get the feeling that he would have told you even if you hadn't promised to keep quiet?"

He shrugged. "I don't know. I never thought about it."

"Think about it now."

"I still don't know."

"But that's not what's bothering you?"

"No, I don't think so."

"Then let's go on. He described Gillette's role in the drug ring. Then what?"

"Then he told me about Mallardi, and about how the government was keeping him on ice until they built the bigger case. And then—"

Suddenly he froze.

"What is it?" she demanded. "What did you remember?"

"He knew about Mallardi!"

"Of course he did. He was there to keep an eye on Gillette, and Mallardi was part of the ring."

Becker shook his head impatiently. "No! He'd been incommunicado for more than a week, and yet he knew Mallardi had been transferred to Mars Base!"

"You're onto something, Counselor!" she whispered excitedly. "Keep going!"

Becker concentrated on the morning's conversation with Montoya.

"There's something else, too—it's just at the edge of my mind!" Suddenly his whole body sagged from the effort. "Damn! I can't quite remember it!"

"All right, calm down," she said. "Let's attack it logically. You spoke to Montoya about the drug ring. He knew Mallardi had been transferred. What else did he know that he shouldn't have known? That there were no autopsies performed?"

"No, that wasn't it."

"That Gillette is back in deep space?"

"He knew that, but given his cover story, it's something he should have known. No, it wasn't about the drug ring."

"About Jennings, then?"

"Yes, I think so."

"What? Something about the trial, perhaps?"

"No, he didn't know I represented Jennings. It was something else, something—I've got it! He made some reference to Jennings saying that killing Provost and Greenberg was for the good of the planet, or for planetary security, or some such thing."

"So?"

"Jennings never said that aboard ship. He never told anyone why he committed the murders until after he was arrested and incarcerated."

"And if Montoya was on the drug case, he'd have no reason to know that!" Jaimie chimed in.

"I'm starting to wonder if the man I spoke to really *was* Montoya," said Becker, an enormous sense of weariness coming over him now that he had ransacked his memory and pulled up the necessary details.

"I'm wondering the same thing myself," she replied. "If he was Internal Security, I should have found something in his record to indicate it."

"He said it was there if you knew where to look."

"He said a lot of things, Counselor, and we know that at least two things were lies. Let's see if *anything* was the truth."

She activated her computer again, placed a call to Bethesda Hospital, and started reeling off a number of equations that made no sense at all to Becker. He was about to ask what she was doing when she turned to him and placed her finger to her lips, and he recalled what she had said the night before about how the machine was unable to differentiate his voice pattern from hers.

A moment later she looked up and nodded to him.

"You can talk now."

"What are you doing?"

"Checking your friend's story," she replied. "He said that Gillette was assigned to Bethesda, didn't he?"

"Not precisely. He said that large quantities of drugs were disappearing from Bethesda, and that they suspected Gillette. He never specifically said that Gillette was stationed there."

"Well, let's see," said Jaimie as a number of lists appeared on the screen. "Yeah, Franklin Gillette worked there from 2061 to 2063." She turned back to the computer. "Computer, produce a list of medical stores unaccounted for during the period of Franklin Gillette's employment at Bethesda." The screen changed instantly, and she frowned. "Too easy, Counselor. Too damned easy."

"What do you mean?"

"See that?" she said, gesturing to a column of figures that ran down the left side of the screen. "That's supposed to be a list of how many drugs turned up missing during the time

Gillette was there." She paused. "You're looking at fifty million dollars or more."

"I know."

"You still don't see, do you?" said Jaimie. "If the military is trying to cover it up, how come I was able to call up the exact figures? Why weren't they hidden or classified?"

"Because they want you to see them," said Becker with a strange feeling in the pit of his stomach.

"And they want me to see them—" she began.

"Because they want us to believe Montoya's story," he concluded. "And since we know part of Montoya's story is phony, I think we'd better assume that the whole damned thing is one big fabrication."

"They went to an awful lot of trouble to set it up," said Jaimie.

"Yes, they did," agreed Becker. "And I bought it lock, stock and barrel."

"Shall we find out just how badly they want you to believe it?" she suggested.

"I don't understand you."

"Watch and don't speak," she said, and spent the next thirty minutes carefully avoiding a number of traps and viruses, at the end of which Gillette's Swiss funds, totaling some eight million dollars, had been transferred to one of Jaimie's own accounts.

"I don't know what this proves, except that you're one hell of a thief," said Becker when the last manipulation was completed.

"It proves they're willing to spend eight million dollars to make you believe their story," answered Jaimie. "They could have made that a bogus account with no money in it, but they knew that sooner or later someone would inspect it."

"It could also be Gillette's account," said Becker without much conviction.

"I've done everything I can with this computer," she said. "But when I get to one with a keyboard, I'll bet you ten dollars to a nickel that there isn't any drug ring and that Gillette doesn't even know this account exists."

"You really think you can prove that with the proper computer?" he asked dubiously.

She nodded. "Half the game is knowing what you're looking for."

"So if you can get to a more sophisticated machine, you can tell me for sure if Gillette and Mallardi were implicated in a drug ring?"

"I can do more than that," she said confidently. "I can even tell you if the man you spoke to this morning was really Anthony Montoya."

"Then we'd better get you to a computer."

"I've got a great one at home."

He shook his head. "We're not going home yet."

"Why not?"

"Because if this whole thing is as phony as I think it is, the only two leads I've got are MacCarron and Montoya, and they're both here."

"You think MacCarron's a part of it?" she asked.

He shrugged. "If we've been set up, then he's definitely part of it. He was the only link you could find to Montoya."

"I don't know. . . ."

"You think I'm wrong?"

"No."

"Then what?"

"If we've been set up, then I think MacCarron and Montoya are probably hundreds of miles away by now."

He shook his head. "There's always a chance I might want to speak to Montoya again. It would be stupid for them to turn up missing while we're still in Illinois—and whoever's behind this may be a lot of things good and bad, but stupid isn't one of them." He paused for a moment, then walked decisively to her closet, pulled out her coat, and tossed it to her. "Come on."

"Where are we going?"

"To find you a computer."

He had the doorman summon them a taxi, then had it drive them two miles into the center of Lake Forest. They got off at a major intersection, then walked a block until they came to a computer store.

"Here we are," announced Becker.

"You think they're just gonna let me walk in and start playing with one of their machines?"

"That's exactly what I think—especially after we flash some money and tell them you're looking for a new modem. Great Lakes Naval Base is just a local call from here, so why should they object to your trying it out?"

"No reason."

"You look uneasy."

"I'm just not used to direct approaches."

He smiled confidently at her and led her into the store, then stood aside while she told a salesman exactly what she wanted. He led her to a shelf containing dozens of different modems. She selected one, and he attached it to a computer for her.

"Let me just play with it for a couple of minutes," she said. "I'll let you know when I'm through."

"Do try to make your calls local," said the salesman. "I'm afraid we must charge you for any long-distance calls, even if you decide not to purchase the modem."

"I understand," said Jaimie, her fingers starting to race across the complex keyboard.

Becker engaged the salesman in a conversation concerning the previous football season and how the Bears might plug the holes that had cost them their divisional championship, gradually moving across the showroom so that Jaimie could work in relative privacy. About ten minutes later he realized that he had gotten so caught up in the discussion that he hadn't seen Jaimie deactivate the machine and detach the modem.

"It's a very nice instrument," she said, handing it back to the salesman.

"If it's not powerful enough, we have one that will transmit at a 38,400-baud rate."

"No, this one seemed fine. Do you mind if I think about it for a little while?"

"Certainly not," he assured her. "Take all the time you need." He picked up a thick packet of brochures from a nearby desk. "Here are the specifications and prices on every modem that we handle. If you find one in here that you think you might prefer, we can set up another test." He paused. "The 76,000 series also offers two excellent choices if you have a lot of data to download."

Jaimie thanked him and buried her nose in the spec sheets as they left the store and went next door to a coffee shop, where they walked past several diners, including two officers from nearby Fort Sheridan, and took a table in the back.

"Well?" Becker asked anxiously.

"We were right!" she said.

"You found something?"

"Not just something, Counselor—*lots*!" she replied. "Now that I know where to look, everything is much easier to find."

"Such as?"

"There never were any drugs missing from Bethesda, and there is no record of drug abuse aboard the *Roosevelt*. Also, Lieutenant Mallardi never left school because of substance abuse; there's no record of his ever having taken drugs either in college or the service."

"You got all of that from Great Lakes?" he asked dubiously.

"Of course not," she replied. "The phone in the hotel's ladies' room is still rigged; I went through *it*, so nothing will show up on the computer store's phone bill."

"Even so, that's a lot of data for just six or seven minutes," he said, impressed.

"I just took a quick peek," said Jaimie. "When I get someplace where I can do some downloading, I'll give you more data than you know what to do with." She paused. "I confirmed something else, too."

"What?"

"The money in Gillette's foreign accounts just appeared magically one day a few weeks ago, totally untraceable—and if *I* can't trace it, nobody can."

"If there was no drug ring, the military had to put it there," said Becker.

"Of course."

He stared at her. "You're looking at me as if I'm missing something."

"You are."

"What?"

She paused. "There's only one reason that money was there, Max."

"Oh?"

She nodded. "They knew someone would find it sooner or later, and an empty account wasn't going to fool anyone. The Brussels account is real, too: it's got another four million in it. I think," she concluded, "that it means they're willing to pay us twelve million dollars to keep quiet."

"Twelve million? That's crazy!"

"Lower your voice," she cautioned him. "You're starting to attract attention."

He turned and saw that a number of diners, including the major and colonel at the next table, were staring at him.

"You must be wrong," he said more softly.

"That's your first reaction, Max; now think about it. How much did it cost to get you this far? How many people did they have to shift around the galaxy? How many computer records did they have to tamper with? If whatever they're hiding is *that* important, what's another twelve million dollars to them? This isn't some *mafioso* protecting his source, Max; this is the military. They've got access to *billions*! They probably spend twelve million on paper clips every half hour."

"I've got to think about this," said Becker.

"Well, don't think too long," she said earnestly. "We've got to decide what to do next."

"That's easy enough," he replied. "I've got to speak to MacCarron or Montoya—or whoever he is—again."

"I don't think that would be very wise, Max."

"Why not? They already know I'm here."

"You ask to talk to Montoya again and they might get the idea you don't believe what you heard the first time."

"I don't."

"Max, these aren't amateurs you're playing with. Someone has gone to an awful lot of trouble to make you think there was a drug ring on the *Roosevelt*. You come back and demand the truth, and they just might eliminate you."

He shook his head. "This is the United States military you're talking about, Jaimie. I'm a part of it. If I stumble on something I'm not supposed to know, they'll just order me to keep quiet."

"Then why have they spent so much money and effort misdirecting you?"

He shrugged. "I don't know."

"I'd sure want to know the answer to that before I told them I didn't believe them."

"You're paranoid, Jaimie."

"It ain't paranoia if they're really out to get you," she said seriously.

"These are my people," he said. "I'm fourth-generation military. I've spent my whole life in the service. They're obviously covering something up, but they're not about to kill me."

She stared at him for a long moment.

"Have it your way," she said at last.

"All right," he said, getting to his feet. "Is MacCarron on duty now?"

She nodded.

"I'll be back in a minute."

He walked to a public vidphone, had the screen scroll the directory under "H" until he found the number of the Great

Lakes Naval Hospital, and then put a call through to MacCarron. The switchboard transferred him to Security, which first denied that MacCarron was stationed at Great Lakes, but then, when he pointed out that he was a major, pretended to run a search through the base for him, and finally announced that a connection would be patched through momentarily.

Finally MacCarron's face appeared on the screen.

"Major Smith," he said, surprised.

"You're a hard man to contact," said Becker.

"Sometimes Security gets carried away with its own precautions," said MacCarron apologetically. "What can I do for you?"

"I need to speak to Benares again."

MacCarron frowned. "I thought your business with him was finished."

"I just need to go over one or two details I neglected this morning."

"I don't think that's possible."

"There's another thousand in it for you if you can get me in this afternoon."

"I don't know...."

"Please," said Becker. "I'm leaving town tonight, and I only need to see him for just a minute or two."

"I'll have to see who's on duty and get back to you," said MacCarron. "Where can I get in touch with you?"

Becker read off the number of the vidphone. "I'll be here for another twenty minutes."

"Right. I'll get back to you before then."

MacCarron broke the connection, and Becker walked back to the table.

"Can you get another thousand in cash in the next half hour or so?" he asked.

"No problem," she said. "Everything went smoothly?"

"Yes."

"Well, maybe I was wrong. Where are you meeting him?"

"I don't know," said Becker.

"What do you mean, you don't know?"

"He's calling me back in twenty minutes to let me know the arrangements."

"He's calling you *here*?"

"Yes. I gave him the public vidphone number."

She got to her feet and grabbed him by the arm.

"Let's get the hell out of here, Counselor!"

"What's the problem?" he asked, confused, as the assembled diners once again stared at him.

"Maybe nothing," she said as they walked out the front door.

"Then where are we rushing to?"

"Just humor me!" she snapped, leading him across the street and into a women's clothing store.

"What do you think—that he's going to try to murder me in a public restaurant?" demanded Becker.

"Stranger things have happened," she said. "Now keep your voice down, or they might throw both of us out of here."

Becker stationed himself by a window and spent the next ten minutes pretending to wait patiently while Jaimie methodically examined every coat and jacket they had in the junior sizes.

"Definitely paranoid," he whispered as she passed by him on her way to the next row of jackets. "MacCarron's probably calling back right now."

As he was speaking, a nondescript blue car pulled up to the restaurant and a small, well-dressed man got out. He entered the building, then emerged a moment later and climbed into the car, which sped off and disappeared around a corner.

"You see?" whispered Becker. "MacCarron probably sent someone to pick me up, and since I wasn't there, he'll—"

Suddenly half a dozen people burst out of the restaurant, gesticulating wildly, and a moment later a trio of police cars pulled up, followed by an ambulance. Becker and Jaimie watched from the clothing shop as the gathering crowd was kept back, and a tall, slender man in a colonel's uniform accompanied two paramedics who carried another man on a stretcher. They loaded the stretcher into the back of the ambulance, and after a moment's hesitation the colonel decided to ride with the blood-soaked patient.

"That's the colonel who was at the next table," whispered Jaimie, as the ambulance sirens faded in the distance and still more police cars pulled up. She turned to Becker. "Do you remember who he was sitting with?"

"No."

"A major." She paused. "After you left, they would have been the only two officers in the restaurant."

"You're sure?"

She nodded. "You were saying something about paranoia?"

Becker sat in his hotel room, staring at his suitcase. "I can't believe it," he repeated.

"Well, you'd better *start* believing it," said Jaimie.

"The military doesn't kill its own."

"Then obviously it doesn't consider you one of its own, Counselor."

He shook his head. "It doesn't make any sense. Why should they want to kill me—and even if they did, why not do it when I was at the hospital, when there wouldn't have been any witnesses? What do I know now that I didn't know this morning?"

"You know they were lying to you," she replied patiently. "And you told them so when you asked to see Montoya again."

"But I don't know *why* they were lying!"

"Maybe they aren't aware of that."

"This is crazy!"

"You get no argument from me, Counselor. I've always thought people who go around killing other people were crazy." She paused. "The question really isn't Sane or Crazy, you know," she continued at last. "It's True or False. And it's true that they're trying to kill you."

"I've got to find out what the hell is going on," he said.

"Not smart, Counselor," said Jaimie. "You don't confront the people who are trying to kill you before you've done *lots* of preparation."

"Well, I can't just sit here in a Chicago suburb, waiting for them to find me," he said irritably.

"I agree," she said. "Besides, they'll probably have those calls I made traced in another six or seven hours. We'd better be long gone by then."

"I've got to go back to Washington," said Becker after some consideration. "That's where all my contacts are. It's the only place where I can function."

"Function? You mean as a lawyer?"

He shook his head again. "As a fugitive. If I'm going to find out who's trying to kill me and why, Washington is the place to start."

"Okay," she replied with a shrug. "Makes no difference to me. Their computer experts may suspect I'm helping you, but nobody is gonna be able to prove it. Washington's as good a place as any other, and at least I'll have access to my own computers."

"All right," he said, getting to his feet. "I think the first thing to do is go to the airport."

"Which one?"

"O'Hare. Why?"

"You're not thinking like a fugitive, Counselor," said Jaimie. "They have to know by now that they killed the wrong man. That means they're going to be watching all the Chicago airports and supertrain stations. I think we'd be a lot better off driving to Milwaukee and catching a plane from there."

"Good idea," he agreed, and then paused. "Won't they be watching the Washington airports and stations, too?"

"Of course."

"So how does flying out of Milwaukee help us?"

She smiled. "We'll fly to Baltimore and rent a car from there."

"I don't like showing my identification for the car."

"Then we'll take a bus."

"Let's play it by ear," he said. "If I can figure out a way to get a car, I'd much rather do that. They may be watching the bus stations, too." He sighed. "I don't suppose it'll make all that much difference once they know I'm alive."

"No sense telling them you're in Washington."

"They'll know that soon enough," he answered. "I was trained as a lawyer, not a covert agent. I don't imagine I'll be able to keep my whereabouts secret for more than a day or two. The trick is for me to find out why they want to kill me before they can find me. It's as simple as that."

"*Nothing's* as simple as that, Counselor, but I get the point."

"I don't suppose you have any phony ID with you?"

She shook her head. "I can print it up at home, but I don't have a laser printer with me—and I don't think it would be safe to go back to that computer store."

"I don't know," he mused. "It's less than a block from where they killed the major. They'd never think we'd be dumb enough to hang around there."

"They'd be right," she said firmly. "There are probably hundreds of cops and soldiers combing the area right this minute. I don't know about you, but *I'm* sure as hell not going back there."

"Well," he said with a shrug, "there's no sense in my going without you. Let's get this show on the road."

He stood up, picked up his suitcase, and walked to the door.

"You know," she said, just before he opened it, "there's a better way than renting a car."

"Oh?"

"I've still got a bundle of cash. Why don't we just take a cab?"

"All the way to Milwaukee?"

"No, that's so unusual it would call attention to ourselves. But why not change cabs every fifteen or twenty miles? Then we don't leave an ID record anywhere."

"Makes sense," he said, nodding his approval.

They stopped by Jaimie's room long enough to get her luggage, then checked out of the hotel. Becker paid with cash, hoping that that plus his bogus name might buy them a little time.

They took a cab north to Waukegan, then took another cab to Racine, just north of the Wisconsin state line. From there to Milwaukee took two more cab rides and another hour, but at last they reached the airport, where they booked passage to Baltimore as a Mr. and Mrs. Maynard Smith. They paid with cash, took their tickets, and immediately boarded the plane.

Jaimie slept during the flight, while Becker again went through his ritual of scrutinizing his fellow passengers, trying to decide which, if any, had been sent to kill him. He kept turning the events of the day over and over in his mind, trying to put all the pieces together and make some sense out of them. After a frustrating ninety minutes, he had come to only two conclusions: some person or persons in the military had ordered his death, and he had no idea why.

It was dark when the plane touched down in Baltimore, and he nudged Jaimie gently.

"Are we there yet?" she asked sleepily.

"Yes."

"I'll be glad to get home and sleep in my own bed," she said, yawning and stretching her arms.

"A couple of hours and we'll be there."

"Oh, that's right," she said, suddenly alert. "We're in Baltimore."

Jaimie stood up in the aisle, then noticed that Becker was still seated.

"Aren't you coming?" she asked.

"You go ahead. I'll be along in a couple of minutes."

"What's the matter?"

"If they've done their homework, they know I'm traveling with a black woman. It makes more sense to go through the gate separately."

"Good idea," she said. "It's been a long trip. I think I'll freshen up at the first ladies' room we come to. You can pick me up there."

He nodded and she began following their fellow passengers into the airport. Then he checked his wristwatch, waited another sixty seconds, and walked to the front of the plane.

As he exited the plane he studied the waiting area, looking for anyone in a military or police uniform, but couldn't spot anything out of the ordinary. He quickly reached the door to the women's restroom, suddenly felt very nervous standing out in the open, and decided to spend a couple of minutes in the nearby men's restroom.

He entered the empty room, walked up to a sink, and began rinsing his face off. As he was looking at his face in the mirror, wondering how it had come to look so haggard in just two days, he saw a tall man enter the restroom and approach the adjoining sink. He was about to reach for a towel when the man's overcoat fell open and he saw the handle of a pistol.

His mind raced back to basic training, some fourteen years ago. Twenty-three ways to disarm a man. He couldn't remember any of them. Six blows guaranteed to kill or incapacitate. He didn't know where to deliver them.

Time seemed to freeze as he studied the man, looking for a weakness in the man's approach, wondering what he would do if he found one. Bits and pieces began coming back to him. A heel in the groin. But to do that he'd have to turn around and put his enemy on the alert. All right, then. A blow to the nose, pushing up, driving the bone and cartilage into the brain. It would never do. He was bent over, with his back to his enemy; there was no way to sight his target as he spun around.

The man was four steps away, then three, then two.

Becker looked for a weapon—a loose soap dish, a glass, anything. He couldn't find one.

Suddenly a large hand reached out and grabbed him by the shoulder.

"Yes?" he said calmly, ignoring the hand and continuing to rinse his face.

"Major Becker?"

"You've made a mistake," he said, still rinsing his face. "My name is Smith."

"Why don't you just come along quietly with me, Major Becker," continued the man, "and we can avoid a scene."

"I told you—my name is Smith," replied Becker. "Who are you and what do you want?"

"You're Major Maxwell Becker," said the man patiently. "Almost everyone else is waiting for you to show up in Washington, but I had a hunch that you might try to get home via Baltimore."

Suddenly Becker let his body go limp for an instant. The man instinctively leaned forward to support him with both hands, and Becker suddenly pivoted and caught him flush on the jaw with an elbow. The man grunted and staggered back and Becker, following up his advantage, pushed him as hard as he could. The man, already off balance, slammed against a wall and fell groggily to the floor.

Becker pounced on him, quickly appropriated his gun, and then backed away, panting heavily.

"All right," he gasped. "Who are you?"

The man stared up at him and said nothing.

"They're already trying to kill me," continued Becker. "If you don't tell me what I want to know, I might as well give them a reason."

"Go fuck yourself," said the man sullenly.

"I'm not kidding," said Becker. "You were going to kill me. I'm certainly willing to do the same to you."

"Fire a shot and you'll have the airport security down here in ten seconds."

"What were *you* going to do about them?"

"I'm just here to take you into custody."

"Who are you—police, military, who?"

The man stared at him silently.

"Fine by me," said Becker, cocking the pistol and wondering if he would actually use it.

"Just a minute," said the man. He carefully withdrew a wallet from his lapel pocket and tossed it to Becker, who caught it with his free hand and flipped it open.

"Lieutenant William Donald Ramis, Space Service Security," read Becker. He folded the wallet and placed it into his pocket. "Okay, Lieutenant Ramis, suppose you tell me just what the hell is going on?"

"You're a wanted man," said Ramis. "You could save yourself a lot of trouble by giving me back my gun and surrendering to me."

"That might save *you* a lot of trouble," replied Becker. "I don't see that it would do a thing for me." He paused. "Who are you working for?"

"You saw my ID," said Ramis.

"Perhaps I should reword that. Who told you to kill me?"

"My orders are to bring you in. You were to be killed only if there was no alternative."

"Why don't I believe that?"

"Believe anything you want," retorted Ramis. "Those are my orders."

"Bullshit. If the military wanted me alive, they would have tried to arrest me instead of kill me this afternoon in Lake Forest."

"I don't know anything about Lake Forest. I just know what my orders are."

"Who issued them?"

"The space service."

"The space service didn't tell you to get me. An individual did. I need a name."

"Do your worst," said Ramis adamantly. "I'm through talking."

"Look," said Becker angrily, "I'm a loyal American citizen,

and an officer in the United States military. I've never committed a subversive act in my life. Suddenly my own people want me dead. I just want to know why, and if you can't tell me, I want the name of someone who can."

"I can't tell you that," said Ramis. "But I'll make a deal with you."

"What kind of deal?"

"Give me back my gun and I'll give you a four-hour head start before I report what happened."

"I don't believe you," said Becker.

Ramis merely shrugged and made no reply.

"On your feet." Becker cast a quick glance at the door and wondered how much longer he could count on being alone with Ramis in a public restroom. He decided that he'd settle for thirty seconds.

Ramis stood up, hands slightly raised, and faced Becker.

"Walk over to the toilet stall and face the door," ordered Becker.

Ramis did as he was told, and Becker, mustering all his strength, brought the pistol down on the back of the tall man's head. Ramis collapsed with a grunt and began trying to stand. Becker hit him again, and he finally lost consciousness.

Becker placed the gun in his pocket, then dragged Ramis' body into the stall, placed him on the toilet seat, and then shut the door. He checked himself in the mirror, was surprised that he looked so calm and well-groomed, and then walked out the door into the long corridor leading from the arrival gate to the baggage-claim area.

"Where were you?" demanded Jaimie, who was standing outside the women's restroom.

He related what had happened as they walked quickly toward an exit.

"You should have killed him," she said when Becker was through. "He could wake up at any minute."

"I can't kill an officer for following his orders."

"He only had one order," she said firmly, "and it didn't have anything to do with arresting you."

"What makes you so sure?"

"He came alone. If they wanted to take you into custody, they'd have sent at least two men, in case you put up a struggle. He was here to kill you, plain and simple."

"Then why didn't he do it the second he walked in?"

"Airport security. Too much publicity." She shook her head. "He would have walked you out of the airport, taken you to a nice quiet spot, and pulled the trigger." She paused. "Did you remember to take his gun?"

"Got it right here," said Becker, patting his pants pocket.

"Good. You're getting better at this all the time."

"Word from on high," he said wryly. "Well, what's next? I don't suppose it can hurt to rent a car, since Ramis will let everyone know I was here anyway."

"And then you'll drive it all the way to Washington so they'll know for sure where you are?"

"Well, a taxi's no good. They keep a record of every address they go to."

"How about a bus?" she said. "No ID and no addresses. We simply get off at the terminal and walk out."

"They'll be watching the terminals."

"Well," she said, "we're a little old for hitchhiking."

"What about a series of three or four cabs," he suggested as they finally walked through the airport's exit door, "the same as we used to get from Chicago to Milwaukee?"

"It's a lot harder to find cabs at night in the Maryland countryside."

"We could hotwire a car."

"I'm game if you are," she replied. "But I have to warn you that I don't know how to do it."

"You can't hotwire a car?" he said. "What the hell kind of criminal are you?"

"A sophisticated one. I can repair a computer; I just can't fix a car."

"Me, neither," he admitted. "All right, we'll take a bus and get off at the stop before Washington, and then take a cab to some generic downtown location."

They found the bus depot without difficulty, and were soon speaking in low tones in the back of the almost-empty vehicle as it sped through the moist night air toward Washington, D.C.

"What do you plan to do when we get there?" asked Jaimie as the bus neared the city limits.

"Ramis is probably awake by now, so I can't go to my apartment or my office, that's for sure," he replied. "I suppose I'll rent a hotel room under a phony name and go from there. What about you? Can you get to your computers?"

She nodded. "Nobody should be looking for me until morning. I ought to be able to get in and out by then."

"Then take this," said Becker, handing her Ramis' wallet, "and see if you can find out exactly who he works for."

"Right," said Jaimie, taking it and putting it in her purse.

"Where will you be after tomorrow morning?" asked Becker.

"I don't know yet."

"How will I get in touch with you?"

She lowered her head in thought for a moment. "Have you got a Social Security card?"

"Of course."

"Give it to me."

He took it out of his wallet and handed it to her. "What's this all about?"

"Can you remember the last eight numbers of it?"

"Certainly."

"Give me until noon tomorrow to find a place. Then call that number."

"What number—you mean the last eight digits?"

"Right. I'll have it rigged so that they connect you to my vidphone."

"Can you do that?" he asked. "I mean, what if someone else already has the number?"

"Oh, ye of little faith," she said with a smile. "You've been with me for two days now. Do you really think that I can't switch a couple of vidphone numbers?"

"I take it back," he said.

The bus stopped for more passengers, and when a few of them sat down on nearby seats, Becker and Jaimie rode the rest of the way in silence. They got off just outside the city limits and phoned for a taxi.

Becker had the cab drop Jaimie off a couple of blocks from her apartment, then directed the driver to a large hotel that catered to the tourist trade. He paid him off with the last of the money Jaimie had appropriated in Illinois, then walked up to the front desk and requested a single room for an indefinite stay.

"Name?" asked the desk clerk.

Aware that both Becker and Smith would probably light up security boards somewhere in the city, he repressed a smile and gave his name as William Ramis.

"Where is your luggage, Major Ramis?" asked the clerk.

"Somewhere in Oklahoma, I think," he said with a grimace. "The airline says that it'll be delivered sometime tomorrow."

The clerk chuckled, and a few moments later Becker sat down, exhausted, in his twenty-fourth-floor room. It had been a long, grueling, occasionally terrifying couple of days, and he was glad to just take his shoes off and relax.

He commanded the holovision to activate and turned to a round-the-clock news station to see if the incident at the Baltimore airport had been reported yet.

He forgot all about it when he saw the headline story.

Captain Wilbur H. Jennings had decided to enter a plea of temporary insanity in his much-anticipated trial for the murder of two crewmen aboard the starship *Theodore Roosevelt*. In a brief appearance before the press at Bethesda Hospital, he stated that he had no recollection of his actions, deeply regretted the grief he had caused his victims' families, hoped he had not irreparably damaged the space program, and was anxious to pay his debt to society.

12

It was four in the morning.

Becker had been unable to sleep, and clutched for Ramis' pistol every time he heard footsteps in the corridor outside his room. It was when he was pacing around the bed and literally jumped at his own shadow that he decided he simply wasn't cut out to be a fugitive. He dressed quickly, put the gun in his pocket, rode the elevator down to the lobby, walked across the street, found a properly nondescript and unidentifiable vidphone booth, and called Magnussen at his home.

"Yeah?" said a sleepy voice a moment later.

"Turn on your light," said Becker. "I can't see you."

"Who is it?" asked Magnussen, staring blearily into his vidscreen.

"The light," repeated Becker.

"I'll get to it, I'll get to it," mumbled Magnussen. "What the hell time is it, anyway?"

"Four o'clock."

"Christ! In the morning?" A soft light suddenly came to life, and Magnussen continued staring at his vidscreen. "My God, Max, it's you?"

"Surprised I'm still alive?"

"What are you talking about? Couldn't it wait until morning?"

"Jim, take thirty seconds and try to get your brain functioning," said Becker.

Magnussen sat absolutely still at the edge of his bed for a moment, then rubbed his eyes and turned back to the screen.

"All right, I'm awake," he said. "What's up?"

"Good. Now suppose you tell me what's going on?"

"What do you mean?"

"Let's start with Jennings. When I left Washington two days ago, he—"

"You've been out of town?" interrupted Magnussen, surprised.

"When I left town," repeated Becker, "he was quite willing to die in exchange for being allowed to tell his story on the witness stand. Now, suddenly, he's pleading temporary insanity. What kind of deal did you make with him?"

"I haven't said a word to him, Max. He asked for a press conference and they gave it to him. I was as surprised as anyone."

"Okay, *you* didn't get to him. Who did?"

"I don't know if anyone did," answered Magnussen. "He sounded pretty sincere to me."

"And pretty sane?"

"He's pleading *temporary* insanity, Max, not permanent."

"Bullshit. Someone is forcing him to do it."

Magnussen yawned. "Is that what you called about? We really could have discussed this in the morning."

"That's only part of what I called about," said Becker. "The other part is that I may not be alive in the morning, and I want to know why."

"I don't understand you."

"The military has made two attempts on my life today."

"You're crazy! We don't kill our own people."

"Jim, it's not a matter of *if* they're trying to kill me, but *why*."

"I'd heard around the office that you'd gotten into some deep shit, but for our people to *kill* you? I just don't believe it."

"Did they say what kind of trouble I was in?"

Magnussen shook his head. "I didn't even know you were out of town. I figured that maybe you'd been caught shacking up with a general's wife, or something like that."

"I went to Great Lakes to interview a witness in the Jennings case."

"Why should *that* get you into trouble?" asked Magnussen.

"I don't know!" snapped Becker. "When I got there, they'd put a double in his place, and—"

"A physical double?"

"No, just some guy pretending to be the man I wanted to interview. But the second they realized I didn't believe in their actor, someone put out a kill order, and I've been running for my life ever since. I want to know why."

"I swear to you, Max, I don't know anything about it."

"Who would?"

"I honestly don't know."

"Have you ever heard of a hit man named Ramis?" continued Becker. "He works for us. Do you know who gives him his orders?"

"The name's not familiar."

"Shit."

"I can try to hunt this Ramis down tomorrow."

"Don't bother. I know where he is."

"You didn't kill him, did you?"

"No, I didn't kill him."

"Then I can still pull out a dossier on him once I get to the office."

"I may be dead by the time you find it," said Becker, deciding not to mention that Jaimie was also working on extracting Ramis' dossier. "I can't wait for tomorrow, Jim. I've got to do something *now*."

"Like what?"

"I haven't done anything wrong . . . and besides, the Jennings case is settled. I *can't* affect it no matter what I do." Becker paused. "I want you to bring me in."

"Bring you in?"

"Guarantee my safety and I'll surrender myself to the space service. I just want to talk to someone and straighten things out."

"Max, I'm just a lawyer. You sound like you want someone from our Covert Operations branch."

"I don't care who you get. I just want people—my *own* goddamned people—to stop trying to kill me."

"Do you want to come to my place?" asked Magnussen. "We can go in together in the morning. I guarantee no one will try to kill you while I'm a witness."

Becker shook his head. "Jim, if you're on their side, there'll be a killer waiting for me at your house . . . and if you're not, I honestly don't think they'd flinch at killing the both of us."

"If you don't trust me, who can I get in touch with that you *will* trust?"

Becker was silent for a moment as he considered his options.

"The police," he said at last.

"The Washington police?"

"I want them to put me in protective custody until you can set up a meet between me and whoever put out the kill order."

"They stay out of military affairs, Max, unless you commit a crime right under their noses. I don't know if they'll do it."

"Have someone call them and explain the situation."

"We come back to the same problem: who do you trust to make the call?"

Becker sighed deeply, "I don't know," he said. "I honestly don't know."

"How about just walking into the local police station and demanding protective custody?"

"Not a chance," replied Becker adamantly. "They'll think I've slipped a gear and stick me in Bethesda, right next to Jennings. If I'm going to be killed, I at least want my assassin to have to work up a sweat."

"Well, you're going to have to tell me what to do, Max. If you're crazy, I've got to humor you, and if you're telling the truth, I don't want to be responsible for sending the wrong guy after you."

"I know," said Becker wearily. "All right. Call somebody in Covert Operations who's totally unconnected with the Jennings case and tell them to bring me in."

"You mean deliver you to the police?"

"Right. Have them make the arrangements."

"Where can I reach you when it's set up?" asked Magnussen.

"You can't. *I'll* reach *you.*"

"Give me half an hour."

"All right. I'll call you then."

Becker broke the connection, then returned to the hotel lobby. He decided against going back up to his room and instead stopped by the hotel's all-night coffee shop, where he spent the next fifteen minutes reading the sports pages from the previous day's newspaper.

Finally he got up, went back inside, found a different vidphone booth, and called Magnussen again.

"It's all set," said Magnussen.

"What are the arrangements?"

"Be in front of the Washington Monument in half an hour. There's a vidphone booth there. Wait right next to it."

"Who did you contact?"

"Covert Operations."

"Give me a name."

"Colonel Marcus Weldon."

"Never heard of him."

"You're not supposed to have heard of *anyone* in Covert Operations," said Magnussen with a grin.

"What did you tell him?"

"That I had a friend who needed police protection, and that his job was to get you safely into protective custody."

"Did you tell him my name?"

"I had to. Otherwise he wouldn't have agreed. He had to run it through the computer and make sure you were really within the space service's bailiwick."

"Not smart," said Becker. "Somebody's bound to recognize my name."

"These are *our* people, Max."

"These are the people who put a hit out on me."

"What else could I do?" said Magnussen in exasperation. "Look, if you don't trust me, or you've got any doubts, don't show up."

"I have to take the chance," said Becker. "I can't spend the rest of my life in hiding." He paused. "Which police station are they taking me to?"

"I don't know."

"All right," said Becker. "You've done your part. Thanks, Jim."

"I still can't believe this is happening."

"It's happening, all right," said Becker. "And Jim?"

"Yes?"

"Be very careful."

"What's that supposed to mean."

"It means that anyone who talks to me might not qualify as the military's favorite person this week."

"Don't be melodramatic, Max. Nobody's going to shoot me for answering your phone call."

"I hope not," said Becker, breaking the connection.

He flagged down a cab and went directly to the Washington Monument, arriving about fifteen minutes before his saviors from Covert Operations were due.

The vidphone booth was deserted at this time of the

morning, as was the entire area. An overhead light totally illuminated the area around the booth, and he felt too much like a target standing there, so he walked back into the shadows around the base of the monument where he couldn't be seen from the street. He lit a small cigar, checked his watch, and waited.

Five minutes passed, then ten, then fifteen, and finally twenty. He checked his watch again.

He was considering entering the booth and calling Magnussen to make sure he was at the correct location when an unmarked green car slowly pulled up to the curb.

Becker backed further into the shadows and peered out at the car—and suddenly, through the darkness, he saw the light reflected off the barrel of a gun.

The car came to a stop, two large men got out, spent a moment walking around the area of the phone booth while Becker retreated still further, conversed in low tones, reentered the green car, and drove off. Becker waited another half hour to make sure that they weren't going to return, then began walking again. He'd gone perhaps a mile when he stopped at another vidphone booth and dialed the last eight digits of his Social Security number.

"Yes?" said Jaimie's familiar voice. Something, probably a cloth, covered the camera so that he couldn't see her.

"It's me," said Becker.

"How's it going?" she asked.

"Not very well," he said. "They know I'm in town and they're after me."

"How did they find out?"

"I called Magnussen."

"Not smart, Counselor. What the hell did you think *he* could do for you?"

Becker shrugged. "I hoped he could bring me in."

"He's a lawyer, not a spy. He wouldn't begin to know how to go about it."

"I know."

"So he went to someone who *does* know about this kind

of business, and they came after you and tried to kill you," she concluded. "Is Magnussen part of it?"

"I don't think so, but I don't dare contact him again."

"So what are you going to do now?"

"I suppose I'll go back to my hotel," said Becker.

"Dumb," she said bluntly. "They know you're in Washington, and they must know you're not at your apartment. They'll be checking every hotel in town. What name did you use?"

"Ramis."

"*That's* got to light up some computers. You'd better come over to my place."

"Your apartment?"

"My hideout."

"What's the address?"

She gave it to him. It was on the edge of the city's largest slum.

"What if someone's tapping your line?" he asked suddenly.

"Believe me, I'd know it if anyone was trying to listen in."

"I've got another name for you to check out while you're waiting," said Becker. "Colonel Marcus Weldon."

"Space service?"

He nodded. "Covert Operations."

"I'll get busy on it. And Max?"

"Yes."

"Watch your step."

"I'm pretty sure no one's following me."

"That wasn't what I meant."

"Oh?"

"Wearing a white face in my neighborhood at five in the morning isn't the most brilliant disguise in the world."

"I'll be careful," he assured her. "What name should I look for on the mailbox?"

"Just come to the address. I'll know when you've arrived."

"You've got the place rigged already?"

"Booby-trapped is more the word for it. Just enter the foyer and wait for instructions."

"Right," he said. "See you in twenty minutes."

It took him almost fifteen minutes to find a cab this time, and the first two he stopped refused to drive him to the address he wanted. Finally he found a cabbie who rode with a powerful revolver laid on the front seat next to him, and a few minutes later he was passing through a housing project that should have been torn down forty years earlier. He began feeling uneasy, and placed his hand in his pocket, touching the revolver for security.

Finally he arrived at the address Jaimie had given him. He entered the lobby of a four-story building that was in dire need of repair and stood in the musty foyer. A moment later the inner door slid open, and he walked into the interior of the building.

"Up here!" called Jaimie's voice, and he began climbing the stairs, almost tripping twice on the torn carpeting.

"Third floor, Counselor!" she called again, and soon he saw a light coming from her open door.

"Well, I see you made it safe and sound," she said as he entered her apartment. This one was neither as large nor as luxurious as her permanent dwelling place, but it was still far more elegant than the exterior of the building promised.

"I wish you hadn't yelled like that," he said. "Someone could have spotted me."

"Not very likely, Counselor. I'm the only resident."

"Oh?"

"I own the whole building."

"Why did you buy it?" he asked. "Surely you didn't think you'd need a hideout someday."

"I own all but three buildings on the block," she replied. "As soon as I get my hands on them, I'm going to tear down the whole block."

"What'll you put up in their place?"

She shrugged. "I haven't decided yet. Probably a bunch of soup kitchens and free stores for the locals."

"You never struck me as being all that philanthropic."

"I need the tax write-off."

"That sounds more like the Jaimie Nchobe I know."

"Just your typical enlightened slumlord," she replied with a smile. She led him to a sofa in her living room. "Did you have any trouble getting here?"

"Nobody tried to kill me since I spoke to you, if that's what you mean," he said. "For a while I thought I was going to die of old age before I found a cabbie who was willing to come here."

She sat down on an easy chair a few feet away from him.

"By the way, I found out a little about your friend Lieutenant Ramis," she said.

"What?"

"He's a killer, all right," she replied. "He used to free-lance for the CIA. Killed the wrong man in Johannesburg six years ago, went into hiding, and didn't surface until eight months ago, when he got a commission in the space service."

"Who's his immediate superior?"

"Well, now, that's the interesting part," said Jaimie with an amused smile. "He works directly for Colonel Marcus Weldon."

"The guy who just tried to wipe me out?"

"Right."

"That's very interesting," he agreed.

"May I assume that your next question will be: who's in charge of Covert Operations in the space service?"

"You may."

"General Benjamin Roth."

"Never heard of him."

"He's stationed in New York, but given how many of his people are out to kill you, the order had to come from him."

"Then once I talk to Jennings and find out what they did to him to make him change his plea, Roth's the next man I have to see."

"Jennings changed his plea?" she said, surprised.

"Yes."

"To insanity?"

"Temporary insanity," replied Becker.

"When?"

"While we were in Illinois."

"Oh, boy," she said in a small voice. "You'd better forget Jennings and get to Roth, and the sooner the better."

"I want to know why Jennings changed his plea."

"It doesn't matter, Counselor," she said.

"It does to me."

"Don't you understand?" she said. "Jennings doesn't matter anymore."

"Why do you say that?"

"Because even if they thought that killing you was the best way to screw up Jennings' defense—which is a pretty ridiculous thought when you get right down to it—they wouldn't still be after you. They would have stopped the minute Jennings changed his plea."

"Damn!" he said. "I've been so busy running for my life that I haven't even considered that."

"Well, you'd better start considering it right now."

"They've got what they wanted," he said, frowning, "and they're *still* after me. What the hell does it mean?"

She stared at him for a long moment.

"It means we're in *big* trouble, Counselor."

|1|3|

Jaimie fixed Becker a gin and tonic, then made the same for herself and sat back down in her easy chair.

"All right, Counselor. Let's see if we can figure out *why* they still want you dead."

"It can't have anything to do with the Jennings case," he said. "That's as good as over."

"It's *got* to have something to do with it," she replied. "They didn't start shooting until you tried to prepare a plea of not guilty."

"But they've got what they want from him. He's pleading temporary insanity, the case will take all of ten minutes to resolve, and everyone will have what he wanted." He paused. "Except Jennings. I'd have bet my pension that he'd have died before he agreed to temporary insanity."

"Forget about Jennings," she said. "It's *you* they're after. Or, rather, *us*. Why?"

"I don't know."

"I don't either, but they don't mobilize all those hit men without a very good reason. What do we know that's got them in such a panic?"

"Nothing," said Becker.

"That's not so, Counselor," she corrected him. "We know a lot of things. We just have to figure out which is the one they want to kill us for."

"All right," said Becker. "We know that Montoya isn't in Great Lakes. Or, at least, we *think* the man I spoke to wasn't him." He paused, his face masking his frustration. "They don't kill people for that."

"Keep going."

"We know that they created a story about a drug ring, and even went so far as to plant phony data in their computers." He looked at her. "They don't kill people for *that*, either. I mean, hell, the truth is that there's *no* drug ring; you'd think they'd be out to kill people who spread the lie."

"What else?"

"We know that Gillette really is in deep space, and that Mallardi is on Mars. Probably Montoya's there, too." He stared at her helplessly. "So what? Who cares? They didn't have anything to do with a drug ring. As far as we know, they haven't broken any laws or subverted the military. Why should anyone want to kill us because we know these guys are innocent?"

"We also know they killed the wrong man in Lake Forest," said Jaimie.

"You'll never be able to prove the military was involved in it," said Becker dejectedly. "Besides, he was supposed to be me. Which means that when it happened, we already knew something they thought was worth killing us for."

"Well," suggested Jaimie, "let's work backward, then. When did they first try to kill you?"

"When I called MacCarron and tried to arrange another meeting with Montoya."

"In other words, when they suspected you knew Montoya was a fraud."

"Right."

"If Montoya was a fraud," continued Jaimie, "what does that imply to you?"

"That there wasn't a drug ring," replied Becker. "But we already knew that. We found it out on your computer."

She shook her head. "You're answering it the wrong way. *Why* did they try to convince you there was a drug ring?"

"I don't know."

"Yes you do."

Suddenly he stared at her. *"Aliens?"*

"See?" she said. "I told you you knew."

"You're as crazy as *they* are!" said Becker.

"Let's continue to attack it logically," she said, unperturbed. "Why does someone go to all the trouble of fabricating a story?"

"To mislead the investigator," said Becker grudgingly.

"All right. Jennings told you his story. You set out to prove it. And the second you did so, the military moved heaven and earth to *prevent* you from proving it. All the machinery to create this fabrication was immediately set into motion. Hell, they even anticipated you—they sent Gillette back into deep space before you were ever assigned to the case."

She leaned back on her chair and took another sip of her drink. "Now," she went on, "if Gillette, Montoya and Mallardi were sent all over the solar system because they couldn't corroborate the fabrication, what do you suppose they'd have said if you could have cross-examined them?"

"Not that Provost and Greenberg were aliens," said Becker. "That's impossible!"

"Do you remember what Sherlock Holmes once said?" asked Jaimie. "Once you eliminate the impossible, whatever remains, however unlikely, must be the truth." She paused. "Now, you don't know that Jennings' story is impossible. On the other hand, you *do* know that the story about a drug ring is impossible, and so you must eliminate it. What's left?"

"Sherlock Holmes was a character in a goddamned book," protested Becker. "We're talking about aliens in the United States space service, aliens that are virtually indistinguishable from humans. I spoke to some scientists right after Jennings told me his story. You know what they said? They said the odds were trillions to one against it."

"What are the odds against Gillette being involved in a drug ring?" she asked.

"There aren't any odds. We know he wasn't."

"That makes a trillion to one look more palatable, doesn't it?"

He shook his head. "It's ridiculous! And if it *was* so, why would the space service be willing to kill anyone who found out about it? Are you saying that aliens have infiltrated the military up to the highest echelons, and that everyone else is blindly carrying out their orders?"

"I'm not saying anything. There's more to this business than meets the eye."

"You can say *that* again!" muttered Becker.

"I mean," continued Jaimie, "that if they wanted to eliminate everyone who knew about aliens, they'd have started with Jennings, wouldn't they? They'd never have let him speak to you."

"That's what I've been trying to tell you," said Becker in exasperation. "Forget all this alien crap, and let's try to figure out what's *really* going on."

"The only thing we know is going on is that you were purposely misled after you spoke to Jennings. The reasons may be conjecture, but the fact remains."

"Therefore," Becker responded, "the question is: *why* was I misled? I must have learned *some*thing from him."

"You did."

"But what?"

"You know what."

"It's too farfetched to even consider," said Becker irritably.

"I keep telling you: look at it logically. When did you learn whatever it is that you're not supposed to know? When you spoke to Jennings, because that's when they started manipulating witnesses in earnest."

"I have no problem with that," said Becker. "Just with the *information* you think I learned."

"You didn't let me finish," noted Jaimie.

"All right," he said. "Finish."

"When did they try to kill you? *After* you found out that they were misleading you."

"So?"

"So why didn't they try to kill you the minute you walked out of Jennings' hospital room? Whatever he told you could be transmitted to hundreds of others by nightfall. You could have told the press, the military, anyone you wanted." She paused, then continued triumphantly. "The reason has to be that whatever you learned was so farfetched, so unbelievable, that you gave it no credence until you learned that they were misdirecting you."

"Shit," said Becker softly.

"What is it?"

"You make it sound so . . . so *sensible*," he said. "But it isn't. It's the craziest thing I've ever heard."

"Did Jennings strike you as crazy?" she asked. "You've always told me that he seemed as sane as your friend Magnussen."

"Let me think," said Becker, and Jaimie fell silent, watching him intently. He remained motionless for almost a full minute, then looked up at her. "It's a possibility," he admitted with a deep sigh.

"Well, that's a start," she replied. "At least you're not calling it crazy anymore."

"But I've got to talk to Jennings again," he continued. "I've got to find out if he's sincere about changing his plea, or if they've somehow bought or scared him off."

"That's not gonna be easy to do," said Jaimie. "They'll have him locked up under heavy security—and I'd be very surprised if every single employee and guard in Bethesda wasn't walking around with a hologram of you in his pocket."

"Still, I've got to see him once more."

"Does he have a phone or a computer in his room?"

Becker shook his head. "Just a holovision."

"I could intercept one of the local signals and put you on the screen," she said, "but there's no guarantee he'd be tuned to that channel—and even if he was, there's no way we could receive his reply." She considered the possibilities, then shook her head. "No, even if I could get around that, I'd have to use so much power that they'd have us located inside of a minute." She paused again. "Maybe *I* could go to Bethesda."

"No," said Becker adamantly. "They may be clumsy, but they're not stupid. By now they must know that you're involved. They'll be on the lookout for you as well as me."

She shrugged. "Well, it was a thought."

"A bad one."

"So what do you intend to do?"

"I can't get to Jennings until after the trial," said Becker. "Once they put him in a home somewhere, maybe I can sneak in and see him."

"I wouldn't count on it," she replied. "Certainly not anytime soon, while they're still actively hunting for you."

"That's the problem I've got to address in the meantime."

"That's quite some little problem, being hunted by the entire space service," she agreed.

"I've got to find this General Roth and have him call off the hunt."

"What makes you think he will?"

"I don't know," he said wearily. "I'll just have to find some way to convince him that I'm not a threat to national security."

"They'll shoot you down before you get within half a mile of him," she predicted.

"Maybe not. They're looking for a fugitive who's hiding out in Washington, not a man who's stalking General Roth in New York. Hell, I'm not even supposed to know who Roth is, or that he's got anything to do with this. I'm supposed to turn myself in like a proper soldier and get killed right here and now." He paused. "That's my advantage. I'm supposed to be hiding, not hunting."

"How are you going to get out of the city?"

"That's the easy part," he replied. "You've got your various printers here. You can make me a new driver's license and ID cards. I'll leave my uniform behind and go as a private citizen." Suddenly he grinned. "I'll even let you treat me to a new car with some of your ill-gotten Swiss money. That way the registration papers will match my ID, just in case they start stopping cars on the way from here to New York."

"Yeah, it'll probably work," she agreed after a moment's consideration. "But getting to New York is the easy part. Getting next to General Roth is the hard part."

"We'll convince him I'm still here," said Becker. "You can use my ID and make a couple of clumsy efforts to access my computer files—clumsy enough to alert them to the fact that I'm in town, but without letting them pinpoint the location."

"Sounds good to me," said Jaimie. "I'll take a couple of my machines along."

"Will they be able to tell that you're trying to access them from out of the area?"

"They would if I did," she replied. "But I'll leave a machine behind and program it to try accessing your files when it receives a signal from me."

"Okay," said Becker. "Now, what can you tell me about General Roth?"

"Let's go take a look," she said, getting to her feet and leading him into the next room. Once it had been a dining room, complete with imitation chandelier and artificial wainscoting, but she had turned it into an office housing four computers of advanced capabilities.

"Over here, Counselor," she said, leading him to a computer that was in the farthest corner of the room. "By the way, before we start, maybe we'd better take care of the bill at your hotel so we don't alert the gunmen too soon."

"No," said Becker.

"No?"

"They already know I'm in town, and that I'm not staying at my apartment. Why not make them waste some manpower hanging around the hotel waiting for me to show up?"

"Good for you!" she said with a grin. "Every time I think you're hopeless, you come up with a suggestion like that."

"Thinking like a wanted criminal takes getting used to," he replied.

"Not at all, Counselor. You just start each day with the assumption that everyone in the world is out to get you, and you go from there."

"It's getting easier to assume that with every passing minute," he said wryly.

"By the way, are you getting hungry?" she asked. "It's nearly daybreak."

"Let's find out about Roth first."

"Whatever you say," she replied with a shrug, activating the computer.

A moment later the holographic screen displayed the grim visage of a middle-aged man with a shock of thick gray hair and a handlebar mustache.

"That's him?" asked Becker.

"That's him," affirmed Jaimie. "Tough-looking grunt, isn't he?"

"What information have you got on him?"

She hit a few keys, and the image of General Roth was replaced by his military record. He had entered the army as a lieutenant twenty-three years ago, had seen action in Zambia, Pakistan, and Paraguay, had transferred to the space service six years ago, and had risen from the rank of lieutenant colonel to two-star general, though his record since then had been classified.

"Where does he work out of?" asked Becker.

Another command, another document.

"Classified?" said Becker, frowning. "How do his people get in touch with him?"

"His people know where to find him."

"Can you break through the red tape?"

"Given a couple of hours," said Jaimie. "But I might not have to."

"Oh?"

"Take a look at *this*."

She hit a final command on the keyboard, and the holograph of a steel-and-glass skyscraper appeared.

"What's that?" said Becker. "It looks like the Diamond Tower."

"It is. He lives there."

"I thought apartments like that sold for four or five million dollars."

"He had a rich papa," she replied with a smile.

"How did you find out about this?" asked Becker.

"Believe it or not, I checked the vidphone directory," replied Jaimie. "His job may be classified, but evidently he has no objection to people knowing that he's a military bigwig with a lot of money. Besides," she added, "the security in the Diamond Tower is probably every bit as good as the security at his office. He's gonna be a hard man to sneak up on."

"What floor is he on?" asked Becker, still staring intently at the building.

"The hundred-and-fifteenth," she said. "There are one hundred and forty, counting the restaurant on the roof."

"Got anything else on him?"

"Not yet," she replied, deactivating the computer. "But I will before we pay him a visit." She paused. "How about some breakfast now?"

He nodded. "Why not?"

"I have to warn you, though—this kitchen isn't quite up to the quality of the one I left behind."

"How many futuristic devices does it take to scramble some eggs and make up a pot of coffee?"

"Probably more than I have," she said. "Cooking isn't one of my strong points."

"I was wondering if you had any weaknesses," he said, following her into the kitchen.

"Oh, I've got lots. I just hide them well."

"That you do. Somehow I feel safer taking on Covert Operations than having you as an enemy."

"That's only because nobody's taken a shot at you for a few hours. Don't forget that you've got the whole goddamned space service out there looking for you."

"You know," he admitted, "I *had* forgotten it for a few minutes. Doping this out with you seems like an intellectual puzzle. It's still difficult to realize that my own people are really trying to kill me."

"Don't worry, Counselor," she said, opening the refrigerator and removing a carton of eggs. "If you survive my cooking, you can survive anything."

"How comforting," he replied dryly.

"Anyway," she said, "we'll eat breakfast, forge some false IDs, wait for the dealerships to open up, and buy a car." She paused. "Something big and blue, I think."

"It's your money," he said with a shrug.

"Not yet, it isn't."

"What are you getting at?"

She flashed him a grin. "Given all the trouble he's put us to, I think the very least General Roth can do is pay for our car."

14

Becker had never liked Manhattan. It was too big, too tall, too polluted, too crowded for him. He always felt claustrophobic walking the streets that seemed to exist only to separate the myriad of skyscrapers. Once upon a time the Empire State Building had been the tallest structure in the world; now Manhattan possessed more than two hundred buildings that towered above it.

Jaimie loved Manhattan for many of the same reasons that Becker felt uncomfortable there. A creature of the cities, she saw it as a Mecca of opportunity; its labyrinthine paths and multitude of hiding places made her feel secure rather than uneasy; and its populace appealed to her predatory instincts.

The city was undergoing its annual face-lifting, the developers reclaiming three or four blocks on the west side while an equal area on the east side was allowed to fall into disrepair, and the poor, the hungry, the pimps and the prostitutes and the pushers, all began their annual migration toward that area which the city fathers felt they could ignore for another twelve months.

They decided to stay at the relatively new Regal Hotel on 58th Street, just a block away from such *doyennes* as the

Plaza and the Park Lane. More to the point, it was only three blocks from the Diamond Tower on Fifth Avenue. It was large—157 stories, and close to six thousand rooms—and characterless, but it always had some vacancies, and Jaimie had made reservations for connecting rooms before they had left Washington. The lower levels of the hotel housed a huge indoor garage, and they parked their new sedan there.

They checked in separately—Jaimie had given Becker's home address as San Francisco and hers as Chicago—then looked about fruitlessly for a bellman who was willing to help unload the car. After waiting for almost twenty minutes, Becker finally found a cart, loaded their suitcases and the two computers Jaimie had brought along onto it, and found a freight elevator, which they took up to the 73rd floor. Once there, they quickly found their adjacent rooms, entered separately, and immediately ordered the connecting door to recede into the wall.

"Well, we're here and nobody's shooting at us yet," remarked Becker. "I suppose that's something."

"Nobody will bother us here," she assured him. "I did a hell of a good job on our IDs. If anyone checks them out, the names and addresses actually exist, and the people are on vacation."

"How the hell did you find the name of some Chicagoan who was on vacation?"

She grinned. "I invaded the database of one of the local kennels," she replied. "I chose a woman who's visiting her mother in New York and isn't due back for a week. Did the same thing in San Francisco: you're a businessman who plans to spend fourteen to seventeen days traveling the East Coast." She paused. "So if the military figures out that we're in Manhattan and starts running all the visitors' names through a database, we're in the clear. My name won't be duplicated, because the woman is staying with her family, and your name won't show up in Manhattan for another week."

He stared at her. "You know, sometimes you scare the hell out of me," he said at last.

"Competent women do that to some men," she replied with a smug smile.

"I'm not only an officer in the military," he continued, "but as a lawyer I'm also an officer of the court. I wonder just how many laws you've broken since we teamed up."

"Probably no more than you."

"Don't remind me."

"There's always an alternative," she said.

"Oh?"

"Turn yourself in and give me the name of a good funeral home."

"Thanks," he said wryly.

"If you're through feeling sorry for yourself, how about helping me set up my computers?"

"Why not?" he said with a shrug, walking over to the cart and unloading it. "By the way, are these things likely to get us into trouble with the hotel?"

"Why should they? Lots of people take their computers with them, especially if they're on business trips."

"They don't take anything *this* complex," he said, gesturing to the machine he had just placed on a table.

"How many maids are gonna know the difference?" she shot back. "Trust me, Counselor."

He shrugged. "You're the computer expert."

"Hold that thought," she said, making various connections at the back of the computer.

It took them ten minutes to set both computers up and unpack their luggage. Then Becker took the cart down the hall, deposited it in the freight elevator and returned to his room.

"Hey, Counselor," said Jaimie from her own room.

"Yeah?"

"I'm hungry."

"Do you want to order from room service?" he suggested.

"No. It costs too much."

"Don't tell me you're spending your own money."

"I'm not . . . but I don't like being ripped off anyway."

"All right," he said. "Where do you want to go?"

"There's a very nice little restaurant on 56th Street that I always hit when I'm in town. It's expensive, but at least you get your money's worth—and it's only a block from the Diamond Tower."

"I suppose I need to dress up for it."

"Well, not a tuxedo, but something a little better than you're wearing."

He sighed. "I'll be ready in five minutes."

"Make it ten," she said, starting to close the door between their rooms. "You need a shave."

He took a quick shower, then shaved and donned a conservative gray business suit. This done, he walked to the door connecting their rooms and knocked on it.

"Are you ready?" he called out.

"Just a minute," said Jaimie.

A moment later the door opened and Jaimie entered his room, wearing an obviously expensive dress.

"What are you staring at?" she demanded.

"You look . . . different."

"Is that good or bad?"

"Good," said Becker. "You look very elegant."

"I'll never get used to high heels," she said disgustedly. "Stop staring. You're making me nervous."

"I'm so used to seeing you in blue jeans and sweatshirts, this is going to take a little getting used to."

"Get used to it in the elevator," she said, opening his door and stepping out into the corridor. "I'm starving."

"Right," he said, falling into step behind her.

They walked to the elevator and spent a few moments waiting for it to arrive.

"You know, you're a fine-looking woman when you make the effort," he remarked.

"I'm not gonna have to lock the door between us, am I?" she asked sharply.

"No."

"Good."

"I was just saying that you look—"

"I know what you were just saying," she replied uneasily, "and I wish you'd stop."

It dawned on Becker that this was the very first time he'd ever seen her uncomfortable, regardless of the situation, and he didn't say another word until the elevator let them off at the upper lobby.

"Looks like a convention," he commented as they passed a number of people wearing plastic badges.

"Three of them, actually," she replied. "I saw them listed at the desk when we checked in: car dealers, librarians, and sporting-goods manufacturers. The car dealers will provide us with an unexpected bit of camouflage."

"I don't think I follow you," said Becker.

"They've got a lot of sleeping rooms at the Regal, but not that much convention space. The car dealers are using the function rooms from nine at night until three in the morning. That means we won't look out of place no matter when we come and go."

"We'll raise more eyebrows for your being black and my being white than for going out at four in the morning," replied Becker. "This is New York, remember? Everyone goes out in the middle of the night when they're on vacation here."

"Well, at least having the car dealers scheduled all night long can't hurt," she replied.

They walked out into the thick, polluted air and began walking along 58th Street.

"Where did all the panhandlers go?" asked Becker, looking around curiously.

"They obviously haven't paid off the cops on this block,"

said Jaimie. "I saw them all over 59th when we drove in. Why did you ask?"

He shrugged. "Just looking over all my possibilities for approaching Roth."

She shook her head. "They'll never let a beggar into the Diamond Tower."

"How about a charity collector?" suggested Becker. "You know, for starving children in Zambia or Nepal?"

"I don't like it."

"Why not?"

"Because if Building Security says no, they've already seen you, and that makes your next approach all the more difficult."

"We could call them and see if it's permissible."

"If you want," she said. "But I can't believe it's gonna be that easy."

They turned onto Fifth Avenue, walked past a row of posh jewelry and clothing stores, and then turned onto 56th Street a couple of minutes later.

"Here we are," she said, walking up to a soot-covered canopy that had once been a metallic gold.

"Looks expensive," remarked Becker as they entered a small foyer that was filled with eighteenth-century gilt furniture.

"Not to worry, Counselor," she said. "It's my treat. Or General Roth's, anyway."

"You're going to put him on his guard."

"Not a chance. Even the bank won't know I've appropriated some of his money until the end of the month."

"I still feel badly about it," said Becker. "After all, *he's* not the enemy."

"He's the one who put out the hit on you," she said. "If he's not the enemy, I'd like to know who is."

"So would I," muttered Becker, as the maître d' approached them and led them to a tastefully secluded table in the back of one of the two dining rooms.

"He acted like he knows you," said Becker when they were studying their menus.

"He does," replied Jaimie. "But he'd act like that just the same. It's his job. Now tell me what you want and let me practice my French."

"You speak French?"

She nodded. "And Kiswahili, and Japanese."

"Why Swahili and Japanese?" he asked.

"Japanese for the same reason as French: not all computer users speak English, but the bulk of them speak one of the three languages."

"And Swahili?"

"My father came from Uganda. I learned it as a child."

"You're a woman of many accomplishments," he said. "Most of them illegal, but an awful lot, anyway."

She laughed. "Am I being complimented or insulted?"

"I never insult ladies who pay for my dinner," said Becker.

"Good. What will you have?"

He ordered a pea soup, duck in a fruit sauce, and a salad, and she deftly translated their orders into French so that their waiter could go to the kitchen and translate them back into English.

"These are such elegant surroundings that it's difficult to remember why we're here," confided Becker with a smile, after the waiter had left. "I'm almost tempted to suggest that we catch a play before breaking into General Roth's apartment and threatening his life."

"It sounds like fun," she agreed. "But there will be a lot more people wandering around the Diamond Tower before midnight than after. I think we'd better go over there as soon as we're through with dinner. And Counselor?"

"What?"

"Don't order dessert."

"Why not?"

"Because there's bound to be a coffee shop or two at the Tower, and if we decide to sit down and discuss our options while we're there, we might as well do it over dessert as over coffee. It'll buy us a little more time, just in case the place is crowded and they're trying to turn the tables over every few minutes."

He nodded. "Makes sense . . . though I just got a look at the dessert cart here. I hate to miss it."

"You're too fat already."

"Thanks."

"Just being honest."

"You lie to everyone else," he noted. "You might tell a little white lie to me every now and then."

She shook her head. "We're partners, Max—and I never lie to my partner. If I start lying to you, I won't stop."

He sighed. "Fair enough."

"Then get that unhappy look off your face. Here comes Jacques with our soup."

"You know him, too?"

"No. I call them all Jacques. No one's ever corrected me."

"Then you can't possibly mind if I call him Henri?"

She smiled. "Suit yourself."

"What's so funny?"

"His French is atrocious. His real name's probably Murray."

"That's okay," grunted Becker. "My French is even worse than his. I couldn't understand a word you said to him."

"Let's see what kind of soup he's bringing us. It may turn out that you weren't the only one who couldn't understand me."

The soup was as ordered, and they spent the next hour enjoying the meal. Becker couldn't believe the size of the tab, but Jaimie paid it cheerfully and left a substantial tip as well. Then they were back out on the street, heading toward the Diamond Tower.

When they reached it, Becker decided that it looked even more impressive in person than on holovision. No less garish, but more impressive. The arched entryway was studded with false but glittering diamonds, and the lobby displayed a sparkling diamond pattern on its immense floor. The building took up no more than fifty feet of Fifth Avenue frontage, but once inside it spread out, covering most of the short block between 56th and 55th Streets. Pricey stores lined the various upper and lower lobbies, five levels of them including a pair of open restaurants and a trio of bars.

Various electronic information boards, their LED lights constantly flashing, directed the visitor to his destination. The first five floors were commercial, the next twenty were the parking garage, the next thirty were offices and exclusive retail outlets. From the 56th floor to the 139th, the building was residential. There were four large apartments on each floor from the 56th to the 100th, and two truly grandiose apartments on each floor above the 100th.

"Oh-oh," said Jaimie as she and Becker stopped to read the board. "Here's the rub. Visitors are not allowed above the 56th floor."

"That's got to be wrong," said Becker. "They've got a restaurant on the top floor."

She read further. "Elevator Number 36 goes nonstop to the rooftop restaurant."

"What's to stop us from taking the elevator that goes to 115?" he asked.

"Take a look," she said, nodding her head in the direction of a bank of residential elevators. "Each passenger has to have his ID okayed before the elevator will let him on. My guess is that you have to go through the whole process again to get off."

He shook his head. "That can't be right. How do these people have friends over for dinner?"

She shrugged. "It doesn't say anything about it on this board."

"Let's hunt up another one," suggested Becker. "There's got to be something about it near the residential elevators."

They strolled toward the three banks of residential elevators, pretending to window-shop as they went. Finally they came to another electronic board.

"Here it is, Counselor," announced Jaimie, pointing to the operative instruction. "You call up on a house phone, they give you a code that they then program into the elevator's computer, and you use that to get on. They then change the code and give you the new exit code while you're in the elevator."

"There are a few bugs in the system," remarked Becker softly. "For one thing, if you're visiting a friend on, say, the 88th floor, and I'm in the elevator with you, I know your exit code."

"Getting *in* may be the easy part," she said. "I've got a feeling that you have to go through the whole process again on the way out, and the elevator computer has to be tied to the personal codes. Even if we get up to Roth's apartment, we may not be able to get back down."

"There's got to be a firewell."

"Coded."

"I doubt it. Some old lady panics and forgets her code and winds up burning to death, the Tower is asking for one hell of a lawsuit."

"Maybe," she said. "The problem is, it's all guesswork. We won't know the situation until we actually try to get in."

"Let's narrow the odds, anyway," said Becker.

"How?"

"It's time for that dessert we never had. Let's go up to the roof for it."

"The place is probably reserved six months in advance," noted Jaimie.

"Good. Then we'll have to find our way down, won't we?"

"You really think the firewell staircase is gonna be accessible, don't you?"

"Let's find out."

She shrugged, and they walked over to Elevator Number 36. Two minutes later it came to a stop at the 140th floor, and Becker had to steady himself for a moment before he stepped out.

They found themselves in a small lobby, and Becker gestured for Jaimie to wait in a plush chair while he approached what was obviously the reservation desk.

"Welcome to the Diamond in the Sky," said the elderly man who was standing behind the desk. "Have you a reservation?"

"No. Do I need one?"

"I'm afraid so, sir. Perhaps you might try the Queen of Diamonds on the fourth level of the lobby, or one of our other fine restaurants on the lower levels. Would you like me to call down and see if they have any tables available?"

"In a few moments, perhaps," said Becker. "Do you mind if my companion and I just look around for a few moments? We're from California, and we've been reading about this place for the past three or four years."

"Certainly," came the reply. "As you reach the north end, you'll find a number of telescopes set up for your enjoyment."

"And is there a restroom?"

The man nodded. "Both restrooms are down this corridor," he said, gesturing to his left.

"Thank you," replied Becker. He turned away from the desk and approached Jaimie. "You've got to go to the ladies' room."

"I do?"

He nodded. "It's down that corridor. Keep on going, and see if you can find anything that looks like an exit or a service elevator."

"Where will you be?"

"There are a bunch of telescopes at the north end. I'll walk off in their direction and see what I can find."

"Where do we meet?"

"If the corridors keep on going, we ought to run into each other. Since the restaurant's got a view, I don't see how that can be, so once you've gone as far as you can go, check everything out and come back here."

She nodded and headed off toward the restrooms while Becker walked slowly toward the north end of the building.

He passed three locked doors—two offices and a store-room—and then the corridor bore to his right, and a moment later he came to a truly spectacular window wall. A number of telescopes stood on sturdy metal stands, and he lowered his head slightly to look through one, which was pointed toward the East River. It was too dark to see anything, and he manipulated it until he was able to focus in on the northern end of Manhattan Island. Then he continued walking, checking every door he passed, hoping to find an exit sign somewhere.

At the very end of the corridor, just before he reached what he assumed was the back wall of the restaurant, he found a service elevator, but although he tried to summon it numerous times, nothing happened. Finally he gave up and walked back to the lobby, where he met Jaimie.

"Come on," he said in a voice loud enough to be over-heard by the man at the desk. "I want you to see the view."

As they walked out of earshot, he turned to her.

"Find anything?"

"I found your stairwell," she said.

"You don't seem enthused."

"You can forget about it. As far as I can tell, it's got a computer lock that won't release unless all the power goes off or the temperature in here reaches the high eighties—and you can bet the farm that the moment it *does* release, there'll be bells and sirens you can hear from ten blocks away." She paused. "Did you fare any better?"

"Maybe," he said, as they reached the telescopes. "I found a service elevator, but I can't make it work."

"Let me see it," she said, and he led her down the corridor until they came to it.

"Pressing the button's just the first step," Jaimie announced after a brief examination. "Then you've got to insert an ID card in this slot."

"What kind of ID card?"

"Who knows?"

"Well, it was worth a try," he said. "Let's go back down, and then take an elevator up to fifty-five."

"Why bother? The stairwell system is gonna be the same throughout the building." She paused. "As I see it, Counselor, you've got three options: swipe an ID card from someone in Maintenance who's qualified to use the service elevator, sneak on a residential elevator down in the lobby and hope whoever's on it gets off on General Roth's floor—or wait for Roth to leave the building, follow him, and try to get him alone."

"I don't like any of them," said Becker. "Roth could stay in his apartment for a week; it's certainly big enough. We'd be calling too much attention to ourselves if we tried to take the residential elevator, and the odds against it stopping at the right floor are too high. And a building like this has to have a maintenance staff of several hundred, maybe even a couple of thousand. Where would we start—and if we stole an ID from the wrong guy, how long would it be before he reported it and everyone was on the alert?"

"Well, I just don't see any other way. Maybe if we waited in the lobby and only tried to get on elevators that had military men in them . . ."

Becker shook his head. "There's that second ID code, just before you get off. If Roth knows I'm still alive—and he must by now—he's not going to let anyone off until he knows who's in the elevator."

"In that case, I'm fresh out of ideas."

"Let's go back to the hotel and think about it," said Becker. "If we have to, we'll try stealing some maintenance man's ID, but I'm not happy with it."

They walked back to the little lobby, summoned the elevator, and were down in the main lobby about two minutes later.

They were halfway back to their own hotel when he suddenly turned to her.

"You said the stairwell lock was geared to a temperature in the high eighties?"

"Yes."

"And that all the locks are on the same system?"

"That's right."

"What if we set a fire on, say, the 53rd floor, and were on the 140th when the computer lock read the temperature. Would it open?"

"A heat bomb with a time-delay?" she mused. "Yes, it ought to work."

"Nothing big," said Becker. "We don't want to burn the place down. Hell, I'd be just as happy setting up a space heater. But whatever we do, if I can put it on, say, a twenty-minute delay, that ought to give us time to get to the 140th. We'll do it at ten in the morning, when the restaurant's virtually empty, so no one's around to watch us in the stairwell. Then, when the lock disconnects, we'll just walk down to the 115th."

"What if someone finds the source of the heat and relocks the doors before we can get to the 115th?"

"Once we're in the well, we're home free. It's against the law to have a fire door that can't open from the stairwell."

"Okay," she said. "Let's say we actually get into Roth's apartment. How will we get out?"

"We have to enter secretly," said Becker, "but we don't have to leave secretly. Once I've had my talk with him, I'll point my gun at him and tell him to take us downstairs."

"Where he'll yell for help at the top of his lungs," said Jaimie.

"He won't say a word," Becker replied confidently.

"Oh? Why not?"

"You're going to see to it."

"Me?" repeated Jaimie. "How?"

"I don't know yet—but once we get back to your computers at the Regal, I sure as hell intend to find out."

15

"It's coming through now," said Jaimie, looking up from her computer.

Becker, who had been sipping a beer that he found in his room's well-stocked pay-by-the-item refrigerator, walked over and looked at the screen.

"He doesn't drink, he doesn't drug, he doesn't gamble, he doesn't screw around," she announced. "Or if he does, he's kept it pretty well hidden from his superiors."

"We've got to find some kind of leverage to use against him," asserted Becker. "He'll know we're not going to kill him. We need something to get him to cancel the hit."

"How will he know you're not going to shoot him?" asked Jaimie.

"He's probably got more information about me than I've got about him."

"But he doesn't know that *I* won't kill him," said Jaimie.

"It won't matter. As the head of Covert Operations, he's probably the kind of guy who's willing to die before he'll say two words to us." He gestured toward the computer. "Keep looking for a weakness."

"He's married, he has five grown kids—the boy and two

of the girls are in the service, another girl is a doctor, and the fifth is estranged from her family and hasn't been in contact with them for almost a decade. He doesn't go to church and professes no religion. He is—or maybe *was*—a master of hand-to-hand combat and holds a couple of sharpshooting records."

"He sounds formidable."

"The head of Covert Operations is *supposed* to sound formidable."

"Do he and his wife live alone?"

"I told you—the kids are all grown and gone."

"What about servants? Or, in an apartment that size, how about military aides, or even bodyguards?"

"I can't pull that kind of information from his dossier," replied Jaimie, after hitting a couple of commands on her keyboard with no results. "I suppose if he has instant access to military personnel, it would be here, but the only way to find out if he's got live-in servants is to go there and see."

"That could be awkward. Given his position, he's got to have direct contact with Covert Operations' headquarters. Probably there's a hidden button somewhere in those ten thousand square feet that summons half a hundred armed men, and we're not going to know where it is until someone hits it."

"The frustrating thing is that there's no way to stake out his apartment until the servants, if they exist, go out. We can watch hundreds of maids and butlers and cooks step out of the elevator on the ground floor, but we can't know which floor they came from."

"Isn't there some light display that tells us where the elevator is at so we can see what floors it stops at?"

She shook her head. "I looked for it when we were there, but they don't have it on the residential elevators, only on the ones that go to the business and office floors."

"Then it looks like his wife is our best bet," said Becker. He paused thoughtfully. "Maybe we could kidnap her while she's out shopping, and then offer her back in exchange for some kind of truce."

"Too tricky," answered Jaimie. "Let's say you accost her in the Diamond Tower's lobby, or even at Tiffany's. You've still got to walk her three blocks to our hotel without her yelling for help, or fainting, or running off into a crowd, and you've got to do it without flashing your pistol. Too many things can go wrong. Besides, for all we know, she's got five plainclothes bodyguards trailing her, bodyguards we won't know anything about until they blow us away." She shook her head again. "Much better to beard the lion in his own den. At least we ought to be able to control the situation there."

"She might still be a weak link, though," suggested Becker. "Roth's got to be trained not to give in to threats of violence. But what if we threaten to kill *her*?"

"If you threaten to do something, you'd better be prepared to do it," said Jaimie seriously. "This guy deals with threats every day. If he sees that you've lied to him once, he won't believe anything else you say."

"Well, she's still a possibility. Keep going through his file and see if there's anything better we can use."

She continued calling up information.

"He's a diabetic," she announced a moment later. "Takes insulin shots twice a day."

"Well, that's *something*," said Becker. "If we get there while he's gone, we can find his insulin and withhold it."

"And turn him into a semicomatose zombie who won't remember or feel obligated to honor anything he says to us?"

"Well, damn it, what would *you* do?" snapped Becker.

"I don't know. I don't think we've found the answer yet."

"Then keep looking. I want to confront him tomorrow. Every hour we wait is an extra hour for them to figure out where we are."

"As far as you're concerned, they think you're in Washington," she assured him. "The first thing I did when I activated my computer was send a signal to the machine we left back in Washington. Right about now everyone connected with this business knows you're in D.C., making clumsy attempts to tie into your computer's memory banks and private files."

He made no reply, but instead started pacing from one room to the next, trying to figure out exactly what he would do if he actually made it to Roth's apartment, and realizing that there wasn't a lot in his legal or even military background to draw upon.

"Take it easy, Counselor," said Jaimie. "You're making me nervous."

"That makes two of us."

"Relax. I've got all night to find something. If it's there, I'll have it before we need it."

"I know," he said. "I suppose the problem is that I'm getting so used to running that waiting is getting harder and harder."

"Depending on what kind of alarm system he's got, you may not get a chance to confront him anyway. We've still got a *lot* of work ahead of us."

"You said my scheme would work."

"Oh, it'll probably get us up to the 115th floor," she responded. "But what are you going to do once you get there? Knock on the door and hope he opens it? Kick it in and hope he doesn't have a private alarm system? Pick the lock with all the skills you acquired in your course on torts?"

"I haven't thought about it," he admitted.

"Why don't you spend a little time thinking about it while I keep trying to dig up more data on Roth?" she suggested.

"It would just be a waste of time," he said. "I can't come up with anything until I know how the 115th floor is laid out."

"That's easy enough," she said, walking over to her other computer and activating it. She typed a few brief commands on the keyboard, waited for a coded response, and then typed some more.

"What are you doing?" he asked.

"Telling the realtor in charge of the building that I want to buy an apartment between the 100th and 120th floors. He's responded that there aren't any available at the moment, and I told him to run a credit check through my Swiss account to confirm that I could afford it, and then to transmit a floor plan to me. If I like it, I'll go on the waiting list."

"You didn't use your real name?"

"Of course not?"

"Then how can he check your bank account?"

"The Swiss don't use names; they use numbers."

"So that's what he's doing now?" asked Becker. "Checking your Swiss account?"

"Checking one of them. As soon as he's through, I'll transfer the funds and close out the account so that knowing the number won't do him any good." The holographic screen suddenly came to glowing life. "Ah! Here it comes."

It was a three-dimensional floor plan of the 103rd floor, with a notation that all the floors within her range had identical floor plans.

"Two apartments," she mused, ordering her machine to keep displaying the plans while simultaneously storing them in its memory for future use. "Still, they're mirror images, so it really won't matter which one is Roth's. If you can find a method that works for one, it'll work for the other."

"How will we know which one is Roth's when we get there?" asked Becker.

"He's not in hiding, Counselor," she explained patiently. "His apartment number will be listed in the building directory."

"I'm sorry if I'm asking stupid questions," said Becker. "But I'm new at this."

"I've never broken into the Diamond Tower either," she responded. "But I do know how to use the brains God gave me."

She walked back to her original computer without another word, and Becker stood, hands on hips, examining the floor plan, looking for weaknesses.

The elevator let the residents off in a circular marble foyer, perhaps forty feet in diameter, filled with plaster duplicates of famous statues. There were two doors, almost equidistant along the foyer's circumference between the residential elevator and the doors to the two apartments: the one to the north was the service elevator, the one to the south led to the stairwell. Both apartment doors had computer locks that were tied in to the main security desk on the 55th floor; it would register every time one of them opened or closed.

He studied the apartments. Each had a living room that was closer in size to a ballroom, with a window wall overlooking the city. The master bedrooms had his-and-her bathrooms, and there were three other bedrooms, each with its own bath. There were studies and libraries, dining rooms and breakfast rooms, gymnasiums and kitchens, and a terrace possessing a hot tub. A myriad of places to hide an alarm switch coded to voiceprint, palm print, or retinagram: by the time he could find the switch and figure out how to turn it off, the entire New York metropolitan police force would be on the premises.

He examined the exterior of the apartments. The walls were steel and glass, too smooth and sleek for so much as a handhold—and besides, he still didn't completely believe Jaimie's hint that she had once been a cat burglar. No, the answer had to be in the interior somewhere, and he went back to studying the floor plan.

Well, if there was no way to pinpoint any personal alarm system, they would have to bypass the alarm. How? By accosting Roth outside the apartment. Look and act desperate enough and he'd deactivate the system for them. He might not do it for a man he was trying to kill for his country, but he'd do it rather than get blown away uselessly by a pair of hopheads out for some quick money. *After* they were safely inside the apartment and the alarms were deactivated, there would be plenty of time to tell him who they were.

So, since the elevator was out and breaking into the apartments was out, the problem was how to confront him in the foyer of the 115th floor.

They couldn't wait in the stairwell; if it boiled down to a race, he'd beat them to the door, or simply step back into the elevator. Nor could they use the service elevator; they didn't know what security devices it possessed, and it was every bit as far from Roth's door as the stairwell.

So they would have to be *in* the foyer when he arrived.

All right, thought Becker; what possible reason can two people have for being there?

Fixing locks? No, he'd have his own locksmith for his own security system.

Painters? No, the foyer was all marble and false gems.

And then he looked at the statues again. There was a replica of Michelangelo's *David*, as well as Rodin's *The Thinker* and a trio of others that he didn't recognize.

Becker continued staring at them for a long moment—and suddenly he knew how they were going to get in.

Satisfied, he walked over to where Jaimie was working.

"How's it coming?" he asked.

"Slowly," she replied. "This is some guy, this Roth. If he's got a weak spot in his armor, I haven't been able to find it yet. Probably the best thing we have going for us is that he seems like a normal, healthy, well-adjusted human being."

"I don't follow you."

"I mean that he doesn't seem like the kind of guy who'll throw away his life for no reason at all, so he'll probably pass the buck along rather than let you kill him."

"Pass the buck where?"

"Who knows?" she said. "But he doesn't create assassination orders; he just carries them out. If we're lucky, he'll tell you who originated the order. *That's* the man you want."

"The first man I want is the man who can call the killers

off," said Becker. "Then we'll get back to worrying about why they want to kill me in the first place."

"Well, just remember not to get too close to this guy. He may not be any spring chicken, but he's got three decorations for bravery above and beyond the call, and he used to be the best killer the army ever had, before he moved over to the space service. They even wrote a book about his commando work in the Guays."

"The Guays?"

"Uruguay and Paraguay."

"I'll remember."

"How's *your* work coming?" she asked. "Have you found a way in?"

"I think so."

"You *think* so?" she repeated dubiously.

"With a building like this, I don't think you can know until you've tried it." He paused. "But if your literary allusion was correct, it ought to work."

"What literary allusion?"

"Sherlock Holmes. Every other approach was impossible, so if the building's security can be breached, I've found the only way to do it."

"Do you want to tell me about it, or are you just gonna surprise me?"

He sat down and explained his idea to her.

"It just might work," she agreed when he had finished. "And besides, we don't have any choice. You were dead right about all the other methods: they're impossible."

"I'm glad you agree," said Becker, getting to his feet and walking to the doorway between their rooms. "Now let's get some sleep. We've got a big day ahead of us tomorrow."

"Right," she said. "Let's just hope that we're still alive at the end of it."

16

They were up and dressed by six o'clock, and by 8:30 they had managed to obtain the materials that they needed. Then, dressed like affluent tourists, they walked over to the Diamond Tower with their possessions in a shopping bag from one of the more expensive women's clothing stores that Becker had rescued from the Regal's trash bin.

They immediately walked over to the elevator complex and began studying the charts.

"Can we get there from the 55th?" he asked.

"I'm looking."

"Wait a minute," he said. "Here it is. Elevator 42: it's express to the 45th floor, local to the 55th, and express again to the 140th."

"All right," said Jaimie. "Let's check and see what's *on* the 55th." She went back to the building's commercial directory, while Becker busied himself finding out the exact number of Roth's apartment. They met back at the elevators a moment later.

"It should be okay," she said. "There are six offices on the 55th, so there won't be too much traffic, but there's also a jeweler and an antiquarian book dealer, so we have some excuse to be seen up there."

"Good," said Becker. "Roth's apartment is 11502."

"That should be to the right of the elevator door," she replied.

"All right," said Becker. "We might as well get going, just in case he comes home for lunch."

"I doubt that he will. He's much more likely to eat out."

"Then that gives us seven or eight hours to get ready for him."

"Or his wife, or his servants, or his housepainter, or—"

"Don't confuse the issue," said Becker. "If you want out, just say so."

"I'm not confusing the issue. I'm just pointing out that he's not necessarily gonna be the first guy along."

"Then we'll play it by ear. Got your gun?"

"That's the third time you've asked me since we left the Regal."

He made no reply, but instead pressed a button that summoned Elevator 42.

"We might draw less attention if we take one of the local ones," she said.

He shook his head. "I'd rather know for sure that this one is waiting for me. The locals don't go to the 140th floor, and that's where we've got to be when the alarm goes off."

She shrugged. "Whatever you say."

"*That's* what I say."

The elevator finally arrived, and a moment later they found themselves alone in it as they ascended to the 55th floor.

"All right," he said, clutching the bag firmly in his right hand. "You stay here and keep the door open."

"What if someone comes along and wants it?"

"Just tell them your husband is paying the jeweler, and that he'll be along in just a few seconds."

"And if the party who wants the elevator has come from the jeweler?"

"Then tell him I'm paying the bookseller!" he snapped.

"The elevator can't take six minutes to make its entire run," she said. "We'd be much less visible if I *don't* hold it for you. I can get off with you, and we can summon it a couple of minutes later."

"I'm no expert," he said. "I *think* I'm setting the damned thing for twenty minutes, but what if it's five?"

"You're just being nervous. If you sent it to go off in twenty minutes, it'll take twenty minutes."

He stared at her as the elevator began slowing down. "You're sure you'd rather get off and summon it again?"

"Yes."

"How about a compromise? Wait here for me until someone summons it. If no one does, I'll be back in less than three minutes."

She shook her head. "Won't work. If you hold up the elevator while it's being summoned, an alarm goes off after about thirty seconds." She stared at him. "You want everyone on this floor to know something fishy is going on and to remember your face? Make a mad dash down the corridor to catch the elevator when the alarm goes off."

"All right," he said. "You win."

"Good," she replied, stepping out of the elevator as it came to a stop and the doors slid open.

He followed her, then paused for a moment to get his bearings while the elevator door closed behind him, and headed off toward the stairwell.

They passed the antiquarian book dealer. Then, when they reached the jewelry store, she stopped.

"I'll just pop in here while you hunt for your book," she said in a loud enough voice to be overheard by the saleswoman behind the counter.

Surprised, he watched her enter the store, then realized that she was talking and directing the saleswoman's attention to the back of the shop so that she wouldn't see which direction he went, and he immediately walked to the stairwell. There were a pair of restrooms right across the corridor from it, and he entered the men's room and began assembling the tiny device he had bought at the army surplus shop earlier that morning. It was no larger than a pencil, but if Jaimie was right about where the thermostat was, it would be enough—and it had the added advantage, once it was discovered, of deceiving the police into thinking they were still on the 55th floor.

When he was through rigging it, he activated the tiny device, took it across the corridor, and taped it to the computer lock. When it went off in twenty minutes, it would produce almost eight hundred degrees of heat for about three seconds, before burning itself out. This would serve the double purpose of setting off the alarm that unlocked all the fire doors, and fusing this particular door shut, so that anyone looking for two thieves or vandals would assume they were trapped somewhere on the 55th floor.

He picked up the shopping bag and walked casually back to the jewelry stop.

"All done," he said in a voice that didn't sound exactly like his own.

Jaimie looked up from an emerald necklace she had been admiring.

"Poor dear," she said consolingly. "They didn't have what you were looking for?"

Not trusting his voice, he merely shook his head.

"Well, we still have time to try those two shops on the west side before lunch."

She turned back to the saleswoman, thanked her for her time, and then joined Becker out in the corridor.

"Try not to look like you're dying of some rare disease," she whispered.

"I'm nervous."

"There's no need to be. If the device was a dud, we'll know in half an hour and we'll come back here and remove it before anyone notices it."

"I've spent my whole life upholding the law, not breaking it," he explained.

"Do you cheat on your taxes?"

"Who doesn't?"

"This is the same thing."

"The hell it is."

"All right," she said, reaching the elevator and summoning it. "Do you want General Roth's hitmen to shoot you down in cold blood?"

"No."

"Then this is a necessary preventive step."

"I know."

"Then what's your problem?"

Becker briefly considered her question. "Probably I'm afraid of being caught," he admitted.

"If I were you, I'd be much more afraid of being killed."

"I am."

In fact, thought Becker, he could hardly seem to remember the last minute that he *wasn't* afraid. Suddenly he felt very tired, and leaned wearily against the wall of the building.

They waited in silence for almost three minutes, and he began to get nervous again.

"Where is the damned thing?" he demanded.

"Don't worry," said Jaimie. "It's coming."

"When?"

"Soon."

"What if it's broken down?"

"Then we'll catch the local elevator down to the main floor and still get out in plenty of time," she said. "I pushed both buttons."

"The local could stop fifty times before it gets here."

"And the express could be here in ten seconds. Now just relax."

And, as if in proof of her statement, the doors to Elevator Number 42 suddenly opened, and an instant later Becker and Jaimie were riding up to the rooftop restaurant.

They emerged into a virtually empty foyer. The restaurant

entrance was locked, and a sign stated that it would not be open for luncheon business until 11:30.

"How much longer?" she asked.

He checked his wristwatch. "Just under thirteen minutes."

"No sense standing here as if we're waiting for something," she said. "Let's go check out the telescopes."

They walked down the corridor, and as they came to the window wall, Becker experienced a momentary surge of vertigo.

"I hadn't realized how high up we were last night," he admitted, grabbing Jaimie's arm while he steadied himself.

"I *like* heights," she said, pressing her face up against the window and looking out.

"You would," he muttered.

"I can see a baseball stadium," she said. "Which one is it, I wonder?"

"I don't know."

"And there's the Empire State Building, and—"

She began rattling off a series of landmarks, as excited as a schoolgirl.

"You know," she said after a moment, "you don't really need a telescope at all. Everything's just as clear as can be."

"Wonderful," said Becker.

"You're sure you don't want to look?"

"Maybe in a minute or two."

She shrugged, and went back to identifying parks and buildings.

Finally he tapped her on the shoulder.

"Four minutes," he said, pointing to his wristwatch.

"Relax, Counselor," she replied. "It'll only take us two minutes to get there."

"So?"

"In all likelihood we're the only two people up here, but what if some tourist or maintenance worker shows up and sees us fiddling with the fire door a minute *before* the alarm goes off?"

"How long will it stay unlocked?" he asked.

"They'll pinpoint the floor in five seconds, but they won't relock the doors until they know what's happened, which means they've got to get up there. Even if there's a security man on the floor, we should have two or three minutes before they kill the alarm and relock all the doors."

He counted off 150 seconds on his watch, then took her by her arm and began walking toward the fire door at the far end of the restaurant. When they were still twenty yards away an alarm starting ringing, and, pausing only to make sure that no one else was within sight, he ran to the door and opened it. She followed him into the stairwell and closed the door behind them.

"Well," she said, starting to strip off her suit, "that takes care of Step One. Where's my outfit?"

He rummaged through the bag until he came to the smaller of two one-piece workmen's outfits and tossed it to her. Then he took off his jacket and tie and slipped into the other outfit.

"How do I look?" she asked after folding her skirt and jacket neatly and placing them into the bag.

"Too clean," he said.

"You too," she replied. She rubbed her hands against the wall of the stairwell, then applied them to her outfit. "Better?"

"Much," he said.

"You do the same."

He followed her instructions, then placed his pistol in his pocket and taped a newly-purchased gun to his ankle, hiding it beneath the loose-fitting leg of his outfit.

"Got your gun?" he asked.

"Yes, goddamn it!"

"All right," he said. "Let's get going."

They walked down flight after flight of stairs until they came to the 115th floor. Then Becker withdrew his pistol and carefully opened the door. There was no one in the foyer, and he gestured to her to follow him.

"Wait a minute," she said, and the door closed behind

him, but before he had a chance to panic it opened again and she joined him, carrying a toolkit under her arm.

"What was that all about?"

"The shopping bag," she replied. "Very few maintenance workers buy their clothes there."

"So where are our clothes now?" he asked.

"In the stairwell. It'll be days before anyone discovers them."

"That was stupid. How will we get out of the building?"

"We'll probably draw less attention dressed like this." She paused. "I checked your coat pockets first; they were empty."

"I don't like it."

"You'd like it a lot less if General Roth saw that bag, or found our street clothes folded up behind *Venus de Milo*. Now let's get to work."

He chose the statue that was closest to Roth's door, a reproduction of Michelangelo's *David*, and using a hammer and chisel, carefully broke the right hand off, catching it before it could smash to pieces on the floor.

"Where's our glue?" he asked.

She pulled it out of the toolkit that he had been carrying at the bottom of the shopping bag, then began laying out an assortment of files and paints and portable sanding machines.

"Let me uncap a couple of these so it'll look like we've been working on it for a couple of hours," suggested Jaimie. "And brush a little paint and glue onto your outfit; it looks too crisp and new."

"You do the same," he said, reaching for a brush.

A few minutes later she started filing away at David's right elbow and shoulder.

"What's *that* all about?" he asked.

"It'll make it look like we've already put the arm back on," she said. "It'll seem less suspicious than our magically appearing to fix a broken hand five minutes before he steps out of the apartment or the elevator."

"You mean he might be in there?" asked Becker, gesturing toward the apartment door.

She shrugged. "Who knows? Two-star generals don't have to keep the same hours as lowly majors."

"What if he stays inside all day?"

"Then he'll come out for dinner."

"Maybe he won't."

"He will."

"Why?"

She grinned. "He's *got* to. I can't make it 'til tomorrow morning without a bathroom." She paused. "If you've got to worry about *something*, worry about his next-door neighbors."

"Why? We're covered. We're fixing a statue."

"We're gonna move the first time anybody opens Roth's door. But what if the neighbors come and go three or four times before Roth shows up? We're not going to seem to be making much progress."

"If they look suspicious, you'll invite them back into their apartment and keep a gun on them until Roth shows up and I can talk to him," said Becker.

"I won't kill them," she said. "If Roth attacks me and I have to go to court on a legitimate plea of self-defense, I will . . . but I don't plan to kill someone just because he's in the way."

"I don't want us to kill anyone. I just want some answers."

"And I just want you to know what can go wrong."

"This probably won't come as a surprise to you," he replied wryly, "but I've already envisioned more things that can go wrong than you could come up with in a year."

"My hero," she said with a low chuckle.

"Roth's a hero," said Becker. "I'm just a goddamned lawyer who everybody seems to want dead."

"Not me," said Jaimie. "I'll be just as happy if you live through all this."

"Thanks a lot."

"You're welcome."

They fell silent for a few moments, and then Becker spoke again.

"You know, Jaimie," he said, "I've been thinking."

"Oh? About what?"

"Roth."

"And?"

"We both know he's not the last link in the chain, that he gets his orders from somewhere."

"Right."

"Once we leave here, even if we've got a name, the whole goddamned military is going to be waiting for us—and for all I know, even *that* name won't be the top of the chain. Is there any way you can use his personal computer to tie into his office and see what the actual chain of command is?"

She considered the suggestion briefly, then shook her head. "Probably not. He's got to have some kind of personal code, and if I don't know it, I can't get in."

"Can't you rig the computer to hit every conceivable code?"

"Not unless I know the programming language," she replied. "I could use every word ever spoken on Earth and every number known to man and still not get in."

"Maybe that's what I should be asking him, then."

"The language?"

"Yes."

"Not a chance. He'll give us the wrong one, and we'll set off alarms from here to Jupiter." She paused. "Still . . ."

"Yes?"

"There might be a way, but it's awfully risky."

"Name it."

"If I can get to his computer without his knowing it, I can rig it not to send his signal, but to remember his code."

"What's risky about that?"

"You'd have to let him get the drop on you *and* try to notify his base via the computer. If he used the phone, or just marched you down to security, or shot you, it wouldn't work. And *I'd* have to have about four uninterrupted minutes at the computer."

"Well, if his wife or a servant comes by first, maybe we'll take a crack at it."

"I don't know," she said. "This is an awfully dangerous man. He's capable of killing both of us with his bare hands."

"Well, it was a thought."

They fell silent again, and after a while Becker, who had been kneeling next to the statue in order to look like he was working on it, found his leg muscles tightening up.

"You got a soft drink in there?" he asked, gesturing to the toolkit.

"Two beers," she said.

"Good," he replied. "Toss one over and open one yourself."

"I'm not thirsty."

"Neither am I—but I can't stay in this position any longer, and if someone comes into the foyer, I don't want it to look like we're just sitting around waiting for him. This way we'll simply be taking a break."

"It's early in the day for beer."

"Not if you've been breathing in plaster dust all morning."

She considered his answer, then nodded and tossed him a beer. He sat down with his back propped up against the wall a few feet from the statue, then opened the container.

He was about to actually take a sip when the elevator door opened and General Benjamin Roth stepped out, a briefcase under his arm.

"What's going on here?" he demanded.

Becker leaped to his feet. "We were just taking a break."

"I can see that. But what happened to the statue? It was fine when I left this morning."

Becker shrugged. "I don't know, sir. We got a call about an hour ago to come up and fix it."

Roth looked at the statue and grimaced. "Ugly piece of

work anyway. They ought to throw the damned thing out and give us something more modern."

"I can speak to the management about it if you'd like, sir."

Roth shook his head. "No matter." He paused. "I wonder who reported it?"

"I believe they said it was a woman, sir," chimed in Jaimie. "Perhaps it was your wife?"

"She's out of town. Must have been my neighbors. Probably broke it themselves; they were drinking enough last night." He approached his door. "Well, don't let me interfere with your work."

"We won't, sir," said Becker, withdrawing his pistol and quietly approaching him. "I hope you don't mind if we interfere with yours, though."

"What are you talking about?" demanded Roth, turning to face him.

"I'm talking about blowing the top of your head off if you don't cooperate, General," said Becker. "I'm a very desperate man."

Roth studied his face for a moment. "You're Maxwell Becker," he said at last.

"Yes, I am," said Becker. "And you're the man who has been trying to kill me for the past two days. We've got a lot to talk about."

"Well," said the general, "you might as well come into the apartment and talk in comfort."

"I don't think so."

"You've got me covered. What can I do?"

"You can start by not setting off your security system," said Jaimie.

"Who is *she*?" asked Roth.

"A friend," replied Becker. "General, please turn and face the wall. We're going to have to frisk you."

"And if I don't?"

"Your entire department is out to kill me," said Becker. "How much more harm can they do me if I kill you?"

Roth sighed, placed his briefcase gently on the floor, and turned toward the wall.

"Assume the position, General," said Jaimie, and he leaned his hands against the wall. "Legs farther apart."

"I'm an old man," he said. "I'll fall down."

"You're an old man who's killed more than fifty men in hand-to-hand combat," remarked Becker. "Do as she says."

Roth spread his legs further apart, and Jaimie, looking like she was ready to jump away at any instant, quickly examined him for weapons.

"He's clean," she said, stepping back.

"I hardly expected to be accosted in my own apartment," said Roth dryly.

"We're not in your apartment yet, General," said Becker. "We're outside of it."

"May I turn around and face you?" asked Roth.

"By all means."

Roth turned, and Becker noted that he still had the animal grace of a natural athlete.

"That's close enough," said Becker as Roth took a step toward him.

"I was just getting *this*," said the general, picking up his briefcase.

"There may be a weapon in it," suggested Becker.

"There isn't."

"I don't think we can take your word for that, sir," said Becker. "Please toss it over here so we can examine it."

Roth shook his head. "I give you my word that there's no weapon in it."

"Then why won't you let us see it?"

"That briefcase contains top-secret documents. If you want to see them, you'll have to kill me first."

Becker stared at him for a moment, then nodded. "Fair enough."

"I'll also give you my word that if you allow us to enter

my apartment, I'll deactivate the alarm system before it can give out any warning."

"Do you love your wife, General?" asked Becker.

"Of course I do. Why?"

"Because I give you my word that if you set off an alarm, I'll not only kill you on the spot, but I'll kill her before I leave town."

"You don't know where she is."

"But I have friends who do," said Becker, amazed that he could lie with such conviction. "That's why we picked today to come here—because our friends told us she was out."

"Why would you want to kill her?" asked the general. "She's not part of this."

"Because, no matter what you think and what you've been told, *I'm* not part of this either." Becker pointed his pistol right between Roth's eyes. "I'm not a killer, General. I'd much rather talk to you than shoot you, and I have no desire to kill your wife. But if you do anything further to endanger me, I won't have any choice."

Roth looked into Becker's eyes, didn't like what he saw there, and nodded.

"It's a deal," he said. "Come on in."

Becker shook his head. "We don't get within arm's reach of you, General. First you open the door, then you step aside while my friend enters the apartment, then you go in, and then I go in."

"All right," said Roth with a shrug. He walked to the door, entered his personal code, and stepped back as Jaimie darted in.

A moment later the three of them were inside.

17

"Jaimie, check the place over while the general and I go into the living room."

She nodded and disappeared into the interior of the huge apartment, while Roth walked straight ahead.

"Uh-uh, General," said Becker. "The living room's to your right."

"I have thirty seconds to deactivate the alarm after entering," answered the general. He walked into a room that was originally a bedroom but now seemed to be a study, entered a code on the alarm box that was neatly camouflaged behind some drapes, and then proceeded to the oversized and elegantly appointed living room.

"May I sit down?" asked Roth.

"On any chair that doesn't have a cushion."

"Why that stipulation?"

"Because I don't know what you have hidden beneath any of the cushions."

"This is an apartment, Major Becker, not an arsenal."

"And I'm a lawyer, not a fugitive."

Roth stared at him for a moment, then walked over to a

high-backed wooden chair, and Becker seated himself about ten feet away on a love seat.

"All right, Major Becker," he said. "Why have you accosted me in my own home?"

"Why are you trying to kill me?" demanded Becker.

"I'm not trying to kill you," said Roth coldly. "I've never seen you before today."

"But you ordered Covert Operations to kill me."

"Yes, I did."

"Why?"

"Because you are a dangerous man, Major."

"I'm a lawyer!" snapped Becker. "You guys are supposed to be killing spies!"

"There's a Code Red out on you."

"What's a Code Red?"

"Kill on sight."

"Why did you issue it?"

"I didn't."

"Bullshit."

"It's quite true, Major Becker," said Roth. "Someone in the space service determined you were a Code Red. My job is to carry out my orders, which are to terminate any Code Red."

"What the hell have I done to make me a Code Red?" demanded Becker.

"I was rather hoping you might tell me."

"Stop playing games with me!"

"I'm not playing games," replied Roth. "I have no idea why you are a Code Red. I only know what I am compelled to do to Code Reds."

"This is crazy! You've got hundreds of your men hunting for me, and you don't even know *why*?"

"I might ask the same question."

"I don't understand you," said Becker.

"How can you be a Code Red and not know why?"

"I don't."

"You must. There have only been three other Code Reds

in the past decade. Two of them were in the employ of our enemies, and the other was a homicidal maniac."

"Do I strike you as a homicidal maniac?" asked Becker.

"You have accosted me at gunpoint and threatened to kill my wife," said Roth. "What do you think?"

"I wouldn't even *be* here if your men weren't trying to kill me!"

"You asked me. I answered."

"Look," said Becker. "I'm a lawyer. I've never been involved in a military action. I've never even met an Iraqi or a Paraguayan. I'm fourth-generation military, for God's sake! Why do my own people want me dead?"

"I have no idea."

"But you could find out if you had to."

"I won't."

"It might save your life."

"Major Becker, I let you in here because the alternative was the murder of my wife. That was nonpolitical: you wanted to talk, and I don't want my wife to die. But now you are asking me to betray my employer, which happens to be the United States of America, and I'm quite willing for both my wife and myself to die before I will do that."

"I'm not asking you to betray anyone!" snapped Becker. "I just want a name, someone who can tell me why they want me dead."

"So you can threaten him as you have threatened me?"

"So I can explain to him that I am a loyal American and have never betrayed my service or my country. I am willing to turn myself in if I know that I'll get a fair hearing, that I won't be shot the second they see me."

"That doesn't seem unreasonable to me," said Roth. "If you and your companion will surrender your arms to me, I'll do what I can to help you."

"Why should I believe you?"

"I haven't lied to you yet," said Roth. "I said I'd turn off the alarm system, and I did."

"Your life was at risk," Becker pointed out. "If I give you our weapons, it won't be, and your orders are to kill me."

"Then you tell me: How can I convince you that I'm telling the truth?"

Becker shrugged helplessly. "I don't know."

"You'd better make up your mind quickly, Major Becker," said Roth. "I have appointments to keep, and if I'm late, people will begin checking into my whereabouts."

"What do you know about the Jennings case?" asked Becker suddenly.

"He just announced that he was going to plead temporary insanity," answered Roth.

"What else?"

Roth frowned. "Just that he murdered two crewmen while on a deep-space mission. Why?"

"Because I was assigned the job of defending him," said Becker. "A week ago I didn't have an enemy in the world. Now suddenly I'm a Code Red."

"And you think that it's because of Jennings?"

"It has to be. Except that the only thing he told me is so ludicrous that no one could take it seriously."

"What did he tell you?"

"That the two men he killed were aliens."

"And he believed it?"

"Yes."

Roth snorted. "Sounds like permanent insanity to me, not temporary."

"Except that every potential witness was suddenly transferred off the planet, and two days later I'm your most important assignment."

"It must be something else," said Roth.

"It isn't," said Becker. "The space service even set up a phony drug ring and left it there for me to find, just to make sure I wouldn't believe him."

"Aliens don't look like humans," said Roth. "They would have to pass medical tests, psychological tests, they would be fingerprinted and retinagrammed and—"

"Don't you think I know that?" said Becker. "It's crazy."

"Absolutely right."

"Then why am I a Code Red?"

"I told you: I have no idea."

"There can only be one reason."

"Suppose you tell me what it is?" said Roth.

"If Jennings' story was true—"

"It isn't."

"But *if* it was, what would that imply to you?"

"You tell me, Major."

"If there *were* aliens in the space service, they wouldn't *all* be operating at the lowest levels. Some of them would be high-ranking officers—and one of them doesn't want me to suggest that possibility to anyone else."

Roth snorted again. "It's a paranoid's fantasy."

"All right," said Becker. "If I'm a paranoid, if there's absolutely no truth to Jennings' story, if I bought it because I'm gullible or demented, why not lock me away? Why make me a Code Red?"

"There must be some valid reason," said Roth adamantly.

"Let me offer an educated guess about something, General."

"About what?"

"About the exact moment that I became a Code Red. It was forty-six hours ago, wasn't it?"

The general stared at him. "It was just after lunch two days ago," he confirmed.

"Do you know how I know that? Because that was the exact moment I let the space service know I didn't believe their drug ring story. And less than an hour later, somebody tried to kill me and blew away some innocent major who was having lunch in the restaurant I had just left."

Jaimie entered the living room just then.

"There's nobody else here," she said.

Becker took a quick glance at his watch. He'd been alone with Roth for a little more than six minutes. He shot a questioning look at Jaimie, who nodded almost imperceptibly.

He hoped to hell it meant what he thought it meant.

"All right, General, you've heard my story. Am I crazy?"

"No," said Roth. "You're mistaken about why they want you dead—you have to be—but you're not crazy."

"Do I strike you as a killer?"

"You strike me as a man who will kill if he has to."

"Does your offer still hold?"

"What offer?"

"If I give you my gun, will you take me into custody and personally guarantee my safety until I can speak to whoever put the Code Red on me?"

"What about the young lady?" asked Roth.

"She'll give you her weapon, too."

Roth frowned for a long minute, and finally spoke. "I can't make that decision unilaterally."

"Why not?"

"No Code Red has ever come in before. I'll have to speak to my superiors before I can accept your offer."

"What if they say no?"

"Then I will have no choice but to kill you."

"Will you explain that I voluntarily placed myself in your custody after, in essence, taking you hostage?"

"I will."

"Do I have your word on it?"

"You have my word."

"You didn't ask the right question, Counselor," interjected Jaimie.

"And what would that be?" asked Roth.

"Will your superiors honor your word?" she said. "They're the ones who know why they want him dead; you don't. They might be harder to convince."

"I'll see to it that they do," said Roth firmly. "I won't speak to them by vidphone, but by computer, so that I can keep a record of their answers."

Becker breathed a sigh of relief.

"All right, General," he said, taking the clip out of his

pistol, emptying the chamber, and tossing the weapon to the older man. "I'm your prisoner."

"And you?" asked Roth, turning to Jaimie.

She, too, emptied her gun and laid it on a nearby table.

"You've made a wise decision, Major," said Roth. He got to his feet. "Wait here while I contact them."

"I'd rather accompany you to your computer, General," said Becker. "If you get a weapon first, I want a fighting chance for my life."

"Son," said Roth levelly, "if I decide to kill you, you're a dead man right now. I don't need a weapon."

"Just the same . . ."

"Have it your way," said the general with a shrug. He got to his feet and walked off toward his study.

When they arrived, he stopped and turned to Becker. "I don't want you any closer than the doorway."

"I want to see what you're saying to them."

"When we get to that part, you can come in, but you can't watch me log on or the arrangement's off."

"All right," said Becker, standing in the hallway just outside the office. He dropped to one knee and began fiddling with his shoelace as the general activated the computer, then carefully unwrapped the pistol that he had taped to his ankle earlier in the day as the general concentrated upon his complicated log-on procedure.

"Ready," said Roth. "You can come in now."

"No," said Becker. "You can come out now."

Roth turned and found himself staring down the short barrel of Becker's gun.

"What the hell is going on here?" he demanded.

"I changed my mind."

"That gun is empty. You just took the bullets out of it."

Becker fired a shot into the wall.

"Different gun, General. Please come back into the living room. You seem like a fair-minded man, but I'll still have to kill you if you disobey me."

Roth glared at him furiously, then walked back into the living room while Jaimie sat down at his computer.

"Now what?" demanded Roth.

"Now we wait."

"What for?"

"For my friend."

"What's she doing?"

"Well, to be perfectly frank, I hope she's saving my life."

"I was *trying* to do that," said Roth coldly.

"I believe you."

"Then why are you doing this?"

"Because I don't trust whoever it was that you were trying to contact, and I don't want them to know where I am."

"They'll know ten seconds after you leave, if I'm still alive."

"Then we'll have to bind and gag you."

"I wish you'd try," said Roth with a grim smile.

Suddenly the vidphone rang, and Roth looked questioningly to Becker.

"Let it be."

"My staff knows I'm here," replied Roth.

"But they don't know *I'm* here," said Becker. "Let's keep it that way."

"They'll be suspicious if I don't answer the phone."

"They'll think you're in the bathroom, or out having lunch."

"They'll call back in five minutes," said Roth as the ringing stopped, "and then they'll know something's wrong."

"I have high hopes that we'll be out of here in less than five minutes," answered Becker.

"Have you given any thought to how you're going to get off this floor?"

"We managed to get *on* it," said Becker with less confidence than he felt. "We'll get off it, too."

Jaimie emerged from the office and entered the living room.

"Done?" asked Becker.

She nodded, then turned to Roth. "General, I've destroyed your computer, as well your security alarm and every vidphone in the house except this one," she said, walking over to the vidphone and cutting the cord. "At such time as you take the hit off of us, you'll receive full compensation in the mail."

Roth glared at her, but said nothing.

"What about the general?" asked Becker.

Jaimie looked thoughtfully at Roth. "I think the safest place for him is in the master-bedroom closet. It's quite spacious, so he shouldn't feel cramped, and his wife was thoughtful enough to put a computer lock on it."

"You broke the code?" asked Becker.

"What kind of goddamned genius do you think I am?" she asked. "The closet is open. It'll lock automatically when we close the door."

"All right, General," said Becker. "On your feet. Jaimie, get out of his way."

Roth walked to the master bedroom while Becker was careful to stay considerably more than an arm's reach behind him. They approached the closet, and suddenly Roth stopped.

"I'll give you one last chance to surrender yourself to my custody," he said.

"I thank you for the offer," said Becker, "but the truth of the matter is that while I'm sure you personally are an honest man, I don't trust the military to honor your word." He paused. "Please enter the closet now, General."

"You're making a serious mistake, Major," said Roth, walking into the huge closet.

"Perhaps," said Becker. "But every word I told you was the truth. And I want you to remember one thing."

"What?"

"I could have killed you, and I didn't. Even though you still have hundreds of men out hunting for me, I didn't kill you."

Roth was about to reply when Becker shut the door and a tiny light verified that the lock had been activated.

"Okay," said Becker to Jaimie, "let's get the hell out of here."

"Right," she said, heading down the hallway that led to the front door.

"By the way, what was all that shit about your not being able to crack a computer lock?"

"Why let him know how good I am?" she said. "Better to let him guess what I did before I destroyed his computer."

"You got what you needed?"

She nodded. "And I managed to extract his personal code for the elevator."

"I figured that, or you wouldn't have suggested locking him up."

They walked through the foyer and Jaimie entered the code. The elevator arrived thirty seconds later.

"Now let's go back to the Regal," she said, "and find out who it is that really wants you dead."

"And why," added Becker grimly.

Becker came out of the shower, dried himself vigorously, and donned a robe that the hotel supplied. He shaved, brushed his teeth, combed his hair, and feeling much refreshed, walked through his room and into Jaimie's.

"How about something from room service?" he suggested.

"If you're hungry," she said absently, sitting cross-legged on the bed with her computer facing her atop a chair.

"Aren't you?"

"Not especially."

"I'm still pumping adrenaline," he said. "Damn! We actually pulled it off! I feel great! Maybe I ought to give up the law and join the underworld."

"You'd be a flop, Counselor," said Jaimie without looking up.

"Nonsense."

"Now you're higher than a kite. Five minutes from now you'll be sure Roth and his people will find us before we check out of the hotel. Got to keep an even keel, Counselor."

"Well, I'm still hungry," he said, suddenly deflated. "Do you want anything?"

She shrugged. "Maybe a sandwich."

"What kind?"

"Whatever they've got."

He walked back to his room, ordered a large lunch for himself and a ham sandwich for Jaimie, then started thumbing through the complimentary newspaper he had found outside his door when they got back to the Regal.

With the trial barely more than a week away, the Jennings story got only two paragraphs on page 8. Somehow his press conference, such as it was, had dulled almost all interest in the forthcoming court case. The man had stepped up in front of a microphone, expressed shock and outrage at what he had done, but added that he couldn't remember a thing and needed professional help, and suddenly half a hundred other unsolved and unrepented crimes took precedence.

"Interesting," muttered Jaimie.

"What is?" asked Becker.

"I'll let you know as soon as I can figure it out," she said.

"What's to figure?" he asked. "Maybe I can help."

"You can't," she said. "Leave me alone, Counselor."

He shrugged and went back to his own room. He thumbed through the sports section without much interest, checked the business news with even less, and finally activated the holovision. The airways were filled with interchangeable soap operas and quiz shows and reruns of old sporting events, and finally he turned it off, just as room service arrived with his lunch. He thanked the uniformed waiter who brought it, gave him a substantial tip, and then rolled the cart over to an area he had cleared between two chairs.

"Come on," he called into the next room. "Your sandwich is here."

"Interesting," mused Jaimie again, oblivious to him.

"What the hell is so damned interesting?" he demanded, walking over to where she sat.

"I'm not sure yet," she said. "It's like a puzzle. I've only been working on it for an hour; give me another twenty minutes and I'll have it."

"Have what?"

"I don't know."

"You're not making any sense."

"Neither is *this,*" she said, nodding her head toward the computer.

"Maybe you're doing something wrong."

She stared at him with open contempt.

"No, of course not," he amended. "But what's the problem?"

"If I could define the problem, I could probably give you the answer," she said.

"You sound like a mystic. Have you got a line on Roth's superior or not?"

"Oh, *that,*" she said with a shrug. "He got his orders from General Truman Fischer."

"That's it, then."

"No it isn't," she replied.

"Then . . . ?"

"Just leave me alone for another half hour and I think I'll be able to tell you what's going on."

He shrugged, returned to his room, activated the holovision again, and began eating his salad while watching a replay of the jai-alai match from four months ago. He had given up on that and was watching three well-paid executives make fools of themselves trying to identify Egypt on an unmarked map of the world by the time he reached his main course. He completed his dessert to the whines and moans of an actress who had obviously been in the process of dying for the past three weeks.

When he finished his coffee, he deactivated the holovision again and walked back into Jaimie's room.

"Fascinating," she said.

"That's even better than 'interesting,'" he noted dryly.

"Fascinating's the word for it," she affirmed.

"For what?"

"Five more minutes."

"I thought you only needed twenty," he said. "That was half an hour ago."

"This is *big*, Counselor," she said, finally looking up at him. "Bigger than you can imagine. Now leave me alone for another five minutes and I'll have some answers for you."

"How about if I just look over your shoulder?" he suggested.

"Suit yourself," she said. "Just keep your mouth shut and let me concentrate."

He glanced at her screen, realized that it was conversing with her in no language he had ever seen before, and stalked out of the room again. He stopped by the bathroom, then lit a cigar, turned on his quiz show again, saw three new executives fail to define the word "enigmatic," and turned it back off.

And then Jaimie, her face alive with excitement, entered the room.

"Where's my lunch?" she demanded.

"Right there," he said, gesturing to the ham sandwich.

"That?" she said. "That wouldn't fill a month-old puppy! Call room service and order me a couple of hamburgers, heavy on the onions." He reached for the vidphone. "And make sure they send up ketchup and mustard and lots of pickles."

"Anything else?" he asked sarcastically.

"A nice cold beer," she said. "No, make that two."

"Right," he said, dialing room service and placing the order. "That's a pretty big meal for a girl who wasn't hungry."

"Who says I wasn't hungry?" she replied. "I'm famished!"

"So am I," said Becker.

"You can have half the ham sandwich," said Jaimie, holding it out for him.

"For information," he added meaningfully.

"There's something very strange going on," she said, biting into her half of the ham sandwich.

"Everyone's trying to shoot me," he said.

She shook her head. "No, it's much more complicated than that."

"Would you like to tell me," asked Becker, "or are we going to play guessing games?"

"Don't be sarcastic," she said. "I just put in a hell of a day on your behalf."

"I'm sorry," he said caustically, "but you can appreciate my interest in your findings."

"All right," she said, putting the uneaten portion of her sandwich down. "Like I told you, the man who gave Roth the hit order was General Truman Fischer."

"So you said."

"But that's just the beginning. I traced the chain of command—after all, there's no reason to assume that it originated with Fischer, any more than it originated with Roth—and I came to a loop."

"Loop?" Becker repeated. "What kind of loop?"

"Theoretically, only two people in the space service can give orders to Fischer: General Harry Blackmane and General Wanda Janowitz. Theoretically they're responsible only to the Joint Chiefs of Staff and the President."

"So?"

"So what would you say if I told you that there is a colonel nobody ever heard of that they both report to?"

Becker frowned. "That doesn't make any sense."

"What if I further told you that this colonel—I haven't got his identity yet, just his code name—has the power to issue a Code Red, which is what they've issued on you, even though he has nothing to do with Covert Operations or Internal Security?"

"*Are* you telling me that?" asked Becker.

"That, and more. This guy has free access to the Joint Chiefs, and can bypass the National Security Council and go straight to the President . . . and that, furthermore, he's done it seventeen times already."

"A *colonel* who's not in the official chain of command has had seventeen audiences with the President?" repeated Becker incredulously.

"Over a period of ten years," she said.

"He was a colonel when it started, and he's *still* a colonel?"

"That's right."

"And he's had access to, let me think, *three* presidents?" She nodded.

"It doesn't make sense," said Becker emphatically.

"Sure doesn't. It also doesn't make sense that he wants you dead, but I think he's the guy who initiated the Code Red on you."

"Who the hell is he?"

"I haven't been able to find out, but his code name is Wild Card."

"Never heard of it." He paused. "I wish we'd have known about this guy earlier. We could have asked Roth about him."

"I'll lay you twenty-to-one that Roth doesn't even know he exists."

"Really?" he said, surprised. "Just how well-insulated *is* this Wild Card, anyway?"

"I've done a little checking, using Roth's access code," said Jaimie, "and you'd be surprised how few people in the space service *have* heard of him." She paused. "You could count them on the fingers of one mangled hand."

"What the hell is going on?" asked Becker.

"Something so big that the military doesn't want it to go through normal channels, that's for sure."

"Where does Wild Card work out of?"

"Washington."

"What else can you tell me about him?"

"Nothing, yet . . . but he's a very careful man, and that will help us."

"How?"

"He doesn't believe in putting all his eggs in one basket, or all his files in one database. He's got 'em scattered all the hell over, and he's got some of them circling the world every ten minutes."

"I would imagine he's got them pretty well-protected, too."

She grinned. "It wouldn't be any fun if it was *too* easy."

"You think you can break in?"

"Eventually."

"I hate to point this out to you, but I have a couple of hundred people vying with each other to see who can kill me first. 'Eventually' is not exactly a comforting answer."

"We're safe here for a couple of more days," she said. "I'll have plenty more by then."

"I was kind of planning on going back tonight."

She shook her head. "Along with monitoring all the airports and train and bus stations, Roth will have roadblocks everywhere, and even if we ran them, you have no place to go in Washington. We're much safer right where we are . . . and he can't keep checking every vehicle day after day without having to answer some embarrassing questions. We'll give him two or three days to assume we've gotten out and call off his dogs, and then we'll drive home."

"But I feel useless here," said Becker. "You've got your computer, but all I can do is sit around and wait for you to discover more about Wild Card. *I'm* the one they're trying to kill; I should be *doing* something."

"What would you do in Washington?"

"Something," he replied. "Maybe I'd try to talk to Jennings and find out what they promised him to make him change his plea."

"Get within a mile of Jennings and you can kiss your old age good-bye," she said. "Or did you think the hit stops at the New York City border?"

"All right," he said. "I'll stay here."

"Now you're making sense, Counselor."

"But you've got to teach me to use your other computer."

"What for?" she said. "Wild Card is damned near the best-kept secret in the country. You wouldn't begin to know how to look for him, even if you could speak computerese."

"There must be something I can do."

"There is."

"What?"

"Be a pillar of silent strength and don't nag me when I'm working."

"Fuck you," he growled irritably.

"That, Counselor," she said with a grin, "is one thing you *can't* do."

He glared at her furiously and made no reply. She enjoyed his discomfort for a few moments, then relented.

"All right," she said. "There *is* something you can do . . . but you won't like it."

"What is it?"

"While I'm trying to uncover more about Wild Card, you can do a little detective work on your own."

"What kind?"

"I can show you how to tie into the Library of Congress, and how to access all the facts you need."

"To prove what?"

"To prove that Greenberg and Provost were human beings."

"*That* again?"

"Prove it, and I'll never mention it again."

"I told you—every goddamned scientist I've spoken to says that the odds are billions to one against—"

"Don't quote scientists at me," she said. "Don't give me logic, don't give me reasoned responses. *Prove* that they were humans."

"That's like pointing at a color and telling me to prove it's red and not green."

"There are ways . . . or didn't they ever teach you about light diffraction in school?"

"This is ridiculous!"

"You didn't think it was ridiculous when you laid it out for General Roth this morning."

"I *had* to sound sincere. It was the only story I could come up with."

"I've been listening to you ridicule it for four or five days now," replied Jaimie calmly. "If it's so crazy, prove it."

"How?"

"That's up to you. I can't think of everything."

"What's the Library of Congress got to do with it?"

"You can't leave the hotel," she pointed out patiently. "That means your computer has to do your traveling for you. And the Library of Congress has the biggest English-language database in the world. That ought to make it easy for you."

"What do I look for?"

She shrugged. "Beats me. You're the guy who has to prove it. *I* think they're aliens, remember?"

"You don't really!"

"Who knows? Every time you try to prove they *were* aliens, someone hides your witnesses or tries to blow you away. Maybe you'll be safer trying to prove they weren't."

"When you say it that way, it almost makes sense," he admitted grudgingly.

"All right," she said. "Let me show you how to tie in to the Library's database and—"

She was interrupted just then as the same waiter returned with her lunch. Becker gave him a somewhat smaller tip this time and his posture made his displeasure evident as he walked out of the room.

"Now, about tying in . . ." said Becker when the door slid shut behind the disgruntled waiter.

"Later," said Jaimie. "I'm starving."

Becker watched her eat, wondering how a body that couldn't have weighed ninety-five pounds dripping wet could store so much food. Halfway through her second beer she suddenly stopped, as if she had just filled to capacity.

She relaxed with a cigarette for a moment, then had him set up the less powerful of the two computers on his desk.

"Now, you'll have to use the keyboard," she said, "but once you're hooked in, all the instructions and data will be in English, so it's not a real disadvantage."

"How do I tie in?"

"I'll do that for you," she said, sending an instruction to the modem to dial a certain toll-free number, then going through the rather simplistic logging-in routine.

"That's it," she announced. "Now just respond to its questions or ask your own. I'll be next door hunting down our mysterious friend."

"Right," he said, staring at the screen.

MAY I HELP YOU?

He typed in his response:

Do you have access to newspapers and magazines?

I HAVE ACCESS TO ALL COPYRIGHTED MATERIAL PUBLISHED IN THE UNITED STATES OF AMERICA.

He thought for a moment.

Does that include high-school and college yearbooks and newspapers?

YES, IF THEY WERE COPYRIGHTED.

Do you have access to current military records?

NO.

All right, he decided, let's start with Provost. Where did he grow up? Somewhere in Pennsylvania. Medford? Milford? That was it—Milford.

Can you access high-school yearbooks from Milford, Pennsylvania?

WHAT YEARS?

It was 2065, and Provost had been in the service for a decade or more. So if he joined in his early twenties . . .

2048 through 2053.

There was a brief pause.

ACCESSED.

Bring up all data and holographs or photographs of Jonathan Provost, Jr., from his senior year.

There followed, in quick succession, a class photograph with Provost's face highlighted, a close-up of Provost, and a tongue-in-cheek prediction that he would be the world's tallest racehorse jockey.

Becker studied the close-up. It sure as hell looked like a younger version of the Provost he had seen in holographs when going over the case documents.

All right. Now to find out if there was anything unusual about him then?

Bring up all sporting-team rosters from Provost's senior year.

Rosters for eleven teams appeared. Provost was listed as a first baseman on the baseball team, a member of the relay team in swimming, and the starting defensive back on the football team.

Which clinched it. He couldn't have made the team without undergoing a physical. Unless the aliens were practicing medicine at the local high-school level fifteen years ago, Provost was human.

He got up from the computer and described his conclusion to Jaimie, who didn't even look up from her screen.

"Wouldn't you like to offer me an apology?" he asked sarcastically.

She shook her head, still without taking her eyes from the almost incomprehensible data that appeared before her.

"You haven't proved anything, except that he was a human fifteen years ago."

"You think maybe he metamorphosed into an alien?" suggested Becker sarcastically.

"Not necessarily," said Jaimie. "Prove that he wasn't replaced by one."

"How?"

"You're a lawyer," she said. "Pretend he's your client and you have to prove that he hasn't been replaced by aliens somewhere along the line."

He sighed and trudged back to the computer, feeling like a complete fool and totally unaware of how close he was to striking paydirt.

It took Becker another twenty minutes to follow Provost's career through college. His hometown newspaper noted that he went immediately into the space service upon graduation.

Becker then followed the same procedure with Greenberg, who had not been an athlete, but who had, according to *his* local newspaper, sued a driver who had hit him and broken his leg while intoxicated. The leg required extensive surgery, which meant that Greenberg, too, was undeniably human at age nineteen. Becker traced his life to the day that he entered the service, and found nothing out of the ordinary.

On a hunch, he tried Gillette next, but could find virtually nothing about him between the year he graduated medical school and the day he joined the space service.

Finally Becker walked into the next room, where Jaimie and the computer were exchanging incomprehensible messages at a phenomenal rate.

"What now?" she asked.

"I've gone as far as I can go without accessing military

records, and if I use my own code I'm going to set off half a zillion alarms," he announced.

She stopped typing at her keyboard long enough to walk over to the desk, grab a piece of stationery, and scribble down an intricate three-part identification code.

"This is Roth's," she said. "Assuming that he's still safely locked away in his closet, this should get you access to anything you need." She paused. "In fact, if they've been feeding you false information, Roth's clearance just might get you the truth."

She handed the sheet to him without another word and went back to work on her computer, while he walked back into his own room, broke the connection with the Library of Congress, and dialed an access number to the space service's central computer. He checked the menu that appeared on the screen when he punched in Roth's personal code, and found that he had many more options than when he accessed it under his own code.

He tried to follow Provost's military career, step-by-step, from his induction to his murder, and found only one unusual sequence, a ten-month period when he had been hospitalized for serious injuries after a plane crash somewhere over New Mexico.

Otherwise, Provost seemed to be an average member of the military, no better, no worse. He had been promoted twice, demoted once (for drunkenness, not drugs), had not found a sponsor for Officers' Candidate School, and just seemed to drift along, probably content to serve his time and take his pension. He had put in twelve years when Jennings killed him.

Becker then turned to Greenberg—and discovered, to his surprise, that he, too, had been involved in the New Mexico crash, and had been confined to a military hospital for almost eleven months. His path never crossed Provost's again until both were assigned to serve aboard the *Theodore Roosevelt.*

Becker stared at the screen for a moment, then began typing again:

Give details of plane crash over New Mexico, November 12, 2056.

A SMALL JETLINER CARRYING 203 PASSENGERS CRASHED IN THE VICINITY OF TAOS, NEW MEXICO, ON NOVEMBER 12, 2056, EN ROUTE FROM HOUSTON, TEXAS, TO SAN DIEGO, CALIFORNIA. INCLUDED AMONG THE PASSENGERS WERE 52 MEMBERS OF THE SPACE SERVICE WHO WERE BEING TRANSFERRED TO THE SAN DIEGO SPACE SERVICE BASE.

How many survivors were there?

THERE WERE 14 SURVIVORS.

How many of the 14 survivors were members of the space service?

ALL 14 WERE MEMBERS OF THE SPACE SERVICE.

All the civilians died?

YES.

And 38 members of the space service died?

YES.

You're onto something here, Becker told himself; now think *clearly* before you continue. Don't go too fast or you might miss it.

Please list the survivors.

ALGAUER, HORACE, CPL.

BASKINS, LEWIS JAMES, SGT.

BILLUPS, ERIC Q., PVT.

BRANNIGAN, WILLIAM M., M.D., MAJ.

CRANE, JASON GREELEY, SGT.

GILLETTE, FRANKLIN WILLIAM, M.D., LT.

GREENBERG, ROBERT, PVT.

KELLY, PATRICK A., M.D., CAPT.

MORRIS, JEROME H., PVT.

NAISMITH, JOSHUA JAMES, PVT.

PRETORIOUS, LOUIS ROBERT, M.D., LT.

PROVOST, JONATHAN, JR., CPL.

SMITH, QUENTIN Q., CAPT.

WAYMAN, MARSHALL, SGT.

Becker read the list, blinked twice, and read it again.

Is the Franklin Gillette listed here the same Franklin Gillette who later served as Chief Medical Officer aboard the Theodore Roosevelt *?*

YES.

Repeat: pilot, crew, and all but these 14 passengers died in the crash. Is that correct?

THAT IS CORRECT.

He was so close now he could taste it, and he paused for a moment to consider his next question.

Were all the survivors career military men?

YES.

He stared at the list again and shook his head. Too easy; he had worded it wrong.

Was there any way to ascertain at the time of the crash that all the survivors would be career military men?

NO.

He was right: he had asked the wrong question.

Were any of the nonsurviving members of the space service career military men?

15 OF THE 38 WERE CAREER MILITARY MEN.

All right; *that* wasn't the connection. He tried again.

Did all of the survivors spend the same amount of time in the hospital?

NO. THE SHORTEST STAY WAS 8 MONTHS 17 DAYS, THE LONGEST WAS 12 MONTHS, 4 DAYS.

What were the nature of Franklin Gillette's injuries?

CLASSIFIED.

Classified? Even to a general who was in charge of the space service's Covert Operations branch? Just to be on the safe side, Becker asked the computer to list the injuries of the other thirteen men; all were classified.

"Woof!" exclaimed Jaimie, walking into the room. "I've got to take a break. I'm going blind reading computer code."

"Have a seat," said Becker. "I'm getting close."

"To proving they were human?"

"I don't know."

She pulled a chair up next to him. "Let's see what you've got here."

He explained what he had discovered thus far.

"All right," she said. "You need to find a common factor among the survivors."

"I'm trying to."

"How about age?"

"No. Gillette was much older than Provost and Greenberg."

"Race?"

"We can try," said Becker, feeding the question to the computer.

It replied that there had been eleven Caucasians and three blacks among the survivors.

"Point of entrance?" suggested Jaimie.

"You mean, did they all join at the same place?"

"Right. Or did they maybe take the same schooling after they joined?"

"How could they? You've got officers, enlisted men, and a doctor."

"Ask anyway. It doesn't cost anything to confirm it."

He asked, and the computer responded in the negative.

"Damn!" Becker muttered.

She stared at the screen for a moment, then turned to Becker. "Narrow it down."

"I don't understand what you mean."

"Don't bother with what the survivors have in common as opposed to the rest of the world. Find out what they had in common compared to the thirty-eight who died."

"I've tried race, and length of service, and—"

"You're not thinking clearly, Counselor."

"Oh?"

"A plane crashed. Everybody should have died. Fourteen men didn't. Why not?"

"I don't know," he said helplessly.

"Me neither. So why not assume that they *did* die?"

And suddenly it all fell into place. Becker leaned forward and began typing again.

For purposes of definition, an immediate member of a family is a parent, grandparent, full or half sibling, spouse, or offspring. Do you understand?

UNDERSTOOD.

How many of the 38 dead space service members were survived by immediate members of their families?

38.

How many of the 14 survivors would have been survived by immediate members of their families if they had died in the New Mexico plane crash?

CHECKING . . .

"Come on!" muttered Becker.

NONE.

"Bingo!" said Jaimie.

"That's *it!*" said Becker excitedly. "There were no survivors of the crash! The space service chose the fourteen members who had no families, nobody who could spot the change, and secretly replaced them with doubles who have been in deep cover for a decade."

"Makes sense to me," agreed Jaimie.

He stared at her for a long minute, then grimaced.

"It doesn't make any sense at all. Do you realize what I just said?"

"That there are fourteen aliens in the space service, disguised as fourteen men we know to be dead."

He shook his head. "That's just the tip of the iceberg. Somebody had to set this up. If *they're* aliens, *he's* an alien. People who knew their origins had to train them to pass for human; probably some of those teachers are aliens. They could never pass a physical examination, so every doctor who has examined them during the past decade is an alien." He paused. "Just how the hell many of them have infiltrated our military? Hundreds? Thousands? Are there any humans left?"

"Don't let your imagination run away with you," she cautioned him.

"And what about all those scientists who say that no alien race could possibly look like us?" he continued. "Could they all be wrong? Or are *they* aliens too?"

"Of course they're not aliens," replied Jaimie. "And it would hardly be the first time scientists were wrong about something."

"How can you sit there so calmly?" he demanded. "There's every possibility that we've been invaded and aren't even aware of it!"

"If we're right, they've been here for at least a decade and they haven't tried to take anything over yet," she said. "Maybe they're peaceful."

"I'd have a lot more confidence in their peaceful intentions if people would stop shooting at me," he said. "If *you* think they're peaceful, why don't you take a walk down Fifth Avenue and see if you live to the first stoplight?"

"If we get shot, it won't be by aliens."

"No, it'll be by humans like Roth who don't even know who's giving them their orders." Becker forced himself to be silent for a moment while he sought to regain his composure. "Have you found out anything more about Wild Card?"

She shook her head. "Not much. I still don't have a name for him." Suddenly she sat upright. "But maybe I have a job for him. Pass me the keyboard."

He did as she ordered, staring at her with open curiosity.

Where were the 14 survivors taken for medical treatment and recuperation?

SPACE SERVICE MEDICAL OUTPOST NO. 1.

I thought the space service didn't have its own medical facilities. Please explain.

SPACE SERVICE MEDICAL OUTPOST NO. 1 EXISTED FROM 2053 THROUGH 2057, AND WAS THEN DISBANDED. THE SPACE SERVICE NO LONGER HAS ITS OWN MEDICAL FACILITIES.

Where was Medical Outpost No. 1 located?

CLASSIFIED.

How many medical doctors were on the staff of Outpost No. 1 in the year 2056?

ONE.

She turned to Becker. "Doesn't that strike you as odd? Only one doctor in an entire medical facility?"

"We already know that it couldn't have been a medical facility," he replied. "It was just a front."

"But the computer doesn't know that—or at least, not in those terms," she explained to him. "I know it seems slow to you, but I've got to ask precise questions to get precise answers."

Please supply the name of the highest-ranking non-medical officer stationed at Medical Outpost No. 1.

GENERAL BASIL KINDERBY.

Where is General Kinderby stationed today?

GENERAL BASIL KINDERBY (2003-2058) DIED OF HEART DISEASE SEVEN YEARS AGO.

Please supply the name of the highest-ranking non-medical officer stationed at Medical Outpost No. 1 who is still alive and active in the space service.

CLASSIFIED.

"We're on the right trail, all right," she said, shooting Becker a triumphant smile.

"Now what?"

"Now we do it the long way."

Please supply the name of the second-highest-ranking non-medical officer at Medical Outpost No. 1.

BRIGADIER GENERAL RONALD WALINSKY.

Is he still alive?

BRIGADIER GENERAL RONALD WALINSKY (1999-2060) DIED OF CANCER FIVE YEARS AGO.

"Two generals to look after fourteen patients," she said. "What do you make of that?"

"You know what I make of it."

Please supply the name of the third-highest-ranking non-medical officer stationed at Medical Outpost No. 1.

CLASSIFIED.

"Wild Card?" asked Becker, and Jaimie nodded.

Please supply the rank of the third-highest-ranking non-medical officer stationed at Medical Outpost No. 1.

COLONEL.

Is he still an active member of the space service?

CLASSIFIED.

Is he still alive?

CLASSIFIED.

"That's our boy, all right."

"If he's such a bigwig that he has access to the President, and even generals like Roth don't know anything about him, why is he still a colonel?" asked Becker, frowning.

She shrugged. "Who knows? We'll have to ask him when we find him."

"He could be anywhere."

"The odds are that he operates out of Washington," she said. "Not only is the space service headquartered there, but anyone who has access to the President and has managed to remain anonymous probably doesn't fly into town for his meetings."

"I wish there was a way we could know for sure."

"Maybe there is."

"How?"

"Let's ask the computer."

"You'll just come up with a classified answer again."

"Perhaps. But based on its answers, it seems like it was programmed to conceal rather than mislead."

"So?"

"So let's give it a chance to mislead us," she said, turning her attention back to the keyboard.

Is the third-highest-ranking officer stationed at Medical Outpost No. 1 currently stationed in San Diego?

NO.

Is the third-highest-ranking officer stationed at Medical Outpost No. 1 currently stationed in Washington, D.C.?

CLASSIFIED.

She chuckled. "See? Sometimes even an answer of classified can tell you something."

"You're *sure* he's Wild Card?"

"How many colonels could keep their identity secret from General Roth?" she replied. "He's Wild Card, all right."

Becker got to his feet and walked over to his closet, where he pulled out his suitcase.

"Let's start packing," he said. "If Wild Card's in Washington, there's no sense staying here."

"I told you: it's safer to wait here for a few days."

He checked his wristwatch. "It's just after two o'clock. If we hurry, we can damned near be in Washington before Roth starts cordoning off Manhattan."

"It's not safe for us in Washington."

"It's not safe for us in New York, either," replied Becker. He sighed. "It's not going to be safe for us anywhere in the world unless we can find Wild Card before he finds us."

It took them just under five hours to make it back to her abandoned building in Washington. They unloaded the computers, but then Jaimie insisted that they leave the car a few miles away in a train station's parking lot, assuring Becker that if he parked on the street within a mile of the apartment, the car would be gone the next morning.

"I'm exhausted," panted Becker as she unlocked the door.

"Better than having some cabbie driving around with my address on his sheet," she replied, leading him into the living room.

"What about all the people who saw us walking here?"

"They think I'm a hooker and that you're my john for the evening."

"Doesn't that bother you?"

"Would you rather I told them that I'm a millionaire and that you're the most wanted man in America?" she asked with a smile.

"You don't have to do it for my sake," he replied wryly.

"Want a drink?" she asked.

"Whiskey. Straight."

"Coming right up," she said, entering the kitchen and returning with a bottle and two glasses.

"You've never asked me if I wanted drugs," he remarked as she filled his glass. "It's always liquor."

"I know how to handle booze," she replied. "Drugs make people crazy. You start messing around with military computers, or the system they've got over at Chase Manhattan, and you've got to have your wits about you." She paused. "The two best computer hackers I ever knew got into drugs; now they can't even spell their own names. I made up my mind that I was never going to wind up like them."

"So you've ended up running for your life instead," he commented.

"We're all through running now," she said. "Now we go on the attack."

"Against who?"

"Wild Card."

"Do you know something I don't know?" he asked, frowning. "Like who he is, for example."

"That's what we're gonna find out."

"I'm game. How do we do it?"

"*We* don't do anything for the next half hour," she said, seating herself at the largest of her computers. "*I* do."

"What do *I* do while you're messing with your computer?"

"Lean back. Enjoy your drink. Read a book."

"All your books are technical manuals."

"If I'd known you were gonna have to sit around, Counselor, I'd have picked up a girlie magazine for you—but I didn't, so you'll just have to make do with what's here."

He shrugged, got to his feet, walked over to a bookcase, and spent the next ten minutes browsing through the titles, hoping to find something mildly comprehensible. At last he gave up, returned to his seat, and activated a small holovision set. They were rerunning a three-week-old African track meet, and by the time he'd watched the Kenyan runners come in first, second, and fourth in the 10,000 meters, Jaimie deactivated the set and announced that they were ready to begin.

"I'd like to know what you've been doing first," he said.

"Don't you trust me after all this time?"

"Of course I trust you. I'm just curious. You've been working like crazy for the past thirty minutes. Since my life depends on it, I don't think it's unreasonable to ask what you did."

"Nothing much," she said. "Just invaded the phone company, is all."

"Why?"

"We're looking for Wild Card, aren't we?"

"You're not going to tell me that he's listed under 'W'?"

"You're not being funny, Counselor."

"All right, then, I'll be serious. How will invading the phone company help us find Wild Card?"

"You'll see," she said, handing him the vidphone. "Here you are, Counselor. Time to make a few calls."

"To who?"

"Start with your friend Magnussen."

"I don't think he's part of this," said Becker after a moment's consideration. "I believe him when he says he doesn't know why they're after me."

"Makes no difference," she said. "Rattle his cage. Make threats. And be sure you mention Wild Card."

"But if he doesn't know what I'm talking about . . ."

She grinned. "Then he'll call somebody who does."

"And since you're tied into the phone company, you'll know who he calls?"

"Right. And who *that* guy calls, and the next guy, all the way up the line. As long as they don't leave the area code, we've got 'em."

"What if Wild Card is so insulated that nobody calls him?"

"We'll make sure they do. Start with Magnussen."

He picked up the vidphone.

"Should I blank out the screen, do you think?"

"He'll never pinpoint your location from the background here," she replied. "Besides, we want him to know you're in Washington."

"I thought you'd rigged one of these computers to try breaking into my files so everyone would think I was in Washington."

"It may have worked for a couple of days, but somebody has to have released General Roth by now. Magnussen knows where you were, all right."

He dialed Magnussen's number, then waited until the attorney's face was displayed on the small screen.

"Max!" exclaimed Magnussen. "Where the hell are you?"

"Close enough," said Becker.

"You know that everyone is looking for you, don't you? What the hell did you do up in New York?"

"They were looking for me before I left," said Becker. "Now *I'm* doing the looking."

"What do you mean?"

"Don't play stupid with me, Jim. You know who I'm after."

"Me?" asked Magnussen, confused.

"You? You don't count. You're just a messenger boy. Now let me give you a message for your boss."

"For the general?"

"Don't play games with me, Jim; I haven't got time. You tell Wild Card he's got one hour to call off his men or I'm coming after him."

"Who the hell is Wild Card?" demanded Magnussen in exasperation.

"Just tell him," said Becker. "One hour, or he's a dead man."

He broke the connection.

"Well done, Counselor," said Jaimie. "You sounded sincere." She checked her computer. "He's already on the phone."

"Who is he calling?"

"Your general. Given the chain of command I uncovered,

it'll probably take between five and ten calls before they reach Wild Card."

"It may not stop with him, though," Becker pointed out. "Once he hears what I said, he's bound to get on the phone and issue more orders."

"That's why we're not gonna sit around waiting for the sequence to stop. Pick up the phone again."

"Who am I calling?"

"General Harry Blackmane."

"I've heard that name," said Becker.

"You heard it from me. He's one of Roth's superiors."

"What do I say to him?"

"Same thing."

He made the call, waited long enough for Blackmane to identify him, and then reiterated his threats to Wild Card.

She checked her computer again when he had hung up the phone. "He's being a bit more thoughtful," she said. "Probably wants to find out what you've been up to first." A tiny spot on her screen started blinking. "Ah, there he goes!"

"Who next?"

"Well, there's no sense calling Roth or General Fischer, since they both have to report to Blackmane. Let's take a shot in the dark."

"Who?"

"Janis Robley."

"Didn't she used to be a senator from Alabama?"

"Mississippi," Jaimie corrected him. "But now she's on the National Security Council. If anybody outside the President and the military knows about Wild Card, it's got to be the NSC."

"There are five members. Why her?"

"Because we don't know how tight the other members are with the space service, but my computer says that when she was in the Senate, she voted for every appropriation they requested."

"Okay," he said. "Let's give it a shot."

He dialed the number she gave him, only to get a prerecorded holograph of Janis Robley apologizing for not being able to answer her phone personally.

Becker hung up instantly and turned to Jaimie. "Somehow my message doesn't seem like the kind of thing we want to leave on an answering device," he said dryly.

"Right," she agreed. "Let's try her office. Maybe she's working late."

A moment later a gray-haired woman with piercing blue eyes and a jutting chin appeared on the screen.

"How did you get past my receptionist?" she demanded by way of greeting.

"Never mind that," said Becker. "Do you know who I am?"

"Should I?"

"Wild Card knows. Tell him he's in big trouble if he doesn't call off his men."

"Who are you and who is Wild Card?" she said coldly.

"Just tell him."

"Now listen to me, Major Becker, I—"

He broke the connection.

"'Major Becker,'" he repeated. "Pretty good guess for someone who didn't know me."

"PR agencies get millions of dollars for making people half as famous as you seem to be in this town," Jaimie responded ironically. "Well, I see she's already making a call."

"Now what?" asked Becker.

"Now we wait."

"For how long?"

"Oh, I'd say at least half an hour, probably a little more."

"And then?"

She smiled. "Then the fun begins."

He walked over to a couch and lay down on it. "Wake me when the fireworks start," he said.

"You're kidding!" she said.

"I'm exhausted. I've been running for my life for four days, and I probably haven't had fifteen hours sleep total. You may enjoy this kind of thing, but I'm not built for it."

She stared at him for a moment, then got up, walked into her bedroom, and returned with a blanket, which she spread over his already-snoring form. Then she walked over to her bookcase, picked up an exceptionally esoteric technical manual, and browsed through it for the next thirty minutes. When she was through, she put it back in its place, walked over to Becker, decided to let him sleep another hour, and went into the kitchen to make something for them to eat.

She discovered that she was out of eggs and almost out of coffee, and she scribbled a note telling him she was going out to an all-night supermarket and would be back in twenty minutes. She stuck the note to her computer screen with a piece of tape, then softly opened the front door and climbed down the stairs to the main entrance.

|2|1|

Becker woke up, stretched his arms and legs, got slowly to his feet, and suddenly realized that something was wrong. It had been early evening when they reached Washington, which meant he had surely gone to sleep before nine o'clock—but now the sun was shining through the living-room window.

"Jaimie?" he called hoarsely. "Why the hell did you let me sleep so long?"

There was no answer.

Then he saw the note on the computer screen and walked over to read it.

> Counselor,
>
> You looked so peaceful that I decided to let you sleep another half hour. I'm just popping out to buy us some food; if you wake up before I get back, don't panic: I'll return in just a couple of minutes.
>
> J.

How the hell long had he been asleep?

He checked his watch. Eight o'clock. That meant she'd probably been gone for eight hours, possibly ten.

Which meant that they had her.

And *that* meant that when they broke her—she was a tough little girl, as streetwise as they came, but he never doubted that the military had methods that could break anyone—they'd be coming after *him*.

It was time to get out. Past time.

But he didn't know where to go, and now that he didn't have Jaimie to help him, he knew he'd never be able to set up another means of identifying Wild Card.

So, trying to fight back the sense of impending panic he felt in his stomach, he forced himself to sit down for a moment and consider his options. Then, with a sigh, he walked over to Jaimie's computer, which was still humming and glowing with life.

He sat down at the keyboard, looked at the screen, found the symbols meaningless, and typed in a single word:

Help.

Immediately the symbols vanished, to be replaced by a statement in block letters:

HOW MAY I HELP YOU?

This is not Jaimie Nchobe. This is Major Maxwell Becker. I am not as conversant with computers as Jaimie Nchobe is, so I need help to understand the results of the program you are running.

HOW MAY I HELP YOU?

Did it understand him, or was it just repeating itself mechanically? He stared at it for a moment, then began typing.

You are keeping a log of all phone numbers called by Colonel James Magnussen, General Henry Blackmane, and Janis Robley. Is that correct?

NO.

"No?" he muttered.

What ARE you doing?

I AM KEEPING A LOG OF THE PROGRESSION OF PHONE CALLS BEGUN BY COLONEL JAMES MAGNUSSEN AT 8:43 PM, BY GENERAL

Precision, Jaimie kept telling him. It's only a machine; it will answer exactly what you ask, nothing more, nothing less.

End the progression now.

DONE.

Compare all the phone numbers, and tell me if any appear on all three progressions.

YES.

Which number?

THERE ARE THREE: 934-12998, 227-25256, AND 227-80003.

Who belongs to each number?

QUESTION UNCLEAR.

Of course, he thought impatiently; people don't belong to numbers. Numbers belong to people. He reworded the question.

In whose name is 934-12998 registered?

GENERAL TRUMAN FISCHER.

No, that wouldn't be Wild Card. He was Roth's immediate superior, the man who had okayed the kill order, but it wouldn't have been initiated by him.

In whose name is 227-25256 registered?

GENERAL WANDA JANOWITZ.

He tried to remember what she had to do with the chain of command, and finally it came to him: Jaimie has said that she and Blackmane should have been at the top of the chain, but that both of them actually reported to Wild Card.

He took a deep breath, then played his final card.

In whose name is 227-80003 registered?

COLONEL LYDELL STUART.

Colonel, not General?

THAT IS CORRECT.

Please supply Colonel Lydell Stuart's address.

The address was a Georgetown brownstone.

Is 227-80003 the last number in each progression?

NO.

Is 227-80003 the last number in ANY progression?

IT IS THE LAST NUMBER IN THOSE PROGRESSIONS BEGINNING WITH JANIS ROBLEY AND COLONEL JAMES MAGNUSSEN.

What number did Colonel Lydell Stuart call in the General Harry Blackmane progression?

100-10000, EXTENSION UNKNOWN.

In whose name is 100-10000 registered?

THE WHITE HOUSE.

If Becker had had any lingering doubts that Lydell Stuart was Wild Card, that took care of them.

Thank you, computer. I am going to deactivate you now. What order must I give you to retain this program's information in your memory?

TYPE PROGRAM 106-JAMIE-MB-4.

He typed in the program code.

NOW TYPE RETAIN.

Retain.

NOW YOU MAY DEACTIVATE ME WITH NO LOSS OF DATA.

He turned off the computer, walked over to the window, and looked out, half expecting to see a group of uniformed men storming the apartment. But the street was empty, and he decided he had a few more minutes before he had to disappear.

He walked over to the phone, picked it up, and dialed. When the connection was made, he found himself looking at a lean, clean-shaven man with graying black hair that formed a distinctive widow's peak over his forehead.

"Hello, Wild Card," said Becker.

Lydell Stuart looked unperturbed.

"Very good, Major Becker. You have been a source of continual surprise to me during the past few days."

"I assume that's a compliment," said Becker dryly.

"You may take it as such." Stuart paused. "You've caused me a considerable amount of trouble."

"Not half of what I'm going to cause you before I'm done."

"Why don't we meet and discuss matters?"

"Why don't you release my friend, and perhaps I'll consider it."

"I'm afraid I can't do that, Major. She's the only hold we have on you."

"Are you suggesting a trade?"

"Not until we find out what she knows."

"She won't be worth trading for once you get done with her," said Becker.

"We're not monsters, Major Becker," said Stuart calmly. "We have painless ways of extracting information."

"You also have painful ways of trying to stop its dissemination," noted Becker. "Your goons have been trying to kill me for the past four days."

"They are not 'goons,' Major. They are members of the same service that you belong to, and they are every bit as loyal to it as you are."

"That's because it's never gone out of its way to kill them."

"Putting a Code Red on you was a matter of policy, Major," said Stuart. "There was nothing personal involved."

"I feel much better just knowing that," said Becker. "Now you listen to me, you son of a bitch. When I started looking for you, all I wanted to do was talk, to try to reason with you. But now you've kidnapped someone whose only crime was that she helped me survive. You turn Jaimie Nchobe loose within thirty minutes or you're a dead man."

"I can't do that, Major."

"You've had your warning."

"I am very well protected, Major."

"You won't be by this evening," said Becker. "They'll all be too busy reading the newspapers."

"It would be very unwise of you to go to the press with what you know, or think you know, Major," said Stuart.

"Are you threatening me, Colonel?" said Becker with a harsh laugh. "What will you do—put out a hit on me?"

"I'm trying to prevent you from making a very serious mistake."

"From where I sit, the most serious mistake I could make would be to trust anyone connected with you."

"If you'll come in right now, I'll cancel the Code Red," said Stuart. "We have to talk."

"We've *been* talking," said Becker. "But one of us hasn't been listening." He glared at the face on the screen. "You bastards lied to me and misled me and tried to kill me. Why should I believe you?"

"You have no reason to, other than my word."

"Your word isn't exactly coin of the realm," said Becker. "Let Jaimie Nchobe go as a show of good faith, and maybe I'll consider it."

"I can't do that, Major."

"Then put your affairs in order, Colonel," said Becker. "Sign your will, kiss your wife good-bye, and take a last good look at your children—because after I've exposed what's going on, I'm coming to kill you."

Becker reached out and broke the connection.

|2|2|

James Magnussen finished his coffee, left a tip at his table, picked up his check, and walked up to the cashier's desk, his briefcase tucked under his arm.

It had been a long morning. He'd been completely cut off from whatever was going on with Becker, but he couldn't help noticing the taut faces around him and hearing the nervous voices conversing in low whispers. Whatever the hell was happening, his old assistant was in a peck of trouble, and from his own sporadic phone conversations with him, he had half concluded that Becker had gone off the deep end.

None of which made his work any easier. The fact that Jennings had changed his plea made the case easier, but as a lawyer he knew that an easy case could be lost on a technicality just as quickly as a difficult one—and that with an easy case there was only one man to blame. So he threw himself into his preparation and tried to ignore all the hustle and bustle going on about him.

Ordinarily he ate in the commissary, but today he felt he just had to get away for a while, so he had taken his lunch at a favorite restaurant. He wanted no company, no conversation, just an hour to examine his paperwork without distraction. He had spent fifty-five minutes of that hour, and now, somewhat refreshed, he was ready to drive back to his office.

He walked to the parking lot, opened the door to his car, and got behind the wheel. It was just after he activated the ignition that he felt the end of the revolver placed against the back of his head.

"You really ought to get in the habit of locking your car, Jim," said Becker's voice from somewhere behind him. "You never know who you'll find in it."

"Max?"

"That's right."

Magnussen started to turn, but the gun was pressed harder against his head.

"Just keep your eyes on the road," said Becker.

"Are you going to kill me?" asked Magnussen nervously.

"If I wanted to kill you, you'd be dead already," said Becker. "Start driving."

"Where to?" asked Magnussen, pulling out onto the street.

"I'll give you directions," said Becker. "Turn left at the corner, and then go straight for three stoplights."

Twice during their circuitous course Becker had Magnussen slowly circle an entire block, just to make sure they weren't being followed. When he was sure that no one was tailing them, he ordered Magnussen to drive out of town to a small forest preserve.

"All right," said Becker, when they arrived at an empty parking lot. "Stop the car and get out."

Magnussen did as he was told and stepped out onto the gravel, his hands above his head.

"Put 'em down," said Becker. "We don't want to attract any attention."

"I'll settle for all the attention we can get," replied Magnussen, lowering his hands. "I don't like the thought of being killed and left here."

"I told you I haven't sought you out to kill you, Jim," said Becker calmly.

"Then why *am* I here?"

"Because you're the only man I know that I think I can trust."

"You've got a hell of a funny way of showing it."

"Would you have come if I hadn't threatened you with a gun?" asked Becker.

"No," answered Magnussen. "No, I don't think so."

"You'd have reported me to your superiors."

"Probably. You know that half the space service is out looking for you, don't you?"

"Only half?" said Becker with an amused smile. "Well, it's early yet." He put his gun into a pocket. "Don't make me pull it out and use it, Jim," he continued. "Just hear me out and nobody will get hurt. Now let's go sit over on that bench, where we won't be so conspicuous."

"What the hell did you do, Max?" asked Magnussen, leading the way to the bench and sitting down. "You mention a code name I've never heard of, and suddenly, even though no one has told me directly, I get the distinct impression that you're Number One on the service's Most Wanted list."

"I am," answered Becker, seating himself opposite Magnussen, but leaving enough distance between them so that he could withdraw his gun before Magnussen could reach him.

"But why?"

"You wouldn't believe me if I told you."

"Aliens again?"

"That's right."

"Max, there aren't any aliens!" exclaimed Magnussen.

"Then why is the space service trying to kill me?"

"I don't know—and if you think it's because of aliens, then *you* don't know either."

"They kidnapped Jaimie Nchobe last night."

"Who the hell is Jaimie Nchobe?"

"A friend of mine." Becker paused for a moment. "She saved my life more times in the past four days than I can count, and now those bastards have got her locked away somewhere and are probably torturing the hell out of her."

"If that's so, you should file a protest," said Magnussen.

"With who?" demanded Becker ironically. "Everyone who outranks me is trying to kill me."

"Except me."

Becker nodded. "Except you. That's why I chose you, Jim."

"You want me to try to find this Wild Card?"

Becker shook his head. "I already found him."

"He really exists?" asked Magnussen, surprised.

"He exists," said Becker. "I know who he is, and I know where he lives."

"By that same token, shouldn't he, with all the resources he's probably got at his disposal, know where to find you?"

"Right now he thinks I'm hunting up a friendly journalist. He's probably staked out every major newspaper and magazine office on the East Coast."

"Then let me ask you again," said Magnussen as a large truck raced by. "What do you want from me?"

"I can't go to the press," said Becker. "I'm a marked man. Besides, they wouldn't believe me. The space service would see to that. But if anything happens to me, they might listen to *you.*"

"Max, I don't believe you either."

"You will, soon enough." Becker reached inside his jacket and brought out a large brown envelope. "I'm giving you this because you're an honorable man, and once you've examined it you'll do what's right."

He slid the envelope down the bench to Magnussen.

"What's in it?" asked Magnussen.

"Everything you'll need to corroborate my story," said Becker.

"Paper or disks?"

"Disks. They contain proof that the space service purposely misled the defense in the Jennings case, that they planted false evidence of a drug ring, that they hid any witness who might have corroborated Jennings' testimony, and that they tried to kill me and Jaimie Nchobe when we found out what they were doing. It also lists their covert chain of command, culminating in Wild Card."

"Can this stuff be independently corroborated?" asked Magnussen.

"Once you know what you're looking for, get yourself someone who's good with a computer—and I mean *good*—and you can corroborate every word of it."

"Including the fact that there are aliens who look identical to humans?" asked Magnussen.

Becker nodded. "The clues are subtle, but the conclusion is inescapable. It's an operation that's been going on for over a decade, Jim."

"I still don't believe it."

"You will, once you examine what I've given you."

"*You're* no computer expert," said Magnussen. "How did you tumble to it?"

"Jaimie Nchobe's the expert. And they've got her, Jim; they grabbed her right off the street last night."

"Why?"

"The same reason they're after me. She knows too much."

"She knows who this Wild Card is?"

"Everything *but* that—though she's probably met him by now."

"These disks," said Magnussen, holding up the envelope, "how are they formatted? What kind of machine and system do I have to use?"

Becker shrugged. "I don't know."

"You don't know?"

"She's the expert, not me. Before I left her apartment today, I told the machine to make a record of everything we had discovered, everything she had done." He paused. "Evidently it took me literally, because it filled up three disks."

"That's fifteen books' worth of data!"

"It includes all her false starts."

"It could take forever to find what I'm looking for!"

"Get yourself an expert," repeated Becker. "Everything you need is on those disks."

Magnussen stared at Becker for a long moment.

"All right, Max," he said. "Let's say for the sake of argument that you're telling me the truth, and that my expert extracts what you say he'll extract. What do you want me to do with it?"

"Nothing, for the time being," said Becker. "In fact, I want you to lock those up in a safe place and forget about them for at least a week."

"Then what?"

"Then, if I don't contact you, you can safely assume that I'm dead, at which time I want you to extract the data in absolute secrecy."

"And then?"

"And then make a million copies and send it to every newspaper and journalist in the country," said Becker. "Don't make the mistake I made and assume that one of your superiors can give you a logical, comforting explanation for what you've discovered. All that'll happen is that they'll kill you and bury the data even deeper this time."

"Why wouldn't they kill me if I release it to the press?"

"Once the cat is out of the bag, why should they bother?" replied Becker. "They'll have bigger problems than you to deal with, believe me."

"Why didn't you do it yourself?"

"I told you. By the time I knew half of what's on those disks, General Roth already had a couple of hundred men trying to kill me. The only way you can handle this is in total secrecy. You can't let them know what you've got until you're ready to make your move."

Magnussen looked from Becker to the envelope and back to Becker again.

"All right," he said with a sigh.

"I'm counting on you, Jim. If anything happens to me, you're the only person who can alert the public to what's going on."

A red sports car whizzed by, and Magnussen pretended to cough and covered his face with his hand.

"God! I've been holding this envelope for five minutes and I'm getting as paranoid as you!"

"Remember what I told you a few days ago?" said Becker. "You aren't paranoid if they're really out to get you."

"Well, they seem to be really out to get *you*," said Magnussen. "What will you do—go into hiding?"

"Hiding won't solve anything. Sooner or later they'll find me."

"So what *do* you plan to do?"

"I've got to get to Wild Card."

"If he's behind a ten-year deep-cover operation that's as big as you imply, he's got to be pretty well-protected."

"I'm sure he is. But he's got Jaimie, and he's got all the answers, and he's the only man who can take the hit off me."

"How are you going to convince him to do that?"

"I'm not sure."

Magnussen frowned. "I won't be a party to murder, Max."

"Would you rather be a party to treason?"

"Of course not."

"Then protect those disks, and don't worry about what I'm going to do." Becker glanced at his wristwatch. "You'd better be getting back before they start wondering what happened to you."

"Yes, I'd better," said Magnussen, getting to his feet.

"Hide the disks before you go to your office."

"I will."

"You know of a good safe place for them?"

"I think so," said Magnussen. "It's—"

"Don't tell me," interrupted Becker. "If I don't know, Wild Card can't pull it out of me."

They began walking toward Magnussen's car.

"Where shall I drop you?"

"You're going back alone," announced Becker. "We've already been together for too long. If anyone sees me getting out of your car, you're a dead man."

Magnussen came to a complete stop.

"What's the matter?" asked Becker.

"I think I just realized the magnitude of what I'm getting into," he replied. "And I don't like it."

"I'm sorry. I didn't know who else I could turn to."

"I'll do it," continued Magnussen. "If there's even a chance that what you said is true, I've got to. But I can't begin to tell you how much I resent the position you've put me in."

"It couldn't be helped."

Magnussen resumed walking, and a moment later he reached his car. He opened the door, placed the disks carefully on the passenger seat, and then climbed in behind the wheel. He slammed the door, started the motor, and rolled down the window.

"If you had half a brain, you'd be on the first flight to South America, Max."

"They'd just find me."

"It's a big continent," said Magnussen. "Bigger men than you have managed to lose themselves in it."

"They've still got Jaimie," said Becker with a sigh. He paused. "And . . ."

"And what?"

"And I'm so goddamned close to all the answers, I can't quit now."

"Even if it kills you?"

Becker patted his pocket.

"If I die, I won't die alone," he said with more confidence than he felt. "Good luck, Jim."

"The same to you, Max," said Magnussen, putting his car in gear. "I have a feeling that we're both going to need it."

So do I, thought Becker grimly. *So do I.*

|2|3|

Becker gave Magnussen a five-minute head start, then took a bus into the city. A pair of transfers put him in the Georgetown area, and he began approaching Colonel Stuart's house on foot. When he got within two blocks of it, he stopped to consider his next move.

Stuart would doubtless guess that he was coming in civilian clothes, since his major's insignia made him a marked man. Furthermore, he had to have taken some steps to protect himself. Probably there were military personnel within the house itself, plus some sniper positioned within sight of the front door. A direct approach was out of the question.

Suddenly two boys, not quite in their teens, walked by, dribbling and tossing a basketball between themselves, and he summoned them over.

"Yeah?" said the shorter of them. "What do you want?"

"I need your help," Becker replied.

"You don't live around here," said the boy. "Why should we help you?"

Becker pulled out his wallet and showed them his space service identification card.

"I work for the government," he said. "I'm on a secret mission right this minute."

Suddenly the boys' faces came alive with interest.

"What's going on?" asked the taller boy.

"Do either of you know Colonel Stuart?" asked Becker. "He lives two blocks from here."

They both shook their heads.

"Well, he's a very important officer, in charge of all kinds of undercover work," continued Becker. "We've just received word that some agents from Paraguay may be planning to kidnap him."

"Really?" gasped the taller boy, obviously impressed.

Becker nodded. "They won't move until dark, but we need to know how many of them there are. My face is known to them, but they won't pay any attention to a couple of neighborhood kids who just happen to be walking past."

"Are they wearing Paraguayan uniforms?" asked the smaller boy.

Becker shook his head. "No, they're much too smart for that. They'll either be wearing U.S. Space Service uniforms, or else they'll be dressed in street clothes." He lowered his voice. "What I want you to do is walk up one side of Colonel Stuart's street and down the other side. Keep your eyes and ears open. See if you can spot anyone sitting in parked cars, or hiding on roofs or in between the buildings. If you do, pretend not to notice them. Then report back here to me. And remember—your country is counting on you."

"Yes, sir!" said the taller boy eagerly.

"Just a minute," said the smaller boy to Becker. "If you want us to do your job for you, you ought to pay us something."

"Fair enough," replied Becker. "But only after your mission is accomplished."

"How much?" asked the smaller boy.

"A dollar," said Becker.

The boy shook his head. "If these guys are as dangerous as you say, we ought to get more than that."

"All right," said Becker. "Five dollars."

"Each," said the smaller boy.

Becker nodded his agreement, and the two boys began walking in the direction of Stuart's brownstone, talking and tossing the basketball as they went. They were back ten minutes later, barely able to contain their excitement.

"Well?" said Becker.

"You were right!" exclaimed the taller boy. "There are three of them sitting in cars, and Jimmy thinks he saw another one on the stairs leading to the basement of the building that's directly across the street from Colonel Stuart."

"Thanks, boys," said Becker. "You did well."

"When are you going to take 'em?" asked the taller boy.

"After it's dark."

"Can we watch?"

Becker shook his head. "Can't have anyone frightening them off. Besides, we don't want any shooting in a residential neighborhood. Probably we'll have Colonel Stuart go out for dinner and take them after they start following him." He paused. "You won't read about it in the papers or hear about it on the holovision, because this is a secret operation, but your country owes you a debt of gratitude."

"And *you* owe us ten dollars," said the smaller boy.

"Right," said Becker, handing a five-dollar bill to each boy. "And a bonus," he added, giving them each another dollar.

They walked off, whispering furiously to each other, while Becker began retracing his steps. Obviously he couldn't approach Stuart at home, and in the long run that might be all for the best, since he certainly didn't have Jaimie incarcerated there. On the other hand, he certainly couldn't enter the Pentagon or the Space Administration Building, even in civilian clothes, without showing some kind of identification, and the one Jaimie had made for him wouldn't get him into a top-level military headquarters. Also, too many people in either building could recognize him on sight, even if he had a false ID and wore his street clothes.

Still, there was no way he was going to be able to hide in the back of Stuart's car—always assuming that he had one, and wasn't driven to work by some underling—the way he had done with Magnussen, nor did he feel confident about gaining entrance to Stuart's house even after the colonel left for work in the morning. The kids probably hadn't spotted *all* the snipers, and he didn't dare approach the house until he knew where every one of them was hiding.

He considered his various options for a few more minutes, then took a bus back to the outskirts of the vast ghetto that sprawled over more than half the nation's capital. When he got off, he entered a drugstore, asked where they kept their vidphones, and was directed to a row of pay booths. He checked each of them until he came to one that displayed a note stating that the camera was out of order, then entered it and dialed the Space Administration Building.

"Please stand before your camera, sir," said the receptionist.

"I'm calling from a pay booth, and the camera's broken," answered Becker.

"One moment while I check, sir," said the receptionist. There was a brief silence. "Very well; my computer confirms your claim. What can I do for you?"

"I've got to speak to Colonel Lydell Stuart," he said. "It's an emergency."

"Hold on, please."

He waited tensely for more than half a minute.

"I'm sorry, sir, but there is no Colonel Stuart listed here."

"You're quite sure?"

"Absolutely."

"Thank you for your time."

He broke the connection, then called a military access number at the Pentagon, requested Colonel Stuart, and got the same answer.

That didn't necessarily mean that Stuart was stationed

elsewhere, since a number of high-level officers engaged in covert projects could not be reached through the main switchboard, but it did give Becker some slight hope that he might not have to show himself in either of those too-familiar buildings.

Still, wherever he went, he was going to have to take some steps to hide his identity, and so he checked the commercial vidphone directory, wrote down the names of the nearest stores possessing those items he needed, and left the drugstore in search of them.

His first stop was a military surplus store, where he purchased the hat, insignia, and bars of a second lieutenant in the space service. They'd be watching for a major or a civilian; a nice, nondescript lieutenant just might be able to sneak past. He had considered picking up a general's trappings, but decided that would call far more attention to himself; there were a lot more unknown lieutenants walking around Washington than generals.

Then he walked into a cosmetic shop, picked up a black hair rinse, an artificial mustache, and a pair of facial pencils.

His final stop was a toy store, where he bought a small rag doll and had it gift-wrapped. They'd be expecting him to come with nothing but a gun; a large box with a satin bow on it was so out-of-character for a desperate fugitive that it just might put them at their ease.

Finally he returned to the cheap hotel room he had rented before accosting Magnussen. He unpacked his uniform, removed all trace of his rank, and carefully applied all of his various second lieutenant's insignia to it.

Then he entered the bathroom, read the directions on the hair rinse, and began rinsing his light brown hair in it. The first application was uneven, but he soon got the hang of it, and half an hour later his hair appeared coal black.

He then took out the mustache, treated it with the rinse so that it exactly matched his new hair color, and then, carefully applying some cosmetic glue to his upper lip, he gave himself a very thin, elegant mustache. He'd have felt safer with a thick, bushy one, but this changed his face every bit as much without calling attention to itself.

Finally he painted a mole on his chin, just off-center. Again, his first inclination was to give himself a huge scar running the length of his cheek, but he decided to stick to his minimalist approach. Besides, he doubted that he was a good enough makeup artist to create a truly believable blemish.

When he was finished, he studied his face in the mirror, then added his hat and a pair of sunglasses, and finally nodded his satisfaction.

He returned to his bed, where he had laid out his uniform, and carefully put it on a hanger and placed it in the closet. By the time he thought of buying a pair of shoes with lifts in them, the stores had all closed for the night, and he decided to try to get some sleep.

His alarm awoke him at five in the morning, and within half an hour he was on his way to the lot where he had left his car upon returning from New York. It was still there—he had been half-convinced that it would been stolen by now, Jaimie's assurances to the contrary—and he began driving toward Georgetown.

He reached Stuart's house just after six, and continued driving past it. What he needed now was some vantage point from which to observe it, so that he would know when Stuart left, and in what type of vehicle he was riding. He toyed with enlisting a few more neighborhood kids, as he had done the previous day, but by the time they got the information back to him Stuart would be long gone and he would have wasted another day.

Finally, on a hunch, he drove past Stuart's house again, turned left at the corner, and turned left again into the alley that separated Stuart's block from the next one over. He counted the buildings until he came to Stuart's and found what he was hoping to find: a two-car garage.

He picked up speed again, drove a couple of blocks to make sure he wasn't being followed, then circled back and entered the extension of the alley one block down from Stuart's house. There was almost no cross-street traffic, and he found that he had a virtually unimpaired view of the entire length of the alley for a distance of two blocks, until a jog in the street forced a curvature that finally obstructed his view.

Still, if Stuart took his own car, he'd pull out into the alley and turn onto a street before coming to the curve. Becker inched his car ahead until he came to a large apron in front of another private garage. He backed into it, turned his car in the opposite direction, and then parked on the apron, so that nothing except his right rear-view mirror could be seen from more than a few feet away. He adjusted the mirror so that he still had his unobstructed view of the length of the alley, turned off his motor, and waited.

Half an hour passed, then another hour. Becker began getting hungry, then restless, then furious with himself for not planning this better. He was absolutely convinced that he had somehow missed Stuart—after all, owning a car didn't necessarily mean that he used it to go to the office—and then, suddenly, a luxurious blue sports car pulled out of Stuart's garage, headed toward Becker, then took a left when it reached the cross street.

Becker started his own car, raced to the end of the alley, turned to his right, then turned right again and headed back to the cross street.

He caught a brief glimpse of the blue sports car crossing the intersection, increased his own speed a bit, and then took a left and found himself five cars behind the blue car. He was content to remain there until the car turned, and he slowed down to keep pace with the traffic.

After about ten minutes Becker realized that they weren't heading for the Pentagon *or* the Space Administration Building, and felt a momentary panic when he realized that for all he knew, he could be following Stuart's wife to her favorite dressmaker or her own place of work. Then a couple of cars turned at an intersection, Becker found himself only two cars behind the blue sports car, and he was able to see that he was indeed following a man.

Stuart finally turned at a major intersection, and a moment later he pulled into the parking lot of a tall, relatively new, steel-and-chrome-and-glass office building. Becker drove past it, circled the block twice to make sure that Stuart wasn't coming back out, then parked in a private lot a block away, checked his mustache and mole briefly in the mirror, took his beautifully-wrapped package out of the backseat, and left the car with an attendant.

He approached Stuart's building in a brisk, businesslike manner, as if he had every reason to be going there. Once inside, he walked past a pair of uniformed space service officers, paying no attention to them, and walked up to the building directory. There was nothing listed under *U.S.* or *Space* or even *Military,* and finally he gave up and checked the directory of clients. There was no *Stuart,* either with or without the *Col.* in front of his name. Then, on a hunch, he checked *Card,* and found that a Mr. W. Card had a private suite of offices on the 34th floor, which could be entered through Room 3415.

Becker's hand dropped to his side, and he tried to take some comfort in the feel of the pistol through the material of his coat. As he had done two days earlier, he had taped a second gun to his right ankle.

Still, he felt uneasy about barging in until he knew what he was facing, and he was painfully aware of the two officers standing a few feet away from him, so he took the elevator to the 48th floor, then entered the stairwell, walked down thirteen flights, and emerged on the 35th floor, just to get an idea of the way the building was laid out.

He stepped out onto a brightly polished floor, then walked to Room 3515. It was an import-export company named Travis and Sharpe that specialized in shipping wood pulp around the world to various printing plants. He walked down the corridor, passing three unnumbered doors until he came to one marked 3523. Then he returned to 3515, opened the door, and entered the reception area. To his right was a solid wall, directly ahead of him was a large window overlooking the city, and to his left was a harassed secretary pounding away on her computer keyboard while trying to juggle three different phone lines. Behind her a door led to other offices.

He waited politely for a few moments until she had managed to route all the calls to their proper destination.

"May I help you?" she asked in a harassed voice.

"I'm not sure," he said, holding up the gift-wrapped package. "I was told to deliver this to a Major Becker in Room 3519, but I can't seem to find the door to his office."

"Somebody gave you the wrong instructions. There isn't any 3519."

"I'm *sure* that was the number," persisted Becker.

"The next three offices are all interconnected," she explained. "You won't come to another number until you reach 3523."

"Do you own all three offices?" asked Becker.

"Yes."

"Then if I were to go down the corridor to the door where 3519 *ought* to be . . . ?"

"You'd still be in Travis and Sharpe," she concluded.

"Thank you," he said. "I guess I'll have to get better directions. I'm sorry to have disturbed you."

She was too busy answering the phone to acknowledge his apology, so he turned and left the office. Then he walked down to the door that would have been 3519 and tried it. It was unlocked. He stuck his head in, apologized to the executive who looked up from a computer to stare at him, and quickly closed the door.

He made one final stop—this time at the law firm occupying 3523—and asked for directions to the import-export firm while quickly checking the wall to his right. There was no connecting door to 3521.

Now he had some decisions to make. Should he chance going through what was certainly Stuart's outer office—

3415—and hope he could bluff his way past whoever screened Stuart's visitors? He didn't like that option at all; he had alerted Stuart to his presence, and the colonel would certainly have warned his staff to thoroughly check any stranger who wanted to see him. Besides, he had a feeling that no one visited this particular office unless he was expected and had definite business to transact.

That left the three unmarked doors that completed the office complex: 3417, 3419, and 3421.

In which one would he be most likely to find Stuart? 3421, probably; the only way in was to enter Room 3415 and walk through two offices, so it gave him the greatest insulation against unwanted visitors.

How should he approach the task of entering 3421? Carefully test the door and hope that it wasn't wired to the security system? Break right through it, gun drawn?

Or should he try 3419 or 3417, take a hostage or two, and then move on to 3421?

It all depended on the doors—and the only door he felt reasonably sure was not connected to an alarm was 3415. If he *knew* for a fact that Stuart was in 3421, he had no compunction about breaking through it and holding the colonel at gunpoint—but what if he broke into an empty office, or at least one that didn't contain Stuart? The one thing his experience of the last few days had taught him was that Stuart seemed to consider *everyone* expendable—which could well mean that if he broke into the wrong office, he was likely to be blown away along with any hostage he took.

He realized that he just didn't have enough information to make an intelligent choice, so when the elevator arrived he passed the 34th floor and went down to the 33rd. He walked to 3315—a small but prestigious architectural firm—and opened the door.

"Yes?" asked the receptionist, a young man in his early twenties.

"Is there a washroom in this suite of offices?" asked Becker.

"The restrooms are down the hall, on the right."

"I know," said Becker. "But my wife was consulting your firm concerning an addition to our home, and she thinks that she may accidentally have left a rather valuable bracelet in your private washroom."

"Then she's mistaken," said the young man. "We don't have a private washroom. You'd better check with the building management to see if the bracelet's been turned in."

"Thank you," said Becker. "I'll do that."

He left the office, walked to the stairwell, and climbed up to the 34th floor. Then he cracked the door open, and found that he had a clear view of the corridor as it went past Stuart's suite of offices.

Sooner or later people had to start coming and going, he decided. They'd go down the corridor to use the facilities, or down to the main floor to buy coffee or tobacco, or they'd leave for lunch. If Stuart left and returned, so much the better, because he'd be able to pinpoint his office door . . . but even if some of his assistants went out, at least he'd be able to eliminate *their* offices.

He sat down on the cement landing, keeping the door cracked open with a package of his small cigars, and waited. After an hour two men in military uniforms entered 3415, but they left again about five minutes later. Then, at eleven o'clock, a major emerged from 3415 and walked down the hall to the restroom. He was followed a moment later by a lieutenant, and Becker realized that whatever offices they worked in, they all entered and exited through 3415.

Which meant that he really had only two choices. He could present himself at 3415 and try to bluff his way through to Stuart, or he could hope he was right about which office Stuart was likely to possess and enter it from the corridor.

It was an easy choice. He didn't even know what Stuart's operation was called. If there were any code words, any names he had to know, they'd spot him before he ever made it out of the reception office. He'd have to try the more direct approach.

He stood up, brushed himself off, decided that he had no further use for the gift-wrapped doll and left it on the landing, and then entered the corridor and walked directly to the unmarked door that led to Room 3421.

He paused for a moment, making certain that nobody was in the corridor, then pulled out his gun. He tried the door, found to his surprise that it wasn't locked, opened it, and quickly stepped into the office.

Colonel Lydell Stuart was seated at a polished chrome desk.

"Good morning, Major," he said calmly as Becker pointed his gun between his eyes. "Please do sit down," he added, gesturing toward an empty chair. "I've been expecting you."

|2|4|

"Keep your hands where I can see them and you just might live through this," grated Becker.

"I'm quite unarmed, Major," replied Stuart.

"And back your chair away from the desk," continued Becker.

Stuart did as he was told, and Becker checked to make sure there were no alarm buttons that could have been reached with a foot or a knee.

"Are you ready to talk, Major?" asked Stuart.

"Soon."

Becker looked around the office. There was only one door, leading to Room 3419, and he quickly wedged a chair against it.

"All right," said Becker, facing Stuart. "Let's start with what you've done to Jaimie Nchobe."

"She's quite safe."

"Where is she?"

"She's in the building here," replied Stuart, still unperturbed by the sight of Becker's pistol pointing at him. "Won't you sit down, Major? I really *have* been waiting to speak with you."

"Sure you have."

Stuart nodded. "Ever since you followed me to work this morning. In fact," he added, "I was just on the verge of sending one of my assistants to bring you in from the stairwell. It must have been very cold and drafty."

Becker looked his surprise, but said nothing.

"By the way," continued Stuart, "that's really quite an excellent disguise. It got you right past my two officers down on the main floor." He smiled. "Fortunately, my very best officer was posing as the doorman. *He* spotted you."

"Why didn't he do anything?" demanded Becker.

"I told you: we have to talk. I didn't want him to do anything that might have scared you away. I'm sure our demolitions experts have already picked up your gift-wrapped package from the stairwell, but I wonder if you'd assuage my curiosity by telling me what it contained?"

Becker grinned in spite of himself. "A rag doll."

"I *knew* I hadn't misjudged you, Major!" said Stuart delightedly. "They wanted to stop you, but I assured them you wouldn't blow up the building, or even my offices, without knowing where Jaimie Nchobe was." He paused. "But why on earth were you bringing me a doll?"

"I wasn't. I just thought it would call attention to the box rather than to me."

Stuart nodded thoughtfully. "Excellent reasoning. By the way, would you mind not pointing your pistol at me? I trust you to act in your best interests, but I haven't yet explained to you what they are."

"Then you'd better start, hadn't you?" said Becker. "You shouldn't mind one little gun. I've been dodging hundreds of them."

"That was my fault," said Stuart. He dismissed the incident with a shrug. "An error in judgment."

"*Why* did you want to kill me?" said Becker. "Are you one of them, too?"

"One of whom?"

"An alien."

"No, Major. I'm as human as you are."

"But you know who they are and who they've replaced," persisted Becker.

"That's what we're going to talk about, Major."

"I'm listening," said Becker, his gun still aimed between Stuart's eyes.

"Let's begin with the aliens," said Stuart.

"Let's."

Stuart turned to the small computer sitting in the corner of his office. "Computer, activate," he ordered.

"Activated," replied the computer.

"Signal for help and you're dead," interjected Becker grimly.

"I quite understand," said Stuart. "Major, would you like to see what a Chebotti looks like?"

"What's a Chebotti?"

"An alien."

Becker nodded.

"Computer, please produce a holographic image of a Chebotti," ordered Stuart.

Suddenly an image flickered and took shape. It looked like a pockmarked brown grapefruit with three sturdy tendrils growing out of the bottom and four longer, more slender ones growing out of the top.

"How does it see?" asked Becker, studying the image.

"It doesn't—at least, not the way you and I understand seeing," replied Stuart. "It possesses what I can only call a sense of perception, which is, in many ways, more accurate than our vision, and in some ways far inferior to it." He paused. "It locomotes on those three large tendrils that are growing out of the bottom, although bottom and top are relative expressions in regard to a Chebotti. It's just as comfortable walking on a wall or a ceiling."

"Is that a life-sized image?" asked Becker.

Stuart shook his head. "No. Actually, the Chebotti go about two feet in circumference, and when their tendrils are extended, they run about eight feet from top to bottom." He turned to Becker. "Are you ready to put your weapon down yet, Major?"

Becker shoved his gun into a pocket.

"Thank you for that vote of confidence," said Stuart dryly.

"I can pull it out again before you can open your desk drawer," Becker warned him.

"I'm sure you can," said Stuart.

"Keep talking."

"The Chebotti, as you can see, are totally different from Men in all respects. In fact, they don't even breathe oxygen. They're a silicon-based race. They are, as you have doubtless guessed by now, the very same race with whom we had such a disastrous meeting in deep space more than two decades ago."

Stuart paused, then continued. "To this day, we *still* don't know what precipitated the incident, nor do the Chebotti. Despite our propaganda to the contrary, nobody knows who fired the first shot, or why. I suspect it will remain a mystery for all eternity. Do you mind if I smoke?"

"Where are your cigarettes?"

"Cigars. They're in the top left-hand drawer of my desk."

Becker pulled his gun out. "Pick them up *very* carefully."

"Thank you," said Stuart, slowly opening his drawer and withdrawing two large imported cigars. "Would you care for one, Major?"

"Later."

Stuart shrugged. "As you will." He lit the cigar and took a deep puff on it. "Anyway," he continued, "about twelve years ago the Chebotti made covert contact with us."

"Who is *us*?" asked Becker. "The United States?"

"Actually, it was China that first picked up their signals. They made them available to the other three star-faring nations, which agreed to pool their resources and respond with one voice. It took our most powerful computers almost three months to create a common language with them." He smiled suddenly. "I think if your friend Ms. Nchobe had been working for us, we could have cut the time in half."

The smile vanished. "At any rate, we began a dialogue with them. They also had no idea what had precipitated the tragedy. They had come to assess our military and expansionist ambitions."

Stuart set his cigar in a large ashtray, leaned his elbows on the desk, and clasped his fingers together.

"By rights, there should be no problems. After all, neither of our races can use the same type of planets. Oxygen is poison to them."

"Why didn't they just blow us away if they were worried about us?" asked Becker. "Any race that's got the technology to travel from one star system to another ought—"

"Their technology developed along totally different lines from our own," interrupted Stuart. "They have found a means of entering hyperspace and circumventing the law that says one cannot travel faster than the speed of light. On the other hand, if it ever came down to a shooting war, not only are our weapons far superior to theirs, but the tight molecular bonding we developed for use on our titanium hulls since our first meeting with them is virtually impregnable to their weaponry. Basically, they can outrun us and we can outgun them.

"Still," continued Stuart, taking another puff of his cigar, "there are an awful lot of them out there, and they're very well-entrenched in this section of the galaxy—the Spiral Arm, as we call it. We have assured them of our peaceful intentions, as they have assured us of theirs. Still, because of that initial meeting twenty-three years ago, neither of us quite trusts the other." He stopped and looked at Becker. "Can you see where this is leading, Major?"

"I think so—but I don't understand what kind of powers they must possess to pass themselves off as men, or why, given those powers, you'd give them access to our technology."

"They don't have any powers," Stuart assured him.

Becker frowned. "Then I don't understand after all."

"Actually, you were closer to the truth than you realize,

Major," said Stuart. "After we'd been in communication with them for more than a year, we hit upon an agreement—a *secret* agreement—whereby we would put various spy devices in some of their ships. Due to their physical and sensory limitations, their race has become quite advanced in the science of cybernetics, and in exchange for their installing our devices, we agreed to let them place a number of androids in our own ships: fourteen here, and thirty-seven aboard ships from the other three countries. Then—still according to the agreement—after a period of some twenty-five years of mutual observation, when each side was totally convinced of the other's goodwill, we would make the facts of this second contact known to both races, and then we would all be free to spread throughout the Spiral Arm in peace and harmony, neither side taking anything the other side could possibly want." He paused. "I was placed in charge of the day-to-day American operation of what came to be known as Operation Wild Card. I keep in daily contact with my counterparts in Russia, China, and Brazil, and of course our scientists constantly analyze the input from our spy devices. The only computers in America that can access our files are in this building and in the White House, and the same degree of secrecy has been maintained in each of the other three countries. I have retained the rank of colonel in order not to call any attention to myself. Theoretically," he added with a wry smile, "the service will make it up to me when I retire."

"This is an awfully small headquarters for such a big project," noted Becker.

"The tip of the iceberg," answered Stuart. "Although all the businesses in this building are legitimate, the structure itself was designed and erected by the space service. Operation Wild Card takes up five entire levels of the subbasement. That's where we've been keeping your friend Ms. Nchobe." He noticed that his cigar had gone out, and he re-lit it.

"To continue: Everything functioned smoothly for more

than a decade. We took advantage of an air disaster to intro-
duce the fourteen American androids into deep-cover posi-
tions about nine years ago, while simultaneously installing
our spy devices into their ships. Given the delicacy of the
operation, it's truly amazing that we made it for almost a
decade without a serious problem."

"And then Jennings came along," offered Becker.

"And then Jennings came along," agreed Stuart. "The
problem began when he somehow spotted something
wrong with the androids. They'd been passing for human for
nine years, but he saw something nobody else had seen."
Stuart sighed. "I suppose it's a consequence of placing command in the hands of your best and your brightest. Whatever it was he saw, he became convinced that there were
two aliens on his ship—he couldn't know they were androids—and he killed them."

"Was Gillette an android, too?" asked Becker.

"Oh, yes—he had to be," replied Stuart. "The androids
could pass just about any social or psychological test, but a
thorough physical examination would have found them out.
Gillette was the third android aboard the *Roosevelt,* and Jennings was bright enough to figure it out when Gillette jettisoned the bodies into deep space." He paused again.
"Thank God he didn't kill him! Only four of our androids
replaced doctors; they've each been in deep space almost
continuously for the past nine years. We don't dare send an
android out without an android medic to certify his weekly
physicals."

"So there *are* androids currently serving with Gillette
aboard the *Martin Luther King?*"

Stuart nodded. "Four of them."

"And he wasn't put there just to keep him from me?"

"No. It fit in with the drug story, so we encouraged you to
believe we were hiding him, but in point of fact none of the
android doctors spends as much as a month on Earth between missions. Of course," he added, "we've falsified their
records to read otherwise."

Becker stared at Stuart for a moment. "Why didn't you just hush up the whole affair?" he asked at last. "That seems to be your specialty."

"We wanted to. Nobody wanted to see Jennings go on trial—a trial he couldn't possibly win—for making a proper decision to defend our security. But there had been too many witnesses to the killings. We *couldn't* cover it up; it was just too big. When the *Roosevelt* landed and the story broke, we took Jennings into custody and decided that the most efficient form of damage control would be for him to plead temporary insanity."

"But he wouldn't cooperate," said Becker with a smile.

"No, he wouldn't. He was convinced of the validity of his actions, and moreover, he was determined to alert the public to what he considered a planetary threat." He looked at Becker. "That's where *you* entered the picture, Major. We wanted to make the trial look good, and that meant getting him a good lawyer." He grimaced ironically. "How were we to know that you'd actually *believe* his story?"

"I *didn't* believe it," replied Becker. "I thought he was as crazy as you people claimed."

Stuart frowned in confusion. "Then why on earth did you try to make a case for the existence of aliens?"

"Because that was the defense my client demanded," answered Becker. "I thought it was a mistake. When I couldn't convince him to plead insanity, I asked to be taken off the case." He paused. "My request was denied, and I had no choice but to follow my client's dictates until I could convince him that he was better off pleading insanity and throwing himself upon the mercy of the court. *That's* when I stumbled upon the phony drug ring you had so thoughtfully provided for me."

"It wasn't explicitly designed for *you*, Major," replied Stuart. "Part of my job is to anticipate any eventuality, including the fact that someone might take just the action that Jennings took. The drug ring was just the latest in a long line of creations that we hoped would never prove necessary;

the information was changed and updated monthly, even to the deposits which your friend confiscated from our Swiss bank account." He paused. "Just out of curiosity, Major, what gave it away?"

"I bought it lock, stock, and barrel until I visited Montoya in the hospital. Then Montoya—or whoever he really was—said a couple of wrong things."

Stuart sighed. "The human element. I was afraid we might have buried some of the drug data so deeply that you would never find it."

"I never would have. That was Jaimie Nchobe's contribution."

"Still," persisted Stuart, "we couldn't make it *too* easy to find, not if it was to have the ring of truth about it."

"Speaking of Captain Jennings, is he still alive?" asked Becker.

"Of course. Why do you ask?"

"I thought he'd sooner die than change his plea. All he wanted to do was have his day in court and tell his story."

"When it became obvious that you had seen through our ruse, I personally approached Jennings and told him exactly what I have told you."

"And that's all it took?" said Becker unbelievingly.

"He is, after all, a *military* man, not a civilian, and his duty was and is the defense of our race. I explained to him that any action that could *not* be explained by insanity might very well result in the public becoming aware of the Chebotti's existence—and *that*, in turn, might abrogate our agreement with them before we're ready. He agreed wholeheartedly, and changed his plea."

"Before we're ready for what?" demanded Becker.

Stuart sighed deeply. "Ah, Major, now we come to the crux of it." He paused and stared directly into Becker's eyes. "Why do you think this is a military operation rather than a scientific one?"

"You tell me."

"Twenty-three years ago, the Chebotti destroyed a ship containing 873 men and women. Maybe they fired first and maybe they didn't—but we cannot risk the future of our race on their word alone. Our spy devices are learning more about their technology and capabilities almost daily, while we've taken great care to put their androids aboard those ships of ours on which the armaments are all but obsolete." Stuart allowed himself the luxury of a superior smile. "They may be as technologically advanced as we are, but they're not as devious. We are already performing successful experiments in hyperspace, while at the same time I doubt that the efficiency of their firepower has increased five percent. When the time for public disclosure comes, we'll be ready for peace *or* war."

"Interesting," said Becker noncommittally.

"And now that you know," concluded Stuart, "I'm afraid you must make a choice: you can become one of us, or you will never leave this building alive."

"Kill me, and by next week five hundred journalists will know that you're dealing with aliens," said Becker.

Stuart smiled and shook his head. "I don't believe you, Major Becker. You haven't the skill with a computer to manage that."

"You'd better *start* believing me," said Becker. "It was Jaimie's data. All I did was find a place to hide it—and make sure that it'll be disseminated all over the country if anything happens to me."

"Even if you're telling the truth, it makes no difference," said Stuart. "This is a matter not even of national security but of *planetary* security, and in such matters we really do have the authority to control the press. So please don't make meaningless threats."

"If you can keep this out of the media, why did you let me live long enough to get here?"

"We didn't *let* you live, Major Becker, I assure you," said Stuart. "You survived our very best efforts to kill you. Anyone who is good enough to reach this office is quite extraordinary—and while we possess ample cannon fodder, we are always in need of extraordinary men and women. By your very presence here, you've earned the right to become one of us, and to work on Operation Wild Card." He paused. "We all hope that our two races will elect to share in a lasting peace—and if they do, there are numerous governmental bodies charged with working out the details. But if it should come to war, it's *our* job to make sure we don't lose." He stared across the desk at Becker. "What is your decision, Major?"

"What happens to Jaimie Nchobe?"

"I haven't decided," replied Stuart. "She knows an awful lot about us."

"If you kill her, I'll kill you," said Becker. "It's as simple as that."

"I may not have any alternative," continued Stuart with no show of fear.

"You offered *me* a job," said Becker. "Offer *her* one."

"I very much doubt that we could offer a salary that would attract her," said Stuart dryly.

"She doesn't need your money. Give her the right job and she'll work for minimum wage."

"What job did you have in mind?"

"The only thing that excites her is a challenge," said Becker. "She found *you* in less than four days. Hire her to come up with a foolproof way to protect your secrecy."

"Do you think she'd agree to do it?"

"I know she would."

"Very well," said Stuart. "Let's find out." He activated his intercom. "Let me speak to Jaimie Nchobe, and put it on visual, please."

A holograph of Jaimie's face appeared over Stuart's desk. She seemed totally unaware of Becker's presence on the other side of the office.

"Ms. Nchobe, your friend Major Becker has made a suggestion that may prove to be to our mutual benefit." He paused. "Would you consider coming to work for us, with the specific assignment of hiding the existence of Operation Wild Card so well that no one—not even someone as talented as you—can ever find it again?"

"Becker suggested it?"

"That's correct."

"Will he vouch for it when I see him?"

"Absolutely."

"How do I know you won't kill me when I've finished?"

"You have my word on it."

"You've spent the last ten years lying to everybody about everything. Why should I believe you?"

"How can I convince you I'm telling the truth?" asked Stuart.

"You can't. But let *me* tell *you* something that's true, and I don't much care whether you believe it or not."

"What?"

"I've got a lot of friends that you would doubtless call unsavory. By tomorrow each of them will know that you're the one who ordered anything nasty that may happen to me."

"If you feel that's necessary," said Stuart with a shrug.

"I most certainly do." She paused. "What about the money that I—ah—borrowed from Gillette's Swiss account?"

Stuart considered the question for a few seconds. "It's yours, in exchange for a written pledge of silence concerning our existence and the events of the past four days."

It was Jaimie's turn to reflect upon her answer. Finally she nodded. "All right, Colonel. You've got a deal."

"Now, concerning salary . . ."

"Don't worry about it," she said. "I'm sure you'll be more than generous."

"I'm delighted to have you aboard, Jaimie."

"That's Ms. Nchobe, Colonel."

"My apology."

He severed the connection, and as the holograph disappeared, he activated another channel on the intercom.

"Yes, sir?" said a voice.

"Release Jaimie Nchobe and inform me when she's left the building."

"Do you want a tail on her, sir?"

"No. She's free to go."

"Yes, sir."

Stuart turned back to Becker. "Well?"

"That was very generous of you, Colonel Stuart."

Stuart smiled ruefully. "If I took the money back, she'd just steal it again. I suggest, Major, that you impress upon her in the strongest possible terms that it should be considered hush money." He paused, and his expression hardened. "She *must* understand that if she ever tries to disseminate what she knows about Wild Card, she will not survive the experience."

"I'll pass your message on to her," said Becker.

The intercom hummed to life.

"Jaimie Nchobe has left the building, sir."

"Thank you."

"Will there be anything further, sir?"

"I hope not," said Stuart. He turned to Becker. "Well, Major, will there be anything further?"

"No," said Becker.

"Then you'll join us?"

Becker stared at him for a long moment. "Before I answer, I want you to know that I don't like you, and I think your notion of problem solving is nothing but legalized murder."

Stuart looked unperturbed. "You're entitled to your opinion. Now, will you join us?"

"I'll join you," said Becker. "But you should know on the front end that it has nothing to do with your threats, nor do I personally give a damn about what you do or don't do with respect to the Chebotti. I'll leave the tactics and the duplicity to the generals and the admirals."

"Then why *are* you joining us?"

"A few minutes ago you called me an extraordinary man.

Well, I'm not. My concern is for those truly extraordinary men, men like Wilbur Jennings, who have the ability to spot a flaw in the facade you've built and the courage to act upon it. If they're to survive rather than disappear, they'll need a good lawyer."

"One capable of proving them insane beyond the shadow of a doubt?" asked Stuart with a smile.

"That's right."

"You have a long-overdue leave coming to you, I believe," said Stuart. "Why don't you consider yourself on furlough as of this moment? When you report back in a month, I'll have your first assignment for you."

"I've already chosen my first assignment," said Becker.

"Oh?"

"I was assigned to defend Captain Jennings. I'd like to do so."

"You've got it," said Stuart. "Your leave begins when the trial is over."

"You'd better take the bugs out of his room," continued Becker. "I intend to discuss his case very frankly with him." He paused. "I don't want you to have to shoot any of your people who happen to be listening in."

"It'll be done by tomorrow morning." Stuart got to his feet, walked around his desk, approached Becker, and extended his hand. "Welcome aboard, Major."

Becker stood up and stared at Stuart's hand without taking it.

"Is something wrong, Major?"

"There's plenty wrong," replied Becker. "You tried to kill me and publicly humiliate Jennings for doing our jobs well, and you incarcerated and planned to kill Jaimie Nchobe for the crime of helping me to stay alive. I'm not joining you because I approve of you and your policies, Colonel. I'm joining you because it's about time somebody voiced an opposing viewpoint around here."

"Major," said Stuart calmly, "I really couldn't care less what you think about me or my methods. I'm doing a job that has to be done. Hopefully things will turn out well, and all my efforts will prove to have been unnecessary. But if it should turn out that we cannot establish peaceful relations with the Chebotti, then I would gladly lock away a hundred Jenningses and kill a thousand men like you rather than allow us to fight the most important war in human history without being adequately prepared for it."

"You've been spending too much time with your androids," said Becker. "You've forgotten what humanity is all about."

"And you, Major, have spent your entire life with human beings. That is no longer a permanent state of affairs."

Becker stared once more at Stuart's outstretched hand, then saluted and left the office.

He felt the tension leaving his body as he took the elevator down to the ground floor. The outrage, he realized, would take a lot longer.

He walked out the front door of the building, hands in his pockets, and started walking toward the parking lot where he had left the car.

"Jesus, I'm hungry!" said a familiar feminine voice at his side. "How are we gonna beat the bad guys if all our soldiers eat is junk food? I haven't had a good meal since we left New York City."

He looked to his left and saw that Jaimie had joined him and was matching him stride for stride.

"Hi," he said.

"Hi, Counselor."

"Did they rough you up much?" he asked.

"A bit," she said with a shrug. "How much of your soul did you sell to get them to take the Code Red off us?"

"A bit," he answered.

"You can tell me all about it over lunch," she said. "I'm gonna start off with a nice lobster bisque, and then Caesar salad, and . . ." She rattled off a seven-course menu.

"Who's paying for this feast?" asked Becker as they reached the car.

"Why, that nice Colonel Stuart, of course," she said with a grin.

"Does he know it?"

"Is the Pope Jewish?" replied Jaimie.

|2|5|

The officers of the tribunal stared at Jennings and his attorney.

"The charges and specifications having been read, does the Counsel for the Defense choose to enter a plea at this time?"

Becker rose to his feet.

"We do."

"And how does the defense plead?"

Becker looked briefly at Jennings, who nodded almost imperceptibly.

"To all charges and specifications, we enter a plea of not guilty by reason of temporary insanity."

Magnussen, fresh from destroying the envelope that Becker had given him in the park, rose to state that the prosecution was willing to accept the defense's arguments.

The trial of Wilbur H. Jennings, former captain of the *Theodore Roosevelt*, was concluded in eleven minutes. Then Becker, all thoughts of his furlough banished from his mind, returned to his new office, rolled up his sleeves, and *really* went to work.

THE BEST IN SCIENCE FICTION

THE TOR DOUBLES

Two complete short science fiction novels in one volume!

Buy them at your local bookstore or use this handy coupon:
Clip and mail this page with your order.

Publishers Book and Audio Mailing Service
P.O. Box 120159, Staten Island, NY 10312-0004

Please send me the book(s) I have checked above. I am enclosing $＿＿＿＿
(please add $1.25 for the first book, and $.25 for each additional book to
cover postage and handling. Send check or money order only—no CODs.)

Name ＿＿＿＿＿＿＿＿＿＿＿＿＿＿＿＿＿＿＿＿＿＿＿＿＿＿＿＿＿＿＿

Address ＿＿＿＿＿＿＿＿＿＿＿＿＿＿＿＿＿＿＿＿＿＿＿＿＿＿＿＿＿＿

City ＿＿＿＿＿＿＿＿＿＿＿＿＿State/Zip ＿＿＿＿＿＿＿＿＿＿＿＿

Please allow six weeks for delivery. Prices subject to change without notice.

THE BEST IN FANTASY

MORE BESTSELLERS FROM TOR

☐	53308-9	THE SHADOW DANCERS: G.O.D. INC. NO. 2 by Jack L. Chalker	$3.95
☐	53309-7		Canada $4.95
☐	55237-7	THE PLANET ON THE TABLE by Kim Stanley Robinson	$3.50
☐	55238-5		Canada $4.50
☐	55237-6	BESERKER BASE by Fred Saberhagen, et al	$3.95
☐	55238-4		Canada $4.95
☐	55114-1	STALKING THE UNICORN by Mike Resnick	$3.50
☐	55115-X		Canada $4.50
☐	55486-8	MADBOND by Nancy Springer	$2.95
☐	55487-6		Canada $3.95
☐	55605-4	THE HOUNDS OF GOD by Judith Tarr	$3.50
☐	55606-2		Canada $4.50
☐	52007-6	DARK SEEKER by K.W. Jeter	$3.95
☐	52008-4		Canada $4.95
☐	52185-4	NIGHT WARRIORS by Graham Masterton	$3.95
☐	52186-2		Canada $4.95
☐	51550-1	CATMAGIC by Whitley Strieber	$4.95
☐	51551-X		Canada $5.95
☐	50764-9	LION IN THE VALLEY by Elizabeth Peters	$3.95
☐	50765-7		Canada $4.95
☐	50775-4	THE AMBER EFFECT by Richard S. Prather	$3.95
☐	50776-2		Canada $4.95
☐	51060-7	GOOD BEHAVIOR by Donald E. Westlake	$3.95
☐	51061-5		Canada $4.95

Buy them at your local bookstore or use this handy coupon:
Clip and mail this page with your order.

Publishers Book and Audio Mailing Service
P.O. Box 120159, Staten Island, NY 10312-0004

Please send me the book(s) I have checked above. I am enclosing $_____
(please add $1.25 for the first book, and $.25 for each additional book to
cover postage and handling. Send check or money order only—no CODs.)

Name _____

Address _____

City _____ State/Zip _____

Please allow six weeks for delivery. Prices subject to change without notice.

THE BEST IN HORROR